Easy Kill

Eventually an object distinguishable as a finger began to emerge from the damp soil, swiftly followed by another. From nowhere, the first fly appeared and made an attempt to land. Rhona swatted it away.

Gradually the full hand lay exposed. It was badly decomposed but recognisable as female, a small gold ring biting into the rotting flesh of the middle finger.

About the author

Lin Anderson began writing while working as a teacher. *Easy Kill* is her fifth novel, and the fifth to feature forensic scientist Rhona MacLeod.

LIN ANDERSON

Easy Kill

HODDER

First published in Great Britain in 2008 by Hodder & Stoughton
An Hachette Livre UK company

First published in paperback in 2009

1

A CIP catalogue record for this title
is available from the British Library

ISBN 978 0 340 92243 9

Typeset in Plantin Light by Hewer Text UK Ltd, Edinburgh
Printed and bound by Clays Ltd, St Ives plc

Hodder & Stoughton policy is to use papers that are natural, renewable
and recyclable products and made from wood grown in sustainable
forests. The logging and manufacturing processes are expected to
conform to the environmental regulations of the country of origin.

Hodder & Stoughton Ltd
338 Euston Road
London NW1 3BH

www.hodder.co.uk

ACKNOWLEDGEMENTS

Thanks to Dr Jennifer Miller of GUARD and Derek Scott (Training Manager, Scottish Ambulance College), and to David Robertson (Development and Regeneration Services, Glasgow City Council) for sharing his expertise on the Molendinar Burn.

To Detective Inspector Bill Mitchell

I

THE CAR WAS flash, and looked brand new. As it pulled up, the nearside window whirred down.

'Hey you!'

The vehicle had drawn up in the darkest part of the street, avoiding the improved visibility of the safe zone. Better lighting and multiple cameras made the punters nervous.

A hand appeared, waving money at her. Still Terri hesitated.

'Are you fucking working or not?'

Terri took her time approaching, trying to get a look at the man before she committed. She preferred regulars. She knew what they wanted. She knew they would pay.

She was near the car now. Terri stumbled, her ankle going over on one high heel.

'Careful,' he called, suddenly solicitous.

Terri bent to look in. The guy's face was in shadow but he looked harmless enough. Three twenty-pound notes sat on the passenger seat. When she opened the door he scooped up the money, freeing the seat for her.

'There's an alley further along,' said Terri, indicating an opening a few yards ahead.

The man pulled away from the kerb, swiftly and purposefully, throwing a quick glance at a nearby camera.

'Not around here. I like my privacy.'

He dropped the money in her lap.

'What does that buy?'

Terri told him, keeping to the normal rates, not telling any lies in case he was testing her. If he was a regular punter, he would know anyway.

He nodded, seemingly satisfied.

The city lights flowed past in a blood-streaked blur. They were heading out of the centre. Despite her misgivings at leaving the zone Terri felt her body relax, soothed by the combination of Valium she'd taken before coming out and the stuffy heat inside the car.

'You'll have to take me back afterwards,' she said.

He didn't react, his profile impassive.

'I have to get back,' Terri insisted, imagining being thrown out miles away.

'One fuck a night not enough for you?' He smiled, but not at her. 'You need how many? Six? Ten fucks a night?

Terri tensed. Talking dirty was sometimes the fore-play. For those who could not perform it was often the whole play.

'How many?' he insisted.

'I have six regulars on a Wednesday night.'

'Six fucks,' he nodded to himself. 'Not a problem.'

They were approaching traffic lights. Terri decided if they changed to red, she would get out of the car.

He zoomed through on amber.

'Look,' she said. 'We don't have to go any further. There's plenty of places around here.'

The punch, when it came, knocked the air out of her. He put his hand back on the wheel as though nothing had happened.

Terri tried to draw breath into her lungs, gasping and wheezing. 'Please.' She whimpered, retreating as far as she could.

He glanced in his rear-view mirror. 'Say, "I need six fucks a night".'

Now his left hand was gripping her exposed thigh. She yelped.

'Say, "I need six fucks a night".'

She said it quietly.

'Louder.'

Terri repeated it, louder this time.

They were on the Kingston Bridge crossing the River Clyde, going west. A sudden thought struck her, she was heading towards home. She'd told her mum she would visit this weekend, and she wanted to keep her word.

He had fallen silent, intent on the road. Terri slid her hand into her bag and felt for her phone. A spasm of fury crossed his face as a sudden drilling noise indicated an incoming text. Reaching across her, he tore the bag from her hand, lowered the window and threw it out.

He took the next exit without indicating, doubling back towards the city centre. Terri kept thinking that as long as he was driving he couldn't hurt her. She tried to compose herself and plan how to get away. She had been in difficult situations before and survived.

2

THE HOTTEST AND wettest July so far on record had turned Glasgow into a warm bath. Had the skies been blue and the sun shining down on the sandstone city, its citizens would have relished this evidence of global warming. After all, it would save a trip to Spain to top up their tans. For the last week, the skies had been perpetually dark and grey, rain a semi-permanent feature, in all its west coast forms; smirr, Scotch mist (an understated steady drizzle) and full-blown tropical downpour, known locally as stair rods.

This morning it was Scotch mist that clothed the eastern side of the city, its magnificent cathedral and neighbouring graveyard – the Necropolis, affectionately known in Glasgow as the City of the Dead.

Two mounted arc lights brought occasional glimpses of a forensic team moving among the mausoleums and ornate graves of Glasgow's rich departed. In their white suits they could have been spectres, or some alien species looking for evidence of human habitation among the tombstones.

The corpse that had brought them there was once a young woman. Sniffed at by a fox on its night-time forage, nosed by one of the roe deer that grazed the luscious grass, it had finally been found by a shocked jogger, who made a point of running to the top of the Necropolis every morning before breakfast. That was something he wouldn't be doing again in a hurry. The flies had got there before him, lifting in a black cloud on his approach. Flesh flies and bluebottles had arrived minutes after death, to deposit their maggots or eggs in all the natural orifices. A little later, standard houseflies had joined the party.

Dr Rhona MacLeod, chief forensic for the Strath-clyde Force, crouched next to the body, her white-suited figure indistinguishable from the other members of the forensic team. Above her, a pinnacle-shaped gravestone declared this to be the last resting place of one *Edwin Aitken, a merchant of the city, respected father and citizen*, whose family sorely missed him.

The young woman usurping Edwin's grave had no name as yet, and apparently no means of identification. Her clothes suggested prostitution, but there were plenty of girls out clubbing in Glasgow wearing even less.

A skirt of flimsy plastic masquerading as leather was drawn up around her waist, a striped top pulled up to expose her breasts. A black nylon bra, knotted around her neck as a ligature, was the probable cause of death, but there were also six bloody puncture wounds clustered in the shaved genital area. The violence hadn't ended there. The stiletto heel of the red sandal, missing from her right foot, had been inserted in her vagina.

The body had lain in this spot since the early hours of the morning. It had been discovered at eight-thirty and by then patches of lividity, caused as the blood sank to the lower parts, had fused together into larger purplish areas that still blanched under pressure. There was no exact science that could establish the time of death, as there were too many parameters affecting the state of the body. Lividity offered some indication, as did infestation. True flies were holometabolous, metamorphosing through four distinct stages: egg, larva, pupa and adult. Left in the open like this for a couple of weeks, infestation would have reduced the corpse to skin, bone and cartilage.

The area was already cordoned off, the incident tent in the process of being raised, which would stop the inevitable rain from washing away the evidence and hopefully keep any more flies at bay.

DS Michael McNab was Scene of Crime Manager, his dark auburn head visible now alongside that of DI Bill Wilson, Rhona's friend and mentor. Bill's face looked as grey as the neighbouring granite headstones. Michael, in contrast, looked like a man who had just been for an invigorating run.

Rhona glanced up as the nearby bushes parted to reveal another forensic suit, filled out a little more than her own. Chrissy McInsh, Rhona's assistant, looked down at the violated corpse. Compassion clouded her eyes.

'Poor cow.'

'Did you find her pants?'

Chrissy shook her head. 'Probably not wearing any.'

'Or he took them as a trophy.'

There had been eight murders of Glasgow prostitutes in the last ten years, with only one conviction. None had occurred since the safe area had been established. Until now. Three of the previous victims had been found without underwear. One had been dumped naked. Extensive police enquiries had led nowhere, except to establish that the unsolved murders were not likely to have been committed by the same man. Which meant there were eight uncaught murderers walking the streets of Glasgow.

'They are shite, killed by shite; who gives a shite?'

'Chrissy!' said Rhona, shocked by her assistant's bluntness.

'Not my opinion. A quote from one of our police colleagues a few years back.'

'Who?'

'Press didn't say, but I have my suspicions.'

If the victim turned out to be a prostitute, which looked likely, they would have a hard job finding her killer. When a prostitute was murdered, it was nearly always by someone she didn't know. No relationship between the murderer and victim meant the circle of potential suspects was limitless. Men using the services of prostitutes didn't volunteer information, since many had girlfriends, wives and families who didn't know about their little hobby. The public weren't interested, unless the death involved an 'innocent' young woman out jogging or walking her dog.

'Is she a user?'

'Probably,' Rhona replied. 'There are marks on her inner thigh.'

'The press will go for "junkie prostitute found dead in graveyard" and the punters will go to ground.'

There were an estimated 1,200 street prostitutes in Glasgow, compared with 100 in nearby Edinburgh. The high number reflected the poverty, deprivation and drug problems of the west-coast city. Most decent Glasgow citizens wished the problem would disappear. It gave the city a bad name.

'We can't be sure she was a prostitute,' protested Rhona.

'Odds against it don't look good.'

'Morning ladies.' As he approached, DS McNab gave them a big smile, aimed predominantly in Rhona's direction. Chrissy raised one eyebrow at her boss, but Rhona ignored her.

'If you can step aside for a moment, we'll get the tent up.'

'You're a bit late. We've been here twenty minutes,' Chrissy said.

The DS looked Chrissy up and down appreciatively. 'Have you put on some weight? It suits you.'

It was a remark Chrissy would normally have furnished with a cutting reply. Not this time. Rhona saw a flush creep over Chrissy's cheek, and stepped in to defend her.

'Can I have a word?'

McNab was happy enough to speak to Rhona alone, although that wasn't her intention. She merely walked him to where DI Wilson stood with the Procurator Fiscal, whose job under Scots Law was to determine whether a crime had taken place.

Chrissy looked relieved to be let off the hook. So far only Rhona and Chrissy's mother knew about Chrissy's pregnancy. According to Chrissy her mother had taken it pretty well, but hadn't built up the courage to tell the family priest yet, let alone Chrissy's father and brothers. All hell would be let loose when the news broke, especially when the men found out who the child's father was.

At close quarters, Bill Wilson's colour was an even more pronounced grey, a tone more in keeping with a strung-out heroin abuser than a healthy man in his fifties with a loving wife and family. Rhona gave him a worried look, which he chose not to acknowledge. She knew what was eating at Bill, but she wasn't sure who else did. Bill didn't allow worries over his personal life to be discussed on the job.

The Fiscal acknowledged Rhona with a nod, then said his swift goodbyes. Not many Fiscals appeared at murder scenes, particularly when there was little doubt that a serious crime had indeed taken place. Rhona imagined Cameron heading back to his nice air-conditioned office and wished she could return to the peace and tranquillity of her forensic lab. But that wouldn't happen for some time yet.

'A bad business,' said Bill. 'I thought creating a safe zone had made a difference.'

'It had,' replied Rhona.

'Not for this one.'

'What do we want the press to know?' McNab asked.

Bill thought for a moment. 'I've a mind to say nothing about prostitution until we're sure. Let's give them *Young woman found brutally murdered after night out.*'

That way they might get forty-eight hours of public interest in the case, before the truth was revealed. Bill was taking a gamble. He could just as easily get on the wrong side of the press. Alienating them meant no high profile for the case and less likelihood of finding the killer. Female street prostitutes, especially junkies, were the most threatened and abused members of society. No one cared when or how they died.

Rhona looked over anxiously at the crime site and was relieved to see that the tent was up. DS McNab had given up waiting for his private conversation with Rhona and was back on scene. The Necropolis was a hive of activity. Inner and outer cordons prevented the public from getting too close to the *locus* of crime, but the steep rise of the ground offered the more inquisitive a bird's eye view, if they were prepared to climb to the top of the hill, or, even better, scale one of the higher monuments.

Rhona made her way back to the tent. Forensic samples taken from the body *in situ* were vital. History was littered with cases where not enough forensic material had been gathered, leaving the prosecuting lawyer with the job of trying to prove a case largely on circumstantial evidence. If the murderer had left any trace of himself on the body, or the immediate area, she wanted to find it.

Chrissy was already inside, working her way over the surrounding area. She glanced up gratefully as Rhona entered, then went back to what she was doing.

Rhona knelt next to the body. The filtered light of the tent softened the victim's features. The woman's face was still thin, her cheekbones prominent, but the expression appeared more peaceful.

She left the ligature in place. It was better removed in the mortuary, keeping the knots intact. You could tell a lot from the way perpetrators tied knots. Rhona took samples from below the fingernails and bagged the hands. Then she concentrated on the mouth. As she swabbed for traces of semen, she found a small metal crown. Any contact with the crown, perhaps during unprotected oral sex, would have left scrapings of DNA. Rhona sampled it, then moved to the wounds in the genital area. The irregular edges and evidence of tearing and bruising suggested they had been made by a blunt force instrument, like a chisel or screwdriver.

Rhona carefully extracted the shoe and studied the six-inch heel. The end looked similar in dimension to the wounds. She bagged and labelled the shoe and set it with the other exhibits. Vaginal and anal swabs would be taken at post-mortem. Sperm deposits could be retrieved up to twenty days after intercourse had taken place.

Closer examination of the inner thighs suggested the victim was a drug user. Rhona checked the bare arms and found the same. Needle sites weren't the only wounds on the body. There were clusters of sores on the front of the thighs and lower arms.

Rhona called Chrissy over. 'Take a look at this.' Chrissy accepted the magnifier and directed it on the wounds.

'She could be a tweaker,' she said after a few moments' study. Tweaking or skin picking was a common
side effect of using crystal meth or methamphetamine
hydrochloride, where the addict imagined there were
bugs crawling under their skin. Chrissy shook her
head. 'If she did this to herself, she was living in hell.'

Her sampling of the body complete, Rhona examined the surrounding area. The earth was well
trampled with no obvious individual footprints and
no discarded condoms. Chrissy confirmed the same on
her patch.

'If he used a condom, he took it with him,' she said.

When the mortuary crew had bagged the body and
loaded it into the van, Rhona was free to examine
the exposed grave. Until now the prominent smells
had been a mixture of fresh blood and the acrid
odour of urine and faeces expelled through fear,
shock, or death itself. Now that the body had been
removed, Rhona realised she was picking up another scent.

She sat back on her haunches and took a deep
breath. Most of the Necropolis graves were grass
covered, but not this one. Built into the hillside and
fronted by a low stone wall, it lay constantly in shadow.
Here there was no grass, only dark earth and a sprink-
ling of weeds.

Rhona bent closer to the ground. The smell was
definitely stronger there. A terrible thought crossed her
mind. One she hardly dared contemplate.

'Are there any police dogs on site?'

'I think so.' Chrissy looked at her quizzically. 'What's up?'

'Not sure yet.'

Outside the tent the drizzle had developed into stair rods. There was no sign of Bill, and Rhona assumed he had returned to the station to set up an incident room. McNab was standing near the inner cordon, apparently oblivious to the downpour.

Rhona called out to him.

'What's up?'

'I need a police dog. The soil under the body is disturbed and there's a strong scent of decomposition.'

'This *is* a graveyard.'

'The man buried here is too long dead to smell this bad.'

The cynical smile disappeared from McNab's face. 'You think there's something else buried there?'

'Let's see how the dog reacts.'

He nodded, serious now. 'I'll radio one in.'

3

THE DOG WAS already working its nose as it entered the tent. On release it made straight for the grave.

They watched as it grew ever more excited, sniffing and pawing at the surface.

'What do you think?' Rhona asked the handler.

'She smells something all right.'

Rhona checked with McNab. 'Do we need permission to excavate?'

'We'll worry about that later.'

Rhona began to remove the earth cautiously with a small trowel, aware of what might lie beneath. It took a little over four inches to establish that something was buried there and by then the putrid smell was strong enough to gag on. McNab, reading the expression on the handler's face, sent the relieved man outside.

Eventually an object distinguishable as a finger began to emerge from the damp soil, swiftly followed by another. From nowhere, the first fly appeared and made an attempt to land. Rhona swatted it away.

Gradually the full hand lay exposed. It was badly decomposed but recognisable as female, a small gold ring biting into the rotting flesh of the middle finger.

Chrissy muttered 'Jesus, Mary and Joseph' under her breath.

Rhona stood up. 'Okay. Looks like our perpetrator has killed before.'

McNab stared down in disbelief. 'He knew the body was there?'

'He knew all right,' Rhona said with conviction. 'Why else bring his victim to this particular grave?'

'I'd better call the boss.' McNab pulled out his phone.

'Bill's going to love this,' said Chrissy.

By the time Bill returned, Rhona had exposed the face and upper body, both in an advanced state of decomposition, but there was no mistaking the ligature around the neck, fashioned from a bra.

'Our man's got a trademark.'

'If the knots are tied the same way.'

'How long has the body been buried?'

'A shallow grave. Hot weather and plenty of rain. At a guess, maybe a month.'

Bill let a sigh escape. 'There could be more.'

Young women engaged in street prostitution appeared and disappeared regularly. Many were homeless and went unregistered. Most were outcasts of society.

'We should use the dogs. Check the rest of the graveyard for disturbed earth,' Rhona suggested.

She didn't need to look at Bill's expression to know how many man-hours that would need. There were 3,500 tombs in the City of the Dead.

'What about this one?'

'I've contacted Judy Brown at GUARD. I'll help her expose the body and get it to the mortuary.'

'Do we call Sissons back?' Bill said.

'I don't think we need a pathologist to determine death has occurred in this case.'

It was a feeble attempt to be light-hearted. Bill acknowledged it with the ghost of a smile. The truth was you couldn't succumb to constant angst in this work. You accepted the horror and got on with the job, even if it meant developing a ghoulish sense of humour.

GUARD, the Glasgow University Archaeological Research Department, supplied the experts needed for dealing with concealed bodies. Judy Brown certainly had the experience, having worked on mass graves in the Balkans, Angola, and more recently Iraq. Thankfully, after a further period of careful excavation, Judy's trowel hit metal. The iron grave-covering lay a couple of feet below the surface.

'He couldn't have buried another one here even if he wanted to.' Judy's long dark hair was drawn back and fastened with a comb under the regulation hood. Smears of dirt marked her face and mask where she'd brushed aside some stray strands. 'The official graves here are twelve feet deep and brick lined. There'll be more than one member of the Aitken family sharing their patriarch's resting place.'

'I bet he never imagined two scarlet women lying on top of him,' Rhona said.

'I expect he preferred them alive,' Judy replied cynically.

The exposed remains followed the same pattern as the one above ground. A short skirt drawn up, the chest exposed, the ligature and stiletto.

'No pants again. Could they have rotted away?'

Judy shook her head. 'Unlikely in the time this has been in the ground.'

'So he collects them?'

'Or they don't wear them. Certainly makes things quicker.'

Rhona stood up, her knees protesting at the length of time she'd crouched. Judy joined her with a groan of relief.

'What about transport?'

'There's a mortuary van waiting,' Rhona told her.

'Let's get some fresh air, then.'

The evening breeze skimming the hill was a welcome relief from the stench inside. Rhona dropped her mask and took a deep breath. She had been inside the tent most of the day. The penetrating smell would have impregnated her clothes and hair, despite the suit. The only solution was a long hot shower.

McNab was still on duty, although Chrissy had long since gone back to the lab. He supervised the removal of the corpse, then joined Rhona and Judy.

'So, not a mass grave then?'

'Only if you count the Victorian layers,' Judy said.

McNab gave Judy an appraising look and Rhona hid a smile. You could always depend on Michael McNab to eye up the ladies. She was just grateful his eye was no longer on her.

'The dogs pick up on anything?' she asked.

'Not so far. We'll have another go tomorrow.'

'I'd better be getting back.' Judy stepped out of her white suit.

'I wondered if anyone fancied a drink,' ventured McNab.

Rhona shook her head. She did fancy a drink, but not with Michael McNab, and besides, she fancied a shower more.

McNab looked directly at Judy.

'Maybe, but I need to go back to the base first.' Turning, so McNab could not see her face, Judy looked quizzically at Rhona – should she?

McNab was fun and had been pretty good in bed. Rhona hoped her expression conveyed at least that much. She left them to their decision-making and headed for her car, which was parked what seemed like miles away.

Dusk had rendered the Necropolis eerie and silent as the throb of the police generator faded into the distance. Out of the harsh glare of the arc lights, the shadowy gravestones stood sentry on Rhona's walk back to the Bridge of Sighs. Below the bridge, a yellow stream of headlights flowed down the road built over what had once been the Molendinar Burn.

The victim had crossed here to her death, just as other victims had made the more famous crossing in Venice. Rhona's mood was growing as dark as the day. She remembered what Bill had told her once, earlier in her career. The only death to fear, he'd said, was your own. It was a strange thought for him to voice, considering how much he worried about the well-being of his two teenage children, and now his wife Margaret.

A line of police vehicles was parked in Cathedral Square. Once inside her car, Rhona called Chrissy.

'Go home,' Chrissy told her. 'I've logged and stored everything. I'll see you tomorrow.'

Rhona found herself readily agreeing.

She drove westward through the city towards a sky bruised red and blue. It looked both beautiful and ominous.

Rhona found herself craving the small ordinary things of life, as far away from violent death as was imaginable. The sounds of the flat when she would open the door, sometimes a hushed silence, sometimes music. The soft mew of the kitten. Its purr of pleasure as it greeted her arrival. Rhona's skin prickled in anticipation as she slid her key quietly into the lock.

Tonight there was music, but no sign of Tom the cat. She stood for a moment in the hall, breathing in its familiar scents, then went in search of the occupants.

They were both in the kitchen. Sean stood facing the window, listening intently, the kitten cradled in his arms. Something in his stance stopped Rhona from interrupting.

The music was jazz piano, a tune Rhona was unfamiliar with. A padded envelope lay on the table. Nearby was an empty CD case. Musicians often sent Sean samples of their work, hoping for a gig at the jazz club. Rhona assumed this was one of those occasions.

As the track drew to a close, Sean turned, sensing her presence. He placed the kitten on the window seat, where it curled itself into a tiny ball.

'That was Sam playing.'

'Sam?' Rhona's heart leapt.

Sean indicated the envelope. 'The CD arrived this morning.'

Sam Haruna, the father of Chrissy's unborn child, had been forced to flee during Rhona's last big case, uncovering a child-trafficking ring in Nigeria. The men chasing him were both influential and ruthless, and if Sam was still alive he was in great danger.

Rhona picked up the envelope, postmarked London, three days before. 'He must have made it back to London. I have to call Chrissy and tell her. She'll be over the moon.' Rhona pulled out her mobile, but Sean stopped her hand before she could dial.

'I think we should wait.'

'Why?'

'This recording could have been made at any time. It doesn't prove Sam's alive now.'

'Who else would send the CD, if it wasn't Sam?'

Sean didn't have to answer. The Suleiman family were as powerful in the UK as they were in Nigeria. If they suspected Sam was back in Britain, then all his ties were here in Glasgow. His job, his church, his girlfriend. They would do anything to flush him out. The muggy heat of the kitchen suddenly seemed suffocating, as though West Africa had followed Rhona home.

'We can't tell Chrissy until we're sure.'

Sean was right. It would be too cruel, especially now.

'There's something I haven't told you,' said Rhona.

The kitten, sensing her mood, rose and stretched with a plaintive miaow, jumped lightly down and came to rub itself against her legs.

Sean waited.

'Chrissy's pregnant.'

A series of emotions played across Sean's face, and Rhona convinced herself that envy was one of them.

He shook his head in amazement. 'Sam would have loved that.' He corrected himself. 'Sam *will* love that.'

Rhona couldn't meet Sean's gaze. She'd purposefully kept this news from Sean, telling herself it was early days yet. Chrissy didn't want everyone to know. All lies, of course. Chrissy had no problem with Sean knowing about Sam's child. It was Rhona that had the problem. Ever since Sean had expressed his desire to have a child, one drunken night after his father died, Rhona had been torturing herself about it. When she'd challenged him sober, Sean had told her to forget it. That all Irishmen were maudlin in drink. But Rhona couldn't forget it, because the words had been said, and drunk or not, Sean had meant them.

'Rhona . . .'

'I'm going for a shower,' she said abruptly.

Rhona felt Sean's eyes on her back as she left the room. It was at times like this she wished she wasn't in a relationship.

4

LEANNE WOKE AT nine o'clock on Thursday morning, knowing something was wrong. Two sleeping tablets had rendered her practically unconscious, leaving her with a dry mouth and swollen tongue. She always took two when it was Terri's turn to go out. That way she didn't lie awake worrying about her.

The lurch in Leanne's stomach when she saw the empty place in the bed beside her sent her to the toilet. She retched in the sink, then turned the tap full on, rinsed out her mouth and splashed her face. In the poor light of a low-wattage bulb, her frightened face looked back at her, white and distorted. Leanne stared down at the healed sores on the blue-veined tributaries of her inner arms, testament to Terri's determination that they should both get clean.

Leanne gripped the sink, as her legs lost what little strength they had. By rights the two of them should have woken curled together, Terri at her back, arm circling Leanne, hand cupping her breast. Leanne shut her eyes, the pain of wishing like a knife in her guts.

After a moment she straightened up, went for the mobile and rang Terri's number, desperation growing with each unanswered ring.

They'd agreed from the beginning. Stay safe, call if in trouble. The phone slipped from Leanne's hand as the trembling became an uncontrollable shake. A cold sweat swept over her, rattling her teeth. She hugged herself to control the tremors and tried to think through her fear.

Wednesdays were regulars. The stall guy from the Barras market who gave Terri pirated CDs. The old man who smelt of piss and called her Marie. Wednesdays were quiet, never more than six, then home. But Terri hadn't come home.

Leanne tried the mobile at five-minute intervals while she dressed. Each time it rang out, she prayed for Terri's voice to break the endless ringing, only to hang up in despair.

She made herself a heavily milked tea with two spoonfuls of sugar, Terri's cure for just about everything, hoping it would quell the mixture of hunger and nausea that gnawed at her stomach. While she sipped it, she put on the radio and listened to the Scottish news. Dread was replaced with hope when there was nothing that might be linked with Terri.

Outside the flat, warm damp air prickled Leanne's skin, as she headed for Terri's favourite spot. On her right, the distant trees on Glasgow Green stood thick-leafed under a thunderous sky.

The network of dismal streets that made up the east end of Glasgow's red-light district, looked even shabbier in daytime. When Leanne reached the entrance to Terri's alley she hesitated, afraid of what she would find. When she finally plucked up the courage to enter, she picked her way across cobbles slimy with wind-blown rubbish and a scattering of used condoms. As her eyes became accustomed to the dimmer light, she was relieved to see the alley was empty.

Someone had vomited in Terri's doorway, splattering orange gunge on the scored wood of the door. On a nearby wall someone had spray-painted, 'Fuck you!' in red.

Leanne walked the length of the lane, looking for any sign of Terri, but found nothing. On the far wall was the mounted camera that was supposed to keep Terri safe.

Leanne passed the police station on her way to the free food van. Even now, she didn't think of going inside and reporting her fears for Terri's safety. A missing prostitute with a drug problem wouldn't be high on their list of priorities. And she was still hoping that Terri would turn up some time soon.

The van was serving breakfast. The smell of frying bacon hung in the air as Leanne approached. There were half a dozen folk in the queue, two of them women, neither of them Terri. Leanne scanned the faces, registering the ones she knew. Three of the men were strangers, the fourth a regular visitor at the van. She was relieved to see the elder of the women was Cathy, still on the game at forty-five going on sixty, everyone's pal and confidante. Her companion looked barely eighteen and hung on her arm like a wet dishcloth.

'Have you seen Terri?'

Cathy registered Leanne's worried expression immediately.

'No. Why?'

'She never came home.'

The girl beside Cathy was stoned, her eyes glazed. There was a bruise on her cheek the size of a walnut. A cold sore on her lip had lost its scab and was seeping. Leanne realised Cathy was the only thing keeping the girl on her feet.

'She needs some food inside her,' Cathy said. She took a firmer hold on her friend, preventing the girl from swaying. 'You checked Terri's spot?'

'There's no sign of her.'

'Her phone?'

'Not answering.'

Leanne knew what was going through Cathy's head. Terri had bought a fix and was flaked out somewhere until the trip was over.

'She's not using.' Leanne said.

Disbelief flickered across Cathy's face.

'She's not,' Leanne repeated, more to convince herself than Cathy. 'Did you see her last night?'

Cathy thought for a moment. 'In the queue for the food van. Then she headed off like the rest of us.'

They had reached the front.

There were two people serving – an earnest young man with red hair, and an older woman called Liz, who all the girls knew and liked. Cathy ordered two bacon rolls and two mugs of tea.

'How about you?' Liz asked Leanne.

Leanne shook her head. 'I'm looking for Terri. She never came home last night.'

Liz turned to her colleague, who was wrapping Cathy's order.

'You manage on your own for five minutes?'

As soon as Liz emerged from the van, she hugged Leanne. The motherly embrace brought tears to Leanne's eyes. She had to bite her lip hard to stop herself bawling like a baby. Cathy had propped her companion on the steps of the van and come to listen.

'Terri was here last night. Ate a good meal. I saw to that. She left around nine thirty.'

Cathy chimed in, looking as concerned as Liz. 'I'll check the drop-in centre. See if she's been there.'

'And I'll ask everyone who comes to the van. Have you got a photo?'

Leanne took out her purse and extracted the one picture of Terri she had. She hesitated before handing it over.

'I'll stick it in the window. It'll be safe there,' Liz said. 'Has Terri ever gone off before?'

Of course she had. Just like Leanne herself had done. But things had changed since they got clean. Since they got together.

Leanne shook her head. 'Something's happened to her.'

'What about the police?'

Fear gripped Leanne. She'd spent too many nights sweating in the cells and paid too many fines.

'How about if I go?' Liz said.

Leanne looked at the woman's kindly expression and wanted to kiss her. 'Would you?'

'Give me your phone number. I'll go as soon as we finish here.'

When Leanne left the van, Terri's photo was already stuck to the glass with Sellotape. If anyone had seen Terri after the food run, Liz would be the one to find out.

Despite this, Leanne didn't feel any better. A sense of dread was churning at her empty stomach. Instead of going back to the flat, she cut through Bain Street to the Gallowgate, and from there up Barrack Street. Some punters didn't like the brightly lit district and took you somewhere less obvious. The area, close to the brewery, was popular for that reason.

A police car passed her, heading up John Knox Street towards the Necropolis, quickly followed by a mortuary van. Leanne watched their progress with mounting alarm, registering the line of parked police vehicles, and the white shape of an incident tent half-way up the slope of the Necropolis.

Worry brought Leanne to a standstill. What if the hive of police activity had something to do with Terri?

5

Glasgow Pussy – Internet Blog

Wednesday July 28th
There are basically five types of flesh for hire in Glasgow. The first is the cheapest and not always value for money.

Class 1
Known as streetmeat, they can be found hanging around the Finnieston area or by Glasgow Green. Mostly mangy crackheads and criminals, there are two kinds. The dried-up worn-out clits brigade who'll do anything, ANYTHING for the money including crap and pee on request. Then the juveniles. Young, some VERY YOUNG and still fresh. Get them before the smack does. If you fancy beating up a whore, this class is for you. Nobody gives a shit what happens to them, including the police.

6

THE PROFESSIONAL ROUTINES required for a murder enquiry were like the preparations for a family funeral. They kept those involved busy and their minds off the proximity of death. For policemen and women death was, if not an everyday event, certainly a frequent one. Working in a post-industrial city like Glasgow – with a murder rate twice that of London – gave detectives the opportunity to hone their skills, and pathologists an interesting and varied workload. Dr Sissons had been heard to say at some dinner or other that he wouldn't have chosen to work anywhere else.

The incident room was buzzing, exuding a sense of purpose. Although no one would ever admit it, any investigation team would be less than thrilled to be assigned to another prostitute murder enquiry. After all, the previous eight remained unsolved. There was also an underlying belief – in the force, as well as among the general public – that, like a soldier on the front line, a street prostitute knew the dangers when they took on the job. However, the discovery of a second body buried under the first had turned the case into something much more interesting than a violent punter or a pimp taking out his anger.

The strategy meeting had been scheduled for eleven o'clock. Bill had gone home late the night before and come back early that morning. Margaret had been in good form when he'd arrived home. They were making a point of not talking about her illness, at her request. As life continued, if not as normal, then with a semblance of normality, Bill realised they were, as the literature said, 'living with cancer'. Margaret behaved the same, although now she had her bad days, which he recognised and did as she'd asked. Kept quiet and let her get on with it. The strange thing was, Bill felt the cancer was eating at him, rather than her. He was the one who looked ill.

Subsequently, he'd found Margaret surreptitously checking him for signs of fear or worry. A murder enquiry meant longer hours away from home. Bill was afraid to admit that being in the office was less of a strain than worrying about Margaret worrying about him.

The identity of the initial victim hadn't yet been established, but a call from a woman who worked on a charity food van had revealed that one of her regulars was thought to be missing. Liz Paterson had agreed to come to the mortuary later that day to check the identity of the dead woman. Even on a brief description, it sounded like a possibility. No match on fingerprints didn't mean the victim hadn't been working as a prostitute. It just meant they hadn't booked her yet.

Bill lifted the mug of coffee, now cooled to tepid just the way he liked it, and moved towards the meeting room. A guy from IT was already there, firing up the overhead projector. The screen image of the crime, with its gothic gravestones and bloodied corpse, looked like the opening of a horror movie. Once again Bill pondered the setting. Probably the two most important features of any investigation were where the crime happened and how the crime happened. The murderer had persuaded a prostitute to leave the safe area, probably by car. He'd taken her into the Necropolis, which involved parking the car somewhere along the way. How had he convinced her to go there? It was both a sensible and a stupid question. If she was a junkie, she would go anywhere and do anything for a fix. The fashion was to swallow Valium before going out on the street. Valium took the edge off, meant you didn't care what the hell was done to you, and didn't remember much afterwards. It wasn't that long ago a prostitute had been found wandering along a motorway, with her arm severed at the elbow. She couldn't remember whether her assailant had done it, or if it had happened after she had got out of the car.

Bill was startled from his reverie by the arrival of the other participants. DS McNab acknowledged him with a nod, Rhona with an inquisitive smile. He hadn't been able to discuss Margaret's illness with anyone except Rhona, although he had informed his superior officer. Detective Superintendent Sutherland had requested he be kept in the illness loop, as he put it, which Bill had so far studiously avoided.

The Super was next in, accompanied by Dr Sissons and a stranger. The unknown man was tall and broad-shouldered with slim hips, his thick brown hair pulled back in a ponytail. What intrigued Bill most were the clothes. Dressed in a brown suede jacket, open-necked checked shirt and well worn jeans, he looked uncomfortable, like a man in the outfit of an age to which he didn't belong. Bill realised his silent analysis was being matched by the stranger's equally appraising gaze. He held out his hand to Bill.

'Magnus Pirie, Department of Psychology, Strathclyde University.'

Pirie's voice exhibited the lyrical quality of the Orkney Isles. Bill recognised both the accent and the Nordic name, having spent three consecutive family holidays in a rented cottage by the harbour in Stromness. He'd loved the place, even thought of retiring there.

'Professor Pirie,' Sutherland said. 'This is Detective Inspector Bill Wilson, who is in charge of the case.'

The man's grip was firm, his hand warm. Bill had a strong sense from that grasp, and from his clear gaze, that this was a man to be trusted. Pirie released him and turned to Rhona. Bill could tell she was curious and equally impressed.

'I read your paper on the DNA characteristics of bacteria and virus samples,' said Magnus.

Rhona looked surprised. 'I didn't think psychologists were into hard science.'

'My first degree was physics, before I saw the light.'

A proponent of psychology in action was impressive to behold. Bill pondered whether Pirie had checked them all out prior to the meeting. If not, the man could read people like a book.

Superintendent Sutherland waved them to their places. Pirie waited until they were all seated before he took his own.

'Professor Pirie has been making a study of our unsolved cases of murdered prostitutes, eight over the last ten years,' Sutherland reminded them.

'There's no evidence to suggest they were committed by the same man,' Bill said defensively.

'I am aware of that. However, in view of the nature of the current case, I have asked the professor to sit in on these proceedings.' The Superintendent smiled reassuringly at Bill, then signalled to McNab to begin.

While McNab talked them through the crime scene recording, Bill watched Professor Pirie from the corner of his eye. He estimated him to be in his late thirties or early forties, which seemed young to have achieved a professorship. Orkney, Bill knew, had produced more professors per head of population than anywhere else in the UK, so maybe the man's status wasn't so strange after all. Pirie's manner, as he watched and listened to the gory details, was of studied and interested calm. He flinched neither at the images nor the descriptions. Then it was Sissons' turn to report.

'The victim was in her mid to late teens, five feet two inches in height and of slim build. She'd not eaten for some time. Various sites on the body, including the inner thigh and arms, suggested drug abuse. Tests are still being run on the breakdown of those. The sample harvest showed evidence of a number of recent sexual partners with a variety of sperm deposits evident on low vaginal, high vaginal and cervical swabs. There were also traces of condom lubricant. The six puncture wounds on her genital area were made by a blunt-ended object, probably the stiletto heel found inserted in her vagina. That is still to be confirmed by forensics. The wounds were inflicted before death, causing a large loss of blood. However, death was by asphyxiation.' Sissons paused at a small gesture from Professor Pirie, who wished to ask a question.

'Are you able to deduce at which stage in the murder the sexual act occurred?'

'We can't assume that the murderer had sex with the victim,' Rhona said.

Dr Sissons agreed. 'The victim had more than one partner shortly before she died. However, as Dr Mac-Leod rightly says, we cannot assume that one of those men killed her.'

'I appreciate that, but is it possible to deduce whether a sexual act took place after death?'

'Of course, that would be important,' agreed Rhona.

'Crucial, from a psychological perspective. The contact a murderer has with his victim leaves a behavioural trace, just as he leaves chemical and biological traces.'

'Unless significant non-vital injuries have been sustained, you cannot say when sex occurred,' Sissons confirmed.

'I removed the stiletto on site,' Rhona said. 'There was little obvious damage, which probably suggests the victim wasn't resisting by this time. Does that help?'

'Yes, thank you.' The professor fell silent.

Bill had listened to this interchange with growing concern. It wasn't that he dismissed psychological profiling per se, but just because *Cracker* made good prime-time TV, didn't mean it worked in real life.

Sutherland, on the other hand, looked impressed by the professor's contribution. Bill wondered if this was his superior officer's pet project, designed to show Strathclyde force was at the forefront of new developments in detection.

The rest of the meeting continued as normal. Bill revealed a prostitute had been reported missing by a member of a Christian organisation, which provided free food to those in need, and told them that Ms Paterson would be coming to the mortuary that afternoon to view the body.

Rhona began her report on the various samples taken from the scene, and the grim discovery of a second body with similar injuries beneath the first.

The professor interrupted again. 'How well buried was it?'

'Sufficiently to avoid being dug up by marauding animals.'

'Was there any evidence to suggest he might have attempted to bury the second one with the first?'

'No. The Victorian grave has a metal lid a couple of feet below the surface, so there wasn't much room.'

'How long had the first body been there?'

Sissons answered this time. 'We can't be exact because of the degree of decomposition, but probably upwards of a month.'

Pirie was silent for a moment, then said, 'I think there's another nearby, either buried or hidden.'

'Why?' Rhona asked.

'He took the two women to the same place and killed them in the same way. The distinguishing feature between the two murders is his disposal of the body. Organised killers hide their kill, unless they become confident they can't be caught. To have reached that level of confidence, he must have killed before, more than once.'

Bill had already worked that out without a degree in psychology. That's why he had men combing the graveyard and surrounding area. That's why he already had a team headed up by DC Clark on the streets of Calton, and another going through missing persons. Bill realised Pirie was watching him, no doubt reading his expression.

'Nothing I suggest will be new to you, Inspector. Everything I've learned has come from people in the front line, like yourself.'

It was a nice little speech. Suitably deferential. Bill wasn't impressed, but from the look on his face Sutherland was. Bill silently wondered, if Pirie had really meant what he'd just said, then how the hell having him around was going to help at all.

7

'HAVE YOU TIME for a coffee?'

Bill had made a swift getaway after the meeting. Superintendent Sutherland had 'left the professor in Dr MacLeod's capable hands', suggesting she help him in any way she could. Rhona decided to play along, if only to give Bill peace for a while.

'If you don't mind having it back at the forensic lab?'

Professor Pirie's face lit up and Rhona realised that was what he'd wanted all along.

'I'd love to take a look at the evidence you collected.'

'Superintendent Sutherland ordered us to welcome you into the fold.'

He looked discomfited by the remark and Rhona relented. 'A joke,' she said hastily. A good psychologist would be able to tell she was lying. Pirie was a good psychologist.

'I'm sorry if Superintendent Sutherland has made things difficult by asking me in. But I do appreciate the opportunity to study the case.'

It was strange, even eerie, to meet a man who could read mood and manner so accurately.

'I deal in the minutiae. You might learn more from Bill.'

He met her gaze. 'We both deal in the traces the perpetrator leaves behind.'

Rhona wanted to argue that her traces were real and scientifically proven, but for the moment she held her tongue.

Chrissy's reaction when Rhona walked in with Professor Pirie was worth the awkward journey. Rhona's offer of a lift had been met with the news he'd come by bicycle. After discussing the possibility of him following the car, they'd agreed to put the bike in the back. Travelling with the handlebars between them had at least discouraged further conversation.

'This is Professor Pirie . . .' Rhona began.

'Magnus.' He held out his hand to an open-mouthed Chrissy.

'Chrissy's my right-hand woman,' Rhona explained, since Chrissy seemed uncharacteristically tongue-tied. 'Professor Pirie is an investigative psychologist. The Super asked him in to help with the Necropolis murders.'

'Cool.'

'Chrissy is a *Cracker* fan,' Rhona explained.

'And *Wire in the Blood*, and *Prime Suspect* and . . .'

'I think he gets the picture.'

Magnus smiled. 'So am I,' he admitted. 'I only wish I had the same results as my small-screen equivalents.'

'Is there any coffee?' Rhona said to break up the prime-time TV admiration society.

'Of course,' Chrissy looked up at Magnus. 'How do you like it?'

'Black, no sugar.'

When Magnus excused himself to go to the toilet, Chrissy gave Rhona her unadulterated opinion.

'Wow. I wouldn't mind him studying me in detail.'

'You're pregnant.'

'The perfect contraceptive.'

'What about Sam?' Rhona regretted the question as soon as it escaped her lips.

'Sam's dead,' Chrissy said flatly.

Rhona chose her words carefully. 'You don't know that for sure.'

The brazen Chrissy was gone, replaced by a vulnerable one. 'We both know he's dead. So why keep pretending?'

A discreet cough behind them indicated Magnus's return. Rhona wondered how long he had been standing in the doorway, listening to their conversation.

Chrissy turned abruptly away. 'I'd better get on.'

Rhona had hoped to deposit Magnus with Chrissy, but that was no longer an option. She would have to deal with him herself.

Rhona began with the victim's skirt. The plastic material, designed to resemble snakeskin, was spotted with dark splashes of what was probably the victim's blood. Intermingled were lighter coloured areas which might or might not have been seminal fluid.

'The haemoglobin of mammals has the capacity to behave as an enzyme in the presence of hydrogen peroxide,' she explained for Magnus's benefit. 'We use this to test for blood.'

Rhona rubbed a damp filter paper over a stain, then added a drop of leucomalachite. When the colour remained unchanged, she added the hydrogen peroxide, and watched it turn green.

'It is blood, but this is a presumptive test. It doesn't tell us it's human, only mammal.'

Magnus watched as she applied a similar test for the presence of semen.

As Rhona became absorbed in her work, she stopped explaining. The skirt seemed to have become an artist's palette, painting the picture of a life she could barely imagine. At first glance the skirt had no pockets, but as Rhona went over it in finer detail, she discovered an opening at the back, close to the waistband. A twenty-pound note had been slipped inside. Magnus came closer as she carefully unfolded it with her latex-covered fingers.

'If this is a punter's note, he should have left some trace of himself on it, hopefully a fingerprint.'

She was exerting little to no pressure on the note, yet the portion that lay between her finger and thumb began to disintegrate. Rhona dropped the note lightly on the table.

'Was it wet?' Magnus asked in amazement.

'Water wouldn't do that. It has to be a chemical reaction.'

'Drugs?'

'Probably. A lot of notes in circulation have deposits of cocaine on them. But cocaine isn't corrosive. More likely it's crystal methamphetamine. The German Bundesbank had a problem recently with twenty-

and fifty-euro notes disintegrating on touch. Turned out crystal meth was the culprit. When a contaminated note comes into contact with human sweat, it produces an acid.'

'But you're wearing gloves.'

'The reaction had already occurred. I just disturbed it.' She told him about Chrissy's explanation for the tweek marks on the victim's arms and thighs.

'Looks like she was right,' Magnus said.

'We'll see once we get the toxicology results.'

'So what happens about the fingerprints?'

'I think we just lost them.'

When she finished with the skirt, Magnus asked to look at the bra and the stiletto. Rhona wasn't ready to work on those yet, but she brought them out for Magnus to examine. He stood in silence, staring down at them, deep in thought.

'Can I smell them?'

'Provided you don't make contact.'

Magnus picked up the bra with his gloved hands, held it close to his mask and breathed in.

Rhona's initial reaction was surprise, then discomfort, as though she was observing a man indulging a sexual fetish. Then Magnus asked her to smell it too. Rhona decided to humour him. She took her time, breathing in, looking for something other than the scent of cheap perfume and deodorant. The result puzzled her. There was a scent, faint but unrecognisable.

'You can smell him?'

'I can smell something. I have no idea what it is.'

When Magnus left shortly afterwards, he gave her his card and asked for Rhona's contact number.

'When you're not so busy, I'd like us to talk some more.'

Rhona told him her life would be like this for weeks, perhaps – God forbid – months. The lab would be working flat out, with help needed from other labs. Two deaths meant two separate enquiries. Another DI would be brought in to head another team, even though the deaths were related. When Magnus looked concerned, Rhona felt sorry for him and relented.

'Do you know The Ultimate Jazz Club near Byres Road?' Magnus nodded. 'Chrissy and I will be there tonight around seven.'

Free of Magnus's presence in the laboratory, Rhona continued her methodical study of the victim's clothing. Back-to-back murders allowed precious little time to amass and study evidence, which meant they were always one step behind the killer. She needed to find something for Bill, before the killer struck again.

8

Glasgow Pussy – Internet Blog

Friday July 30th
Two mangy crackheads lying one on top of the other. One fresh meat, the other rotting. The police didn't even know the rotting one was missing. Told you. No one gives a shite.

9

BILL ESTIMATED LIZ Paterson to be in her late fifties, with a Scottish accent he couldn't place. She reminded him of a primary teacher he'd liked. Underneath the motherly exterior, Bill suspected the woman had nerves of steel. Serving free food every night to the underbelly of Glasgow, she'd need them.

Liz explained about Leanne and her concern for Terri. 'They're a couple. Terri was, *is*, determined to get them both clean – and she's succeeding.' Liz's voice faltered. 'They're only seventeen.'

Bill absorbed this information in silence. In his experience, getting 'clean' was a promise seldom kept. Drug addicts were no longer in control of their thoughts, their lives or their souls. The devil Bill had been taught about as a child had adapted himself to the modern world. Now he acquired souls chemically.

'And Terri disappeared last night?'

'Yes.'

Bill began to explain the procedure Liz would have to go through.

'It's okay. I've done this before,' Liz said grimly.

Bill left her in the viewing room while he went into

the mortuary. Sandra, the young assistant, greeted him in her usual friendly manner.

'She's all ready for you.' She indicated a draped body lying next to the viewing window.

Someone had done a good job. The face was even younger now that it was cleansed of make-up. The pale, veined eyelids had been gently closed on the terrified eyes. The vicious marks on her neck were concealed by a white sheet. No matter how many times he'd stood in that place, Bill had never grown accustomed to this laundered image of death. Since news of Margaret's illness, he'd sensed death stalking him, a dark shadow that loomed over his entire family. Something he could no longer leave at the office, or here in the chemical cleanliness of the mortuary.

'Okay?' Sandra nudged his arm.

Bill nodded and went through. He wanted to be beside Liz when she identified Terri's body.

Liz stood very close to the glass as the curtain was drawn back. Bill heard her gasp when the face came into view, and his first reaction was to assume the worst.

'I'm sorry,' he began.

'It's not Terri!' she said, a mixture of relief and sorrow evident in her voice. 'It's Lucie.' She gripped his arm to steady herself.

Liz had obviously steeled herself for a particular outcome and had been completely thrown by this one. Bill guided the woman to a chair. She let go of his arm and sat down.

'You know the victim?'

Liz's face had drained of colour. 'She came to the van sometimes with an older guy.'

'Her pimp?'

'Probably.'

'Do you know his name?'

Liz was visibly trying to marshall herself. 'Lucie called him Minty, I think.'

'Craig Minto? Big guy, balding, with a tattoo on his cheek?'

'He was bad to her,' Liz growled.

'Minty's bad to everyone, except himself.'

This wasn't the first time DC Janice Clark had visited the drop-in centre. Dressed in jeans and a loose top, if she didn't blend in exactly, neither did she stand out. She was alone, which meant she was less threatening and more likely to get a positive response. The woman in charge was called Marje Thomson. Janice suspected Marje knew as much about life on the streets as her charges did, except she'd got away – at least as far as here. Marje recognised Janice immediately and gave her an appraising look.

'You'll never get picked up dressed like that.'

Janice pretended offence. 'Why not?'

'No flesh showing. The punters like to see what they're buying.'

Marje laughed, a deep-throated rumble that betrayed a forty-a-day habit. She gestured Janice towards a back door, indicating her need to feed her nicotine craving. The exit led to a small paved courtyard littered with dog-ends, which the rain had mashed to a soggy thin carpet.

Marje lit up and took a deep drag, sending the smoke swiftly to her lungs. 'We send these lassies out every night to get beaten, raped and buggered, but we can't let them smoke on the premises because it's bad for their health.' She shook her head in disbelief and took another draw.

Janice waited until Marje had enough nicotine to relax, then said, 'The female body found in the Necropolis has been identified as Lucie Webster.'

Marje looked shocked. 'Wee Lucie?'

'You knew her?'

'She was a regular here. Not every night, but at least a couple of times a week.' Marje looked puzzled. 'The news said a young woman. It didn't mention she was a prostitute.'

'DI Wilson wanted it that way initially.'

'Oh, I see. Get Joe Public on your side. The same public that heads here after dark looking for a cheap screw with some wee lassie barely out of school.' Marje blew smoke fiercely into the air. The whites of her eyes were yellowed, the irises brown, flecked with gold. Her lip curled, and Janice thought she resembled a lioness furiously defending her cubs. She took another pull at the cigarette, her hand trembling.

'There was a second body buried beneath Lucie.'

Marje's face turned the colour of putty. 'What?'

'They think it's been there at least a month.'

Marje's shock was fast turning to outrage. 'The bastard!'

'Is there any other girl you haven't seen for a while?'

Marje thought for a moment before answering. 'It can't have been a regular. Not if she's been missing a month. Some turn up once or twice at the centre, then we never see them again. They head for bigger pickings down south. Newcastle. Birmingham, London.'

'I'd like to talk to as many of the girls as I can. Warn them what's going on.'

'Sure.' The forgotten cigarette dropped ash at Marje's feet.

'We need your help to get the man who did this.'

Marje scowled. 'Like you got the other eight men who did the same thing?'

Janice knew better than to make excuses. 'The safe area has helped.'

Marje dropped the dog-end and ground it underfoot. 'Until now.'

The small room was home to a two-seater settee, a chair and a coffee table. A corner stand held an electric kettle, a tray with mugs, a jar of instant coffee, some milk in a carton and a pile of teabags.

Marje assured Janice the room would remain private to herself and whoever she was talking to. She was true to her word. Three girls trooped in one after another, accepted a cup of coffee and sat opposite Janice on the settee. If her mother had seen these poor souls she would have wanted to take them home, convinced that good food and motherly love would cure them of life's ills.

Janice gave each of them the same story. They were being told the truth to keep them safe. The word 'safe' rang hollow in her ears each time she said it. To these girls there was nothing more frightening in life than not having the next fix. They would be out on the street tonight, like every other night, to make sure they got it. As to Janice's enquiry about a missing girl, none of the three could offer an answer. They knew Lucie through the centre. They weren't aware of anyone else going missing.

The fourth girl was different. She accepted the coffee with shaking hands, told Janice her name was Leanne, then burst into a terrified babble about her missing friend Terri Docherty. It took Janice ten minutes to get the whole story.

'I thought it was Terri they found in the graveyard, but Liz went to identify the body . . .'

'Liz?'

'She works on the food van. I told her about Terri not coming home and she went to the police.'

'And Terri's been missing for how long?'

'It was her night on. I was asleep. She's usually home by two.'

'So she's been missing since two o'clock this morning?'

'He's got her. I know he has.' Her voice rose in a wail.

'Who's got her?'

'The man who killed Lucie.'

10

MAGNUS PEERED INTO the shallow grave.

The light filtering through the tent made him think of camping with the cub scouts when he was eight years old. The acrid aroma of decomposition and raw earth smelt like the pit latrine they had laboriously dug. Magnus had been frightened of that pit. Frightened of falling into it in the dark. Of drowning in other people's shit. All Magnus could remember about the weekend camp was the smell of those toilets. Now, no doubt, chemical toilets would be used. But not thirty years ago on Orkney.

Magnus breathed in, assimilating and separating all the various odours that occupied the tent. As a child, his father had declared his son to have the scenting capability of a bloodhound. The waves of nausea that often accompanied Magnus's olfactory episodes had eventually lessened, and he'd grown able to concentrate on analysing and categorising the mix of scents that regularly assailed him. Gradually the smells of his island home became familiar and comforting, even at their strongest – a dead sheep in a field ditch, a rotting seal's carcass on the shore.

When he'd moved to Glasgow to attend university, the city had bombarded him with scents of its own. As an adult he'd learned, if not to turn off his intense sense of smell, at least to manage it by ignoring or tuning in to it at will. It was only while in a state of high emotion the full force of Magnus's gift (for he now thought of it that way) showed itself.

Both bodies had been removed from the site. Magnus would have preferred to have studied them *in situ*. He'd surveyed the many photographs taken by the forensic team and the detailed video footage of the crime scene. None of these was as good as being present.

Magnus closed his eyes and put his hands flat against the headstone. The grey granite felt cool and solid under his palms. Many people were disturbed by cemeteries. Magnus had never felt that way. Coming from Orkney, where ancient burial sites were a familiar part of the landscape, Magnus felt at ease near the dead. Although this ostentatious graveyard bore no resemblance to the windswept clusters of carved stones that marked the end of life in Orkney.

Magnus felt a tingle begin in his hands, as the energy trapped in the stone transmitted itself to his body, then onwards and upwards until it concentrated in his lips. In this state of receptiveness, he allowed his mind to roam at will. The scents that surrounded him grew stronger and ever more pungent, hitting him in waves. When people spoke of smelling fear they were right. Fear smelt as individual as the human gripped by it; their natural scent mixed with terror-fuelled perspiration, sexual energy, the acrid aroma of urine and the stench of loosened bowels. Serial killers needed that scent to feed their fantasies, just as vampires fed on blood.

The location chosen by an organised killer was as important as the modus operandi. But the signature of the killer was the most important aspect of all, and the two were not the same.

In each of the recent deaths, the victim had been strangled with her bra, knotted in a particular way. Then the bodies had been mutilated with the heels of their shoes. The modus operandi was strangulation. The signature was the knot and the mutilation.

Magnus imagined the feel of her bra in his hands, recalled the smell when he'd held it to his nose. The murderer's scent was on that item. That, and the shoe. Both had become an extended part of the perpetrator's being. Without a survivor to talk with, Magnus could never know the full narrative between the murderer and his victim. But the level of violence suggested an aggressive offender, who used the victim as a vehicle to reflect his own anger. And anger like that did not dissipate easily.

Magnus let his hands drop by his side and waited for the pulse that beat rapidly in the hollow of his neck to slow. Gradually the world of scent receded and his other senses reasserted themselves. Somewhere in the nearby undergrowth, a female blackbird sang, rich and fluting. Magnus felt a sudden and overwhelming sadness, as he contrasted her simple song of life with the violent death that had occurred nearby.

He spent another hour investigating the surrounding paths, worrying the police officer left to guard the site, with his constant toing and froing. As the summer light began to fade, the Necropolis became a place of shadows, night sounds and scents, just as it had been when the murderer had struck. Before Magnus left, he told the incredulous duty officer he would return around two o'clock in the morning.

The evening commuter rush was still at its peak when Magnus left the City of the Dead. Weaving through the stationary traffic on his bike brought a chorus of irritated horns, which he ignored. Checking his watch, he found he had half an hour before he was due at the jazz club, so he made for the designated red-light area. As he explored the network of streets, Magnus considered why he'd asked to speak further with Dr MacLeod. It hadn't been a sudden decision. His observation of her in the strategy meeting had prompted it. As a physicist, he understood her confidence in her science, but he'd also observed how her use of science was married to an intuitive nature. And intuition, as far as Magnus was concerned, was simply psychology in action.

Descending the steps of the jazz club, Magnus was met by the hum of voices. As his eyes became accustomed to the light, he saw an open space in front of a small stage, circled by clusters of tables and chairs. Most of the current occupants were gathered at the bar. Magnus searched the heads and spotted Rhona sitting on a stool next to her assistant, Chrissy. Magnus stood for a moment, observing their interaction, before making his way across. He'd sensed an underlying tension between them, and wanted to avoid a repeat of the awkward moment he'd generated in the lab.

He wasn't surprised when Rhona sensed his approach, despite having her back towards him. She turned and gave him a cautious smile.

'Professor Pirie.'

'Magnus,' he urged.

'Magnus,' she repeated. 'What would you like to drink?'

'It's my call. After all, I asked to talk to you.'

'Okay,' she conceded. 'I'll have a glass of white wine.'

Magnus turned to Chrissy, who shook her head. 'I'm off home.'

'I didn't mean to drive you away.'

'You haven't.' Chrissy slid off the stool. 'See you tomorrow,' she said to Rhona.

When the drinks arrived, Magnus asked for a cognac glass, tipped his whisky into it, then handed it to Rhona.

'Tell me what you smell.'

'Is this another of your tests?'

'You could say that.'

Rhona obliged him with a sniff, then shrugged her shoulders. 'I smell whisky.'

'This time swirl the liquid around the glass, then move it slowly from right to left under your nose.'

Rhona threw him a glance suggesting there was a limit to her humouring him, then did as he asked, curiosity getting the better of her.

'Now what do you smell?'

She thought for a moment. 'Peat and,' she paused, 'heather?'

Magnus grinned. 'Very good. The peat on Orkney is quite unique. It has very little wood content. Because of the wind, the heather is deep-rooted and resilient. Highland Park aromas reflect where it was made. You have a good nose.'

Rhona didn't look convinced. 'It was a calculated guess.'

'But you did smell those things?'

Rhona conceded. She was softening, meeting his smile with one of her own.

'That scent on the bra. Did you find out what it was?'

Rhona shook her head. 'Not yet. But I did identify the knot he used.'

'And?'

'It was a slipknot, also known as a simple noose. Very effective and you don't have to be an expert to tie it.'

'What about the other corpse?'

'The same.'

Magnus reached down and loosened the lace on his right shoe.

'What are you doing?'

'Let's see who knows how to tie a slipknot.'

The barman came over to ask if they needed a refill. Magnus handed him the shoelace.

'Tie me a slipknot.'

Fifteen minutes later, Magnus had proved his point. Out of ten selected people, only one could tie a slipknot.

'Okay,' Rhona said. 'Not everyone can tie a slip-knot.'

'Could you tell if he was right- or left-handed?'

'You can't necessarily tell, but the chirality, the usual direction of movement, is generally consistent.'

'And?'

'If I was asked to put a bet on it, I would say the man who tied the knot was left-handed.'

'So a left-handed former cub scout with a distinctive if unrecognisable smell?'

He had succeeded in making her laugh. It wasn't something he was in the habit of trying with women. Magnus felt a stirring in his groin and turned towards the bar and his whisky. Flirting with the chief forensic on the case wasn't wise, but the heightening of all his senses through sexual desire could prove useful.

An Irish male voice caused him to turn. A dark-haired man stood next to Rhona, his hand resting on the nape of her neck in an intimate manner.

'Sean, this is Professor Magnus Pirie. He's working on the Necropolis case as an investigative psychologist.'

Magnus took the offered hand. Sean's eyes were a keen blue with a smile lurking at the corners. Magnus realised immediately that this was Rhona's lover, and he envied him a little for that. If this showed on his face, Sean didn't react.

'Pleased to meet you.' Sean turned back to Rhona. 'I'm on at ten. Fancy something to eat first?'

Magnus realised that good manners might result in

Rhona asking him to join them, so he got in before she could answer.

'Don't let me keep you. I'll see you tomorrow at the meeting.'

Magnus looked back from the doorway to watch Sean tip Rhona's chin up and kiss her. The image stimulated the memory of her scent. Not the subtle perfume she wore, but the underlying fragrance of her skin.

II

'TERRI SAID SHE would come.'

'Might come,' Nora's husband reminded her.

Nora lifted the teapot and topped up her mug to avoid replying. David's face had assumed a closed look again. Heartbreak did that to you. Sometimes Nora wondered how she and David operated at all, with joy and happiness such a thing of the past.

She took a mouthful of tea, a functional movement like all the others that made up her day. Reasons to be busy. Too busy to think. Nora pressed a finger to her right temple. Her head was thick from drinking too much wine the previous evening. It had started out with a couple of glasses with dinner. David had had a beer, which had put Nora in dangerous territory. When he'd gone out after the meal, Nora had lingered downstairs, waiting for the phone to ring. By ten she'd drunk the remainder of the bottle. She should have gone upstairs then, but instead of making her drowsy, the alcohol had put her on high alert. She'd found herself focusing on the creak of the wind in the trees outside. She hadn't wanted to give up on the night. Give up hope that Terri would call or turn up on the doorstep, like she'd done on previous occasions.

When the phone had finally rung, the sudden noise was like a knife in her aching head. Nora had snatched the receiver from its cradle and, seeing the caller ID, had expected Terri's voice. But there had been no voice, just a constant swish, like tyres through puddles. Then a thump, then nothing. Nora had immediately dialled Terri's number, but it rang and rang with no answer. Nora hung up, worried and frustrated.

She'd told David the story over breakfast. He'd listened patiently enough, then said it was time she gave up the pretence that Terri was a normal daughter.

'Terri doesn't know what the truth is. Not since she became an addict.'

'She's still Terri underneath,' Nora had insisted.

At that point, David's lips had thinned to an angry line and Nora had known to hold her tongue.

Nora threw her husband a surreptitious look. Sometimes she thought David suffered more than she did. His silence was the silence of the walking dead. He went through the motions of being alive, but in reality he had died when Terri walked out the door, after their last of many attempts to help her get off drugs. Nora, on the other hand, still clung to hope like a life raft; a phone call once a month, if she was lucky, her daughter's voice a moment's oasis in the desert that had become Nora's life.

Nora waited until David left for his job at the Marina, then called Terri's number again. When the result was the same as before, she phoned the provider's helpline. Despite the man's professional tone,

Nora got the impression he wasn't interested in teenage daughters who didn't call home.

'But it was her number. There was a strange background sound, then it went dead,' Nora explained.

'That can happen if the call button is pressed by accident. The caller doesn't realise the call is being made.'

His explanation didn't satisfy Nora. Her state of high alert stayed with her all morning. She went through the chores like a zombie, her mind churning. In their last conversation, Terri had told Nora she was coming off heroin, this time for good. Nora had heard it all before, but there was something in Terri's voice that had fed her hope. She'd never told David about that conversation. She hadn't wanted to see the despair and anger in his eyes, so she'd kept the words to herself, playing them over and over in her head, like a mantra.

At ten o'clock Nora turned on the radio and listened to the Scottish news. The headline about the body of a young woman found dead in a Glasgow graveyard sent her running to the phone. The hotline number given for the public response was busy and Nora was put on hold for five minutes. By the time someone answered, Nora was so frightened she could hardly speak.

'My daughter's missing. She was supposed to call last night.'

A voice asked for her daughter's name and address.

'Terri Docherty.' Nora's face flushed with shame. 'I'm sorry, I don't know her current address.'

'Terri Docherty?' the voice repeated.

'Yes.'

There was a moment's silence, then the voice said, 'Mrs Docherty, I'm going to transfer you to someone who will take details.'

Nora went cold. 'Please God no,' she whispered to herself.

'I'm passing you over to a police officer now.'

Nora sank to her knees, still grasping the phone. A man's voice came on the line.

'Mrs Docherty, this is DS McNab. Tell me about your daughter.'

Two uniformed officers arrived at midday. Nora was in the garden, staring up at the tree house. Terri had spent all her time up there, after her brother died. Separated by only ten months, Philip and Terri had been like twins, although Philip had always led and Terri had followed. Philip's death aged sixteen, from a brain haemorrhage had been like an explosion at the heart of their family, its shock waves weakening the foundations that held them together. The doctor had told them to let their daughter deal with her grief in her own way. Terri's way had been to shut out both her parents, as though the anguish were all her own.

The two officers accepted Nora's offer of tea, and she went into the kitchen and put the kettle on. She wondered how many teas or coffees they were subjected to in any given day and if they merely drank them out of kindness. Nora's hand trembled as she poured boiling water into the teapot and set mugs, milk and sugar on a tray. Through the open door to the sitting room, her visitors sat awkwardly at either end of the sofa, like a couple who weren't on speaking terms.

They waited in silence while Nora went through the ritual of dispensing the tea. The man, who introduced himself as PC Connachie, accepted her offer of a chocolate biscuit. It was the woman, PC Ferguson, who spoke first.

'DS McNab explained that the body found has been identified and it isn't Terri?'

Nora nodded.

'We're here because someone else reported a Terri Docherty missing.'

Nora's hand gave an involuntary jerk, spilling drops of hot tea in her lap. She brushed them off and set the mug on the tray. She pondered for a brief moment, whether it might have been David who called the police, then dismissed the idea.

'Do you know a Leanne Quinn?'

Nora repeated the name. 'No, I don't think so.'

The officer passed Nora a copy of a photograph. It had been scanned, then printed out. The colours were vibrant, almost too bright.

'Is this your daughter?'

Nora stared down at the image of Terri, taken before cheekbones had become the defining feature of her face.

'She doesn't look like that any more.' Nora swallowed hard. She rose and fetched a small photo from a nearby desk drawer and handed it to the female PC. 'My daughter is a heroin addict. This is what she looks like now.' Nora watched as the constable masked her shock at the contrast between the two images.

'The drug eats them up,' Nora said quietly.

'When did you last hear from Terri?' the man asked.

'Nearly a month ago. She said she would be home this weekend.' Nora explained about the strange phone call.

'A handbag was found this morning on the Kingston Bridge,' the man said. 'It had a mobile in it that had been damaged. Leanne Quinn identified the bag as Terri's.'

Nora's hand rose involuntarily to her throat. 'Oh dear God.'

They waited until she had control of herself.

'We're concerned for your daughter's welfare. We suspect she may have got into a client's car . . .'

'A client?' Nora interrupted him. She watched them exchange glances. 'Terri was on benefit, and I put three hundred pounds in her account every month to make sure she had enough.'

It would never have been enough. Not to pay for drugs. Nora had known that all along, though she'd never admitted it, even to herself.

PC Connachie cleared his throat. 'According to Leanne Quinn, she and Terri were working as prostitutes.'

When the officers left, Nora went quickly to the drinks cabinet and poured a large vodka. She swallowed it down before she could change her mind. She didn't want to get drunk, she just wanted to force her heart to keep beating.

Prostitute. She couldn't say the word. Dark images of men jerking against her daughter's thin, wasted body filled her head.

'My baby. My baby,' she muttered.

The vodka hit her stomach and came back up minutes later. Nora barely made it to the kitchen, launching herself at the sink, as the regurgitated alcohol burned its way back up her throat.

When she felt steadier, she went outside and walked purposefully to the tree house. At the foot of the steps was a bench where you could rest against the trunk. Nora leaned back and clasped her hands to stop them shaking. The most important thing was that Terri was still alive. She had to believe that. The police were worried for Terri's safety and were looking for her. A photo would be on tonight's news.

It was such a small and fragile hope to cling to.

Nora thought of David. How would he deal with his daughter's face broadcast to the nation, the details of her heroin addiction exposed? Worst of all, how could David cope with the knowledge that his daughter was a prostitute?

12

THE HANDBAG WAS a designer copy. Something you could buy from a stall at the Glasgow Barras for a couple of pounds, made by some poor soul in China for starvation wages. Inside was a wallet, with sixty pounds in four tenners and a twenty note, and about two quid in change. The various side pouches contained a few receipts, mainly for food, a couple of Tesco vouchers, and a snapshot of Leanne Quinn and Terri Docherty, faces squashed together in a photo booth. There was also a picture of a small brown dog, looking inquisitively up at the camera, which looked as though it had been cut from a magazine.

The mobile phone had been almost completely crushed by the car, which had marked the bag with muddy tyre tracks. It had been given to the Tech department to extract Terri's address book. Bill scanned the subsequent list. Leanne was there and Terri's mum. The rest were men's names, most of them probably nicknames to protect the 'innocent'.

Glasgow men were estimated to spend around 6 million a year on prostitution. More graduates bought sex than those who hadn't had the advantage of a university education. Bill had read all the statistics.

None of which made it easier to understand. He had a daughter, the same age as Lucie Webster. The same age as the missing girl. Bill was sickened by a sudden image of his daughter Lisa, lying on the cold earth, her bra tight around her neck, her body punctured and raped by the heel of her shoe. It made his blood run cold.

'Sir?' DC Clark brought him back to the moment. 'Leanne Quinn's here.'

Leanne scanned the list. As she turned the page, her hand trembled.

'We didn't talk about the punters much. I don't know everyone on this.'

'What about Wednesday nights? Did Terri have regulars then?'

'An old guy. He smelt of piss. He called her Marie. Terri said it was his dead wife's name. She felt sorry for him.'

'What was he called?'

Leanne pointed halfway down. 'Geordie.'

Bill put a cross beside it. 'Anyone else?'

'Cee Dee. He has a stall at the Barras. Gives us free CDs and DVDs. Every Wednesday night.'

'Anyone else?'

'There was a guy every other week. Terri was really upset the first time he showed up.'

'Why?'

'She said he'd been her guidance teacher in secondary school.'

'What?'

'Terri knew him right away, but she said he pretended not to recognise her.'

'Is he on the list?'

'He didn't use his real name. He called himself something out of a book or a film, Terri said.' Leanne found it and pointed. 'That's it I think.'

'Atticus?'

'*To Kill a Mockingbird*,' DC Clark offered.

'I know where it's from,' snapped Bill.

Leanne identified two more. A young guy called Gary, who came up from south of the city twice a month, and a posh bloke calling himself Ray.

Leanne sagged back.

'Did Terri ever say anything about a punter hurting her?'

'They all think you're shite. Some pretend not to, to get what they want. A few get off on pretending to be your friend.' She paused. 'They're all abusive, one way or another.'

Bill was silent for a moment. 'We're advising that the women stay off the streets until further notice.'

Leanne gave a small, strangled laugh.

'Too late for Terri.'

'We don't know that.'

'If she was alive she would have contacted me.' Leanne hugged herself. 'We were getting out. Two more months, that's all we needed.' Her body seemed to fold in on itself.

'Are you okay?'

Leanne's face had drained of colour. 'I'm fine.'

'You don't look fine to me,' Bill said. 'Have you had anything to eat today?'

Leanne shook her head.

'Take her to the canteen,' Bill told Janice. 'Make sure she eats something.'

During a post-mortem, the mortuary harboured a smell Bill would never get used to. He had never been sick, or fainted, or had to leave, but it had been a close shave on occasion. Work on the second body, or what was left of it, had taken time. Time to determine the obvious scientifically. The victim had most likely died of strangulation.

The lower half of the body was in an advanced state of decomposition, but striated marks on the pelvic bones suggested the heel of the shoe had been used to stab the victim. For this one, there would be no gentle closing of eyes, no masking of wounds with the pristine whiteness of a sheet. No one to tell them who she was.

'Female, approximately twenty,' Sissons told Bill. 'Five foot two inches tall. Long blonde hair. Under-nourished.'

A fair description of most of Glasgow's young prostitutes.

'Nothing that could help identify her?'

'You could try dental records. She's had some work done, but it looks pretty old.'

13

THE BRA WAS black nylon with a lace covering, the details of size and make no longer legible on the frayed label. It was clean and smelt primarily of deodorant, although there was something else in the scent she still couldn't distinguish.

Rhona held the bra over paper and used a fine-haired brush to dislodge any loose trace evidence, then taped it to lift any other residue, concentrating on the knot. Trace material depended a lot on the recipient surface and the nature, duration and force of the contact. The murderer had exerted a lot of pressure when he had twisted the rough lace, so he should have left traces behind.

Rhona's careful harvest was rewarded with abundant skin flakes for DNA testing, and something else, which proved to be a little more unusual. She examined the printout of the chemical breakdown of the sample. Sodium chloride, sulphate, calcium, potassium and magnesium. There was no doubt what it was.

Rhona looked up as a pale Chrissy emerged from the washroom, after a bout of morning sickness. It had been like this every day for weeks. Rhona wasn't allowed to say anything, her words of comfort freezing on her lips under Chrissy's glare. Having made up her mind to go through with the pregnancy, Chrissy wasn't looking for sympathy. Rhona had wondered if lab work was triggering the bouts of nausea, or at least exacerbating them. Chrissy had dismissed the idea.

'I'm sick at the same time every morning. It doesn't matter where I am.'

Ten minutes later Chrissy was serving up coffee and hot buttered rolls, the colour back in her cheeks.

'Right, where are we then?'

'Exactly where we were yesterday, with one exception,' Rhona said. 'Magnus was right. There was something unusual on the bra.'

'What?'

'Traces of salt.'

'Salt? You mean table salt?'

Rhona shook her head. 'Not pure sodium chloride. I checked the constituents. This was sea salt.'

Chrissy looked puzzled. 'Why would there be sea salt?'

'You remember the smell Magnus talked about? It was a mix of diesel and salt, the smell you get around harbours.'

Chrissy looked thoughtful. 'It's something, I suppose.'

'There's also the matter of the slipknot.' Rhona told Chrissy the story of Magnus's experiment in the bar.

Chrissy smiled. 'Wish I'd stuck around to see that.'

'I tried to retie the knot, before I began headspace analysis to test for diesel. It wasn't easy tying it with a bra. A single piece of cord would have been much quicker.'

'So the bra was significant.'

Rhona nodded. 'The diesel was red, the stuff used in boats or farm machinery. It's basically the same as heating oil, but contains a colourless marker, quinizarin, and is coloured with CO Solvent Red 24 to distinguish it from the white diesel you get at roadside pumps. Red diesel has a lower tax tariff, which means it's much cheaper.'

'So someone who works with boats, with a bra fetish?'

'Points that way.'

They were prevented from further discussion by the ringing of the lab phone.

Bill's voice was grim. 'We've found another one. She's buried at the eastern end of the graveyard.'

Bill met Rhona at the Bridge of Sighs. In the near distance, dogs and handlers were strung out across the Necropolis.

'We've been over this place twice already. I don't know how the hell we missed her.'

A third of a dog's brain is devoted to scent. Police dogs could be trained to sniff out almost anything, but they weren't infallible.

'How deep is she buried?' Rhona asked.

'Not deep, but she's been there some time. Looks like the gardener's been trimming the grass over her.'

'No wonder the dog didn't spot it the first time.' Rhona wanted to show her support. Bill wasn't personally responsible for every rogue body they found buried in the graveyard.

Bill glanced around the well-kept green lawns that separated the rows of ancient stones and mausoleums. 'How many more are out there?'

'I think we should get GUARD to take some aerial photographs. Recent burials will show in the colour of the vegetation.'

Bill looked impressed. 'Bloody ironic, looking for bodies in a graveyard.'

To cheer him up, Rhona told him about her harvest of skin and salt.

'The boat connection could be significant, if we come up with a suspect. We ran the DNA profiles, identified from the different semen deposits through HOLMES. No matches,' Bill said.

'Maybe we'll get a match from the skin flakes.'

The truth was, if the perpetrator wasn't on the DNA database, and wasn't a regular punter, the chances of finding him at all were remote. Bill departed for the station, where they had three of Terri's regulars waiting to be interviewed.

The tent was up, a forensic team already combing the surrounding area. Chrissy had stayed on at the lab. Someone had to process the mound of material that was threatening to swamp them.

Inside the tent, McNab was in deep discussion with Judy from GUARD. Rhona had a feeling it wasn't about the body, at least not until she walked in. A slight flush crept across Judy's cheek when she spotted Rhona, and Rhona wondered if she and McNab might have indulged in more than an after-work drink. Judy covered her embarrassment by urging Rhona over to view the remains, while McNab slipped past her with a twinkle in his eye.

'I see you and McNab hit it off.'

'He's a funny guy,' Judy volunteered.

'Hilarious.'

Rhona pulled up her mask and knelt on the soft earth. Judy had dug away the surface covering, revealing the putrefied remains of a woman bearing all the hallmarks of the previous two victims; a brassiere ligature, a black high-heeled sandal jammed between what remained of her thighs.

Judy indicated a stack of turf alongside. 'He must have cut the turf, then replaced it when he was finished. You can make out the discolouration of the grass caused by the decomposition.'

Rhona leaned closer to the body. The face was a creamy white waxy colour, the classic image of a 'soap mummy'. A combination of warm wet earth, lack of oxygen, alkaline soil and plenty of fatty tissue had resulted in the formation of adipocere, a process whose advancement could tell them how long the body had been in the ground.

'I'd estimate he buried her approximately four to six months ago,' said Judy.

Which meant the killer had been working his patch possibly as far back as the start of the year.

A shadow loomed over them. Neither had heard Magnus enter the tent, so engrossed were they in their discussion. He wore a forensic suit, his long hair tucked inside the hood. Rhona caught Judy's disconcerted look.

'Judy, this is Professor Pirie. He's a criminal psychologist.'

Judy managed to keep her expression blank, no easy task as Magnus began to sniff the air like a bloodhound.

'Ammonia with a touch of cadaverine and putresine,' Judy suggested with a smile.

'Not an ideal combination,' countered Magnus, holding out his gloved hand to grasp Judy's firmly.

Rhona watched them eye each other up and wondered if Magnus had had time to do his homework on Judy. She got her answer almost immediately.

'Weren't you involved in the excavation of a mass grave at Hatra in northern Iraq?'

Judy looked surprised but flattered. 'Yes, I was.'

Magnus frowned sympathetically. 'A terrible business.' Unlike the Balkans, where mass graves contained men of fighting age, Hatra had been filled with women and children shot through the head.

Magnus stared down at their latest find. 'How long do you estimate she's been there?'

'Four months, at least.'

'The intervals are getting shorter.'

'If there are no more bodies,' said Rhona.

Magnus threw her a worried glance. 'You have evidence of more?'

Rhona felt a twinge of guilt at her need to challenge Magnus. She felt herself needled by his constantly thoughtful air, as though he had inside knowledge of the killer.

'We missed this one. We may have missed others,' she suggested.

Magnus contemplated that in silence. 'I don't think he'll kill here again, since he left the last body above ground.' He turned to Judy. 'Was there anything about this grave that suggested he wanted us to find it?'

Judy thought for a moment. 'There was a turf loose when I got here. I assumed the handler had done that. I could check with Michael,' Judy offered, then looked flustered at her indiscreet use of McNab's first name.

Rhona suppressed a smile. 'Good idea.'

'Office politics,' Rhona told Magnus when Judy left the tent.

'The most interesting kind.' He held her gaze, his expression frank and friendly. Despite Rhona's antagonism, he seemed to want to call a truce. Rhona wasn't ready for that yet.

McNab had the good sense not to come back with Judy, or else she'd asked him not to. Rhona knew him well enough to guess he didn't mind flaunting his new love interest. Judy was another matter, though. Rhona had an urge to warn her colleague – of what, she wasn't quite sure. Her own relationship with McNab had crossed three genres in swift succession – romance, thriller, horror. In that order. She and McNab had resolved their differences during their last case together, but that didn't mean he'd mended his ways.

'DS McNab says the turf was like that when they got here.'

Rhona was irritated to find herself watching Magnus for his reaction. He, on the other hand, seemed oblivious to her interest, muttering to himself under his breath.

'That's why he came back.'

'You think the killer loosened the turf to help us locate the body?' Rhona said. The site was alive with police. The idea hardly seemed credible.

'The more he interests us in his previous crimes, the less time we spend anticipating his next.'

Rhona didn't buy that. 'But to come back here?'

'I was here at two o'clock this morning. Just me and the guard, and he spent most of his time in the incident van.'

Rhona didn't ask why Magnus was visiting the Necropolis at 2 a.m., but it was pretty clear he was of the opinion the murderer could enter and leave after dark at will.

'Any word on the missing girl?'

Rhona shook her head. 'Bill's gone to interview some of her regulars.'

Magnus's face darkened.

'What are you thinking?'

'I think if Terri Docherty's still alive, it won't be for long.'

14

Glasgow Pussy – Internet Blog

Saturday July 31st
If you found your way here, you know what the stakes are.
The next streetmeat is yours to slaughter. Bidding starts at
a grand.

15

LEANNE BOLTED THE door and stood with her back against it, breathing hard, her body crying out for relief from her mounting anxiety and fear. The truth was that she was useless without Terri.

'Please,' she muttered under her breath as she slid to the floor. 'Where are you?'

No locks would deter Minty and his henchmen if he decided to come for his money. She'd left two messages on his mobile, explaining about Terri's disappearance and the fact the police had her handbag with the money and bank card.

Since Terri had taken charge of their finances, they'd paid off most of Minty's loan, despite the huge interest he levied. They'd laughed and joked about how soon they would be free. Free of drugs and free of Minty. How stupid that seemed now. A sob escaped Leanne's throat. Already the dream she'd had with Terri was fading, replaced by a desperate need for something, anything to take away the pain.

She scrambled onto her knees, pulled herself upright and staggered into the bedroom. She would have to get out there early, pick up as many punters as she could, if she was going to keep Minty off her back. The only

way to face that was to take something. She took the
Valium from the bedside cabinet and swallowed four,
then took another two to make sure.

As she got ready to go out, she watched the news.
The original story, about a young girl murdered on a
night out, had been replaced with the truth. Lucie's
face stared out at Leanne, as the horrifying details of
her death were read out. But nothing prepared Leanne
for what followed. The revelation that a second body
had been found buried below the first, sent her into
hysterics. She was crying so loudly, she didn't hear the
first bang on the door. Then Minty's voice broke
through her sobbing.

'Open the fucking door!'

Leanne froze as fists pounded the flimsy wood.

'I said open the fucking door!'

Leanne tried desperately to get her head into gear.
The Valium was kicking in, bringing euphoria to replace the panic. Minty would be a whole lot angrier if
she didn't let him in. But maybe he would think she
wasn't there and would go away? Leanne stood motionless, unable to make a decision.

The next thump sent the door flying, crashing
against the inside wall. Leanne glanced wildly around,
but there was nowhere to hide. Terri had always been
the one to deal with Minty. She hadn't been scared of
him, not the way Leanne was.

Now he was in, Minty was taking his time. Leanne
heard him go through to the living room, then the
squeaking hinge told her he was in the kitchen. If she
ran now, she might just make it down the hall and out

the front door. Leanne glanced down at her half-clothed body and bare feet. Minty would catch her before she got as far as the stairs.

The door swung open. Minty was perspiring heavily from his exertions. He stank of sweat, stale beer and skag. He smiled when he saw her, exposing the space where his two front teeth should have been. Leanne made a useless attempt to cover her exposed top half. But Minty wasn't interested in bare breasts; not yet, anyway.

He snapped his fingers. 'Money.'

Leanne struggled to find her voice. 'I told you on the phone.' She licked her lips. 'The police have Terri's money. I'll make it up tonight.'

He thought about that, his eyes roaming over her. Leanne reached for the top she'd laid out on the bed. Until now, Minty had taken their money and never demanded anything else. Lucie had been different. She had been his to own – a piece of streetmeat he'd controlled and fed off when required.

And Lucie was dead.

The terrifying thought that Minty might be the killer crossed Leanne's mind. Maybe Lucie had done something to piss Minty off, like not handing over her earnings, or spending it all on drugs.

'I have to go to work.' Leanne pulled on the top and sat down to put on her shoes. The tranquillisers were generating a wave of disinterest, as though she were an onlooker rather than a participant in the scene.

Leanne rose unsteadily and had to widen her stance to balance on her heels. In her present state, Minty's approach appeared to play out in slow motion, although it must have taken only a split second. She saw the gleam of the knife as he flicked it open, then he was on her. A hand grabbed her bare crotch under the short skirt and she yelped as his nails dug into the sensitive flesh. Then he used the blade to hook the strapless top and yank it down to expose one breast.

To her fury and shame the nipple grew hard, as adrenalin fuelled by fear fought the Valium for control of her body. Minty swiped the blade past, so close Leanne thought he'd cut her nipple. His face was an inch from hers, his mouth frothed with angry spittle.

'Tomorrow. Got it?'

Leanne forced a nod.

Minty pushed her away and she staggered back, her head reeling. Then he was gone, the door slamming behind him. Leanne sat on the edge of the bed, the room drifting in and out of focus. She longed to curl up and let the drug take over, but she had to stand up. She had to go to work. Minty would be back looking for twice as much money tomorrow.

16

'DOGGING?' Bill said in disbelief.

'We're not talking about walking the dog, here,' grinned McNab.

'I know what we're talking about.'

'The Necropolis is recommended on dogging websites,' Janice said. 'Which goes some way towards explaining the quantity of condoms we've picked up, sir.'

Bill was struggling with such a concept. 'I thought they needed a car for that?'

'It's been a long, hot, wet summer.'

Bill shot McNab a look, ending the joke. 'So someone might have seen him?'

'Dogging involves watching people have sex outdoors,' Janice explained. 'Sometimes joining in. They might not want to advertise what they've been doing, or watching.'

'We could ask the websites to mention the crime,' said McNab, more serious now. 'Encourage any member who has used the Necropolis recently to email Strathclyde Police in strict confidence?'

'Worth a try,' Bill conceded. 'Okay, who have we brought in?'

'The old man, George Wilkins,' said Janice. 'Charles Beattie, alias Atticus, should arrive shortly. He denied everything until we pointed out we had phone evidence of his contact with Terri. He asked to come in rather than be interviewed at home.'

'What about the Barras man?'

'Haven't got hold of him yet. Gary Forbes is being interviewed on his home turf. Posh Ray doesn't answer his phone. We're checking his home address via the mobile company. The other contact numbers are being dealt with by the rest of the team.'

'Okay, let's see Mr Wilkins.'

'I should warn you sir, he's not washed for a while.'

That was an understatement. Bill felt his throat close in a reflex reaction. Someone had opened the window, but the combination of heat and stale urine in the room was overwhelming. If Terri agreed to have sex with this old man, she was either out of her head, or she deserved a medal for services to the community.

'Mr Wilkins?'

A pair of rheumy eyes looked vaguely up at Bill. 'You found Marie?'

Bill sat down and faced him across the table. Janice switched on the recorder and identified those present.

'Who is Marie, Mr Wilkins?'

'Everybody calls me Geordie. Marie is my wife, Inspector. Forty years we've been married.'

'I'm afraid I don't know where Marie is, Geordie. We wanted to ask you about another woman. Terri Docherty. You used to meet her on a Wednesday night.'

'I don't know any Terri Docherty.' He shook his head. 'Marie and me every Wednesday, regular as clockwork.'

Bill changed tack. 'What does your wife look like?'

Mr Wilkins's face broke into a smile. 'A bonnie, bonnie lass. They all wanted her, but she married me,' he added proudly.

Bill turned to Janice and said quietly. 'What do we know about his wife?'

'According to a neighbour, she died three years ago of cancer.'

'Jesus,' muttered Bill under his breath. The old man was staring at him, trying to make sense of what was going on.

'You met Marie every Wednesday?'

Geordie nodded. 'Same place, same time. I wanted her to come home with me, but she wouldn't.' He looked distressed. 'She was always ill at home.'

Forty years of marriage and it had ended like this.

'We think, ah, *Marie*'s gone missing.'

'I know she has,' Geordie said with certainty. 'She got into that car and never came back. I waited and waited.'

'You saw her get into a car?'

Geordie nodded again. 'She shouldn't have done that.'

'What kind of car?'

The old man's eyes filled with tears.

'Geordie,' Bill said softly.

Geordie began to cry in earnest, his body slumping forward. 'She's never coming back, is she?' He turned his fearful gaze on Bill.

'We're going to find her, Geordie, but we need your help. Can you remember what the car looked like?' Bill watched the old man's struggle, anxiety driving his desire to be useful, his memory letting him down.

Finally Geordie said, 'It was a dark colour. Big and flash.'

Bill waited patiently, willing him to give them something more. 'Did you see the number plate?'

But the light had gone out. Geordie was back in his own world, filled with grief. 'He won't hurt her, will he?'

'We'll make sure he doesn't.' Bill could say the words, but he couldn't keep the promise. 'What if DC Clark gets you a nice cup of tea? That might help you remember.'

Geordie's face brightened. 'Any chance of a chocolate biscuit?'

Atticus was waiting in reception. Bill decided to bring him through himself. He wanted a surreptitious look at a guidance teacher who paid for sex with his former charges.

The view from behind the desk was that of a balding man in his forties, dressed in golfing trousers and sweater. The desk sergeant gave Bill a nod and informed him under his breath that the gentleman had been waiting twenty minutes and had already made a complaint.

Bill buzzed open the door.

'Mr Beattie. I'm Detective Inspector Wilson.'

The man rose. 'I've been waiting for twenty minutes.'

'Thank you for coming in so promptly. We appreciate that.'

Instinct had sent Mr Beattie down the path of outraged innocence. Bill's grateful response was causing him to reconsider. The man was intelligent and used to giving orders. Being on the receiving end of authority was unnerving him.

Geordie was still in the interview room. Bill had told Janice to leave the door ajar when she went for the tea. He walked Mr Beattie slowly past so that he could get the full benefit of Geordie's scent, before showing him into a neighbouring room and ushering him to a seat.

'What was that terrible smell?'

'Another one of Terri's customers.'

'I was not one of Terri's customers.' The affronted air was back.

'Your number is on her phone.'

Beattie drew himself up. 'I was Terri's guidance teacher at school. When her older brother died, she became very withdrawn and I tried to help. I gave her my mobile number then. She recently phoned me to ask if I would help her again.'

'How, exactly?'

'She needed someone to talk to. She was trying to get off drugs and change her life. I told her to call her parents. She said her father had broken all contact and forbidden her to visit or get in touch.'

'Did you meet with Terri?'

'No.'

'Terri told someone that you were a regular punter. Every second Wednesday without fail. She recognised you, but you pretended not to recognise her.'

'Then that someone is lying.'

Beattie was growing more confident with every utterance. Even if they could prove he had sex with Terri Docherty, she wasn't a minor and he hadn't committed an offence.

'You are aware that Terri is missing?'

'Of course I am. Her picture is everywhere.'

As well as being on the front page, Terri's photograph had appeared on the big screen in the main train and bus stations and two major shopping centres. This still hadn't resulted in a sighting.

Bill changed his tone. 'I'm sure you understand, given the present climate, how imperative it is we find Terri.'

Beattie looked momentarily mollified. 'I've told you all I know.'

'We'll be asking everyone connected with Terri to volunteer a mouth scraping for DNA purposes, to eliminate them from our enquiries.'

'But I haven't seen Terri since she left school.'

'Then you have nothing to worry about, Mr Beattie,' Bill said.

It seemed to Bill that there was a worse stink in this room than anything coming from next door.

17

NORA STOOD OUTSIDE the drop-in centre, trying to pluck up enough courage to enter. Occasionally one of the young women entering the building threw her a curious glance, but for the most part she was ignored. Sweat trickled down the front of her blouse, dampening the material and making it stick to her skin. She'd grown accustomed to the flashes of heat that clothed her body in perspiration and fired her cheeks. In this state, she could neither think nor speak coherently and longed only for a cold shower to beat on her face and reduce her surface temperature to something resembling normality.

Nora didn't know exactly why she'd come here, but something had driven her to walk the streets her daughter had walked. She'd told David she was visiting her sister Jessie in Largs for the day. Nora wondered if he'd registered her lie, if he even cared how she spent her time, as long as she was there when he returned from work.

She had followed the tourist route map from the railway station to the cathedral, her feet too hot in their thin-soled sandals, her mind still reeling after seeing her daughter's face on the big screen in Central Station.

When the cool air in the cathedral had washed over her, Nora had felt she'd left hell and entered heaven. Sitting under the vast arched roof, she had prayed. To whom or what she had no idea, but those moments had seemed to renew what little strength she had.

The graveyard itself had been off limits, a police barrier erected across the Bridge of Sighs. Nora had stood for a moment, imagining Terri's body buried somewhere up there. The pain this had generated had crushed her chest, stopping her breath. The policeman on duty had offered to help, thinking her ill. Nora had found herself telling the young man that it was her daughter they were searching for.

Afterwards, walking the surrounding streets, she'd tortured herself, imagining Terri standing in every alleyway. She wanted to kill every man who had used her daughter as a commodity, and wondered if even for a moment they had thought of her as a person, as someone's child.

Nora had contemplated her own death many times. When things were at their worst, it was the one thing that kept her going. Then she would mutter to herself, 'If I die, it will all be over.' She hadn't chosen that escape route. Not yet.

Nora glanced at her watch. David would be on his way home. She wondered what he would think when he found the house empty. Maybe he would phone Jessie and discover she hadn't been there? She had never intended going there. Would he worry? Something told Nora that David was past worrying. He was barely alive himself.

The hot flush had passed, leaving her weak but clear headed. Nora waited for the next young woman to arrive, then followed her inside.

The woman who handed her a cup of tea seemed much like Nora herself. Weary of the world, but not yet willing to give up on it. Nora suspected Marje's path in life had been very different from her own, yet they had ended up together, in this little room, with its faint smell of damp.

Nora sipped at the tea, tasting sugar for the first time in a decade, realising the woman thought she was in shock. And who could blame her? How was she to know that this was Nora's state, every hour of every day?

'I'm glad you came.'

The simple welcome brought tears to Nora's eyes.

'You should speak to Leanne.'

'Leanne? You mean Leanne Quinn?'

'Terri's partner.'

Nora wondered if Marje meant they worked together.

Marje observed Nora's puzzled expression. 'They live together.'

Nora absorbed that. 'Oh, I see. Is Leanne here?'

'Not at the moment.'

'But she will come in?' Nora was seized by a sense of purpose. This Leanne cared enough about Terri to report her missing. Nora wanted to speak to her.

The sugar rush had left a strange taste in her mouth. Normally she would have gagged at the syrupy liquid, Marje's version of tea. Now Nora craved more, imagining it to be the source of her new-found energy.

'When did you last see my daughter?'

Marje met her desperate look. 'She came in the other day, Wednesday, to stock up . . .' Marje hesitated.

'Stock up,' echoed Nora.

Marje decided to be frank. 'On condoms. No needles. She and Leanne are clean. Have been for a couple of months.'

Nora concentrated on the word 'clean'. Clean meant drug-free, didn't it? A mental picture of her daughter's bruised limbs brought back the pain. Nora allowed a measure of hope to wash over it. She felt a hand on her arm and looked up to find Marje's concerned eyes on her.

'Why don't you stay for a bit. Leanne usually comes in later.'

The energy had drained from Nora as quickly as it had come. She had a vision of herself. A middle-aged woman sitting in a dingy little room, her clothes damp with perspiration, her feet swollen. The tears finally escaped her eyes.

'It's okay,' Marje was saying. 'We'll look after you.'

Nora felt a pair of strong arms enfold her, a soft, cushioned body press against her own.

18

RHONA AND BILL were sitting in his office, drinking one
of the endless cups of coffee you consumed to keep
your eyes open on a twelve-hour shift. She'd reported
her discovery of crystal meth on the twenty-pound
note found in Lucie's pocket. Both were aware that
crystal meth was available on the streets of Glasgow.
The drug's fast addiction rate and the violence associated with it made it one of the force's biggest problems. Crystal, or Ice, could be made relatively simply.
The profits from such an endeavour could be substantial. Just the sort of business Minty would relish.
They'd brought Minty in many times before, but none
of the girls he ran had been willing to press charges.
And now he'd simply disappeared.

'You can't make money from a dead woman. Minty'll
be leaning on all the others to make up the difference, but
they're still too frightened to give him up.'

'When do I get to examine his place?'

'We should have the warrant by tomorrow.' Bill
rolled his eyes: tomorrow was Sunday. 'No rest for
the wicked, eh?'

They fell into an uneasy silence. Rhona longed to ask
about Margaret, but before she could, Bill said gruffly

'Margaret's doing okay. Balder than me now, but at least she gets to wear a scarf to cover it.' His weak attempt at humour only made things worse.

'How are the kids?'

'Lisa's overprotective, which drives Margaret mad. Robbie's pretending it's not happening.' Bill didn't say 'like his father'.

'You shouldn't be working these long hours.'

Bill looked up at her. 'Margaret understands the job. She doesn't want things to be any different from normal.'

'But they are.'

Rhona's frank reply drew a resigned shrug from Bill. 'The truth is, I'm better working than watching her all the time. I make her more nervous than Lisa.'

Serious illness had been known to destroy marriages. Rhona couldn't imagine that happening to Margaret and Bill, but she could appreciate the stress he was under. Rhona judged it was time to change the subject. 'How's Magnus getting on?'

Bill grimaced. 'He asks a lot of questions. And is yet to prove himself useful.'

'Do I detect a note of resistance?'

'He told me he thought there was another body. I had already worked that out for myself. I just couldn't find it.'

'Do you think the killer led us there?'

'Looks like it.'

'So our perpetrator is now an official serial killer, who will keep going until he's caught, or dies. You don't need a profiler to tell you that,' Rhona said sympathetically.

'You and I both know profiling never brought Sutcliffe, Fred West or Ian Brady to justice. Solid police work did that.'

'And solid police work needs time, which we haven't got.'

'I think you should take a look at this, sir.' Janice had knocked and entered without waiting for a response. Bill swallowed his reprimand when he saw her eager expression and heard the clamour of voices behind her.

'What is it?'

'The IT boys found a set of photographs of the victims online.'

Bad news had travelled fast and the incident room was packed. The noise fell to a whisper as Bill appeared. All eyes followed his to the wall screen and the projected images.

The pictures looked as though they had been taken shortly after death. The latest victim was immediately recognisable, the other two distinguished by location, modus operandi and signature. There was no doubt they were looking at the same gravestone and the wooded area north-east of the Necropolis.

'Could the first one be a crime scene shot?'

Bill's question caused a ripple of shock – could a scene of crime officer have posted confidential material online?

'I don't think so. It must have been taken very soon after she died. Look at the skin and blood colour,' Rhona moved closer to the screen.

The victim who shared Lucie's grave bore a striking resemblance to her. It was almost uncanny. Similar features, hair length and colour, build and age. Had it not been for the different clothes, they might have been the same girl. Dr Sissons would hopefully present his report on victim three at Monday's meeting. Until now she had been an unknown quantity.

'She looks to be the youngest,' observed Rhona. The puffy, mottled face that stared down at them from the screen could almost have belonged to a child.

'We'd better trawl for missing minors,' said Bill.

There was activity behind them, as some of the team moved to carry out his order.

'He likes them young, and he likes them to look the same,' said Rhona.

'And Terri Docherty is seventeen, five foot three and blonde.'

Any hope they'd had that Terri had simply gone AWOL was fast disappearing. Bill was pacing the room, glancing up periodically at the screen.

'Did IT find these by chance, or were they given a lead?'

'A member of the public called in on the confidential line. He said the photos were available via one of the doggers' websites,' Janice replied.

The DI's expression was a mixture of anger and frustration. 'He's playing with us.'

Placing Lucie's body on top of a previous victim, leading them to the burial site, now the release of photographs of the victims shortly after he killed them; everything suggested the perpetrator was keen to control the investigation.

'We should bring Magnus in on this,' said Rhona. Despite her misgivings, unravelling the twisted thought processes of a serial killer was a job for a psychologist.

Bill acted as though he hadn't heard.

'How widely distributed are these photos?'

'IT say they've been viewed or downloaded by a substantial number of the "dogging" community, in the UK and probably North America.'

'So the world and his mother is ahead of us on this?'

'There's something else, sir. A website that may have a link to the crimes.' Janice moved the slideshow forward and displayed the following script.

Wednesday July 28th
Known as streetmeat, they can be found hanging around the Finnieston area or by Glasgow Green. Mostly mangy crackheads and criminals, there are two kinds. The dried-up worn-out clits brigade who'll do anything, ANYTHING for the money including crap and pee on request. Then the juveniles. Young, some VERY YOUNG and still fresh. Get them before the smack does. If you fancy beating up a whore, this class is for you. Nobody gives a shit what happens to them, including the police.

Friday July 30th
Two mangy crackheads lying one on top of the other. One fresh meat, the other rotting. The police didn't even know the rotting one was missing. Told you. No one gives a shite.

Saturday July 31st

If you found your way here, you know what the stakes are.
The next streetmeat is yours to slaughter. Bidding starts at
a grand.

The silence in the room was palpable, all eyes glued to
the screen.

The first message had been posted the day Terri
disappeared. The second could have been written by a
sicko following the case, but the third . . .?

'What the hell does that mean?'

'It's an online auction,' Rhona voiced what no one
else wanted to say. 'He'll carry out and record the next
kill for the highest bidder.'

There were murmurs of disgust and anger.

'It could be a hoax,' said Janice.

Bill shook his head. 'I think it's the next move in the
game.'

19

MAGNUS STARED DOWN at the chessboard. The game was currently in limbo, but he still liked to study the pieces poised for battle, frozen in time. His opponent had departed Orkney for a lecture tour in the United States and Canada on the topic of John Rae, Orkney's greatest son and explorer.

Magnus could forecast from the current position that he was likely to lose, again. Douglas Flett was a powerful opponent. Magnus had learned a lot by playing him regularly over the past three years.

Thinking about Douglas produced a sudden longing for Orkney, its smells and sights. The Raes' family home, The Hall of Clestrain, overlooked Scapa Flow, not that far from Magnus. Rae had been his boyhood hero. Like the young John, Magnus had learned to sail on the ever changing Scapa waters and believed himself capable of great adventures.

Magnus stepped out onto the small balcony that hung above the River Clyde. Here at least he could enjoy the smell of water, although not the sea. He would have to go further west for that.

Glasgow's great river and its extended waterways covered 600 square miles and was served by multiple marinas. Thousands of people sailed its waters or worked with boats that did. Traces of sea salt and diesel weren't significant in narrowing their search for the killer, unless they had a suspect. But it added to the profile that Magnus was forming of the man they sought.

Magnus went back inside, poured himself a whisky and resumed his place in front of the computer screen. If DI Wilson was to take him seriously, he would have to come up with something that made sense to such an experienced professional. Magnus wondered if the older man's antagonism wasn't born of more than just having a profiler foisted on him by a superior officer. He recalled the concerned look he'd seen pass between Rhona and the detective. If the DI did have a confidant, it was probably Dr MacLeod.

Magnus turned his thoughts away from Rhona and towards the large map that hung above his desk. He'd marked all known marinas with a cross. A list of sailing clubs that used these marinas and their race programmes had been easy to find, particularly as many had sites online.

All the murders (at least the ones they knew about) had occurred in the heart of the city, and not that far from the river. Lucie had been known to work both Finnieston and Calton red-light districts, so she could have been picked up in either area. Terri had stuck to Calton. The killer had either charmed or threatened the dead girls to get them to the graveyard. The timing of the kills would be significant. Someone who planned so carefully did not kill on the spur of the moment. The fact that he had salt and diesel on his hands when he strangled Lucie, suggested he'd been near a boat not long before the crime.

Magnus was so engrossed in his preliminary profile, he didn't hear his mobile at first. He got to it just too late and voicemail told him it had been Rhona. He returned her call immediately, before he had time to think about it. When she answered, his body reacted by reminding him of her scent. Magnus found the sensation pleasant, though distracting.

'There's been a development,' she said.

'Shall I come down to the station?'

There was a moment's hesitation at her end. 'Can I come by your place on my way home?'

Magnus had a sudden vision of Rhona in this room. It both excited and perturbed him. 'Of course.' He gave her directions.

'I'll be with you in ten minutes.'

Magnus found himself lighting lamps against the growing dusk, and tidying the papers on his desk – whether through nervousness or an attempt to impress, he wasn't sure. If he were honest with himself, he found Rhona MacLeod intriguing.

Psychologically profiling the women he met was an obsession of his. If they weren't sufficiently complex, he quickly lost interest in any possibility of a relationship. If he found them enigmatic, he spent too much time on analysis. There were times, like now, when Magnus wished he could just 'be' rather than seeking always to understand.

He refreshed his whisky, and opened the balcony doors wide. A soft breeze swept the room. Magnus tried to concentrate on the aroma of the whisky and the mix of scents wafting in from the river, to no avail.

The scent of a woman was as distinct as her finger-prints, despite the modern world's attempt to disguise it with cosmetics and perfume. Sexual attraction was stimulated by image and natural scent. For him, natur-ally, scent was by far the greater influence.

Magnus had once sat in a room with two people who, he'd quickly realised, were sexually attracted to one another. There was nothing overtly sexual about their behaviour, but he could smell their desire. The scent was so strong he'd felt his own body respond. Magnus had never, until that moment, imagined the two men in question to be other than straight. He suspected that, until they met each other, neither had they.

He could only be glad that Rhona MacLeod's sense of smell was not as acute as his own.

Rhona pointed the remote at the car. She always unlocked it well before she reached it, especially at night and particularly in an empty multi-storey car park. The distance to her car from the entrance seemed unnaturally far and she was conscious of her heels clipping the surface and of her breathing. There were only four other vehicles on this level. Most evening users found a place lower down.

Although she knew it was silly, she began to walk faster. The sense that someone was watching her was so strong that she stopped and looked back. The atmosphere was thick with the day's heat, radiating from the concrete, mingling with trapped exhaust fumes. Sweat beaded on her upper lip and between her breasts. Once inside the car, she locked all the doors.

Magnus lived in one of the modern flats by the river. She'd been surprised by the address, having imagined him ensconced in a hundred-year-old sandstone property, with original features and shelves full of books, like an Oxford don.

Rhona had called Magnus from the incident room, in earshot of Bill. Ignoring the command to include Magnus was Bill's way of saying he was on top of the job, despite the Super's suggestion he take compassionate leave until Margaret's course of chemotherapy and radiation was complete.

It was easier for Rhona to liaise directly with Magnus than to ask Janice or McNab to defy their boss's unspoken order openly. Janice had looked relieved when Rhona had said she would bring Professor Pirie up to date. That was one problem solved, at least. And the truth was that Janice, like Rhona, was interested to see what Magnus could come up with; what he would make of the photographs and the messages.

Rhona tried not to look around the room, but directed her gaze towards the open balcony doors and the inky blackness of the Clyde beyond.

'May I?'

'Of course.'

She stepped outside, drawn to an expanse of water, as she had always been from childhood.

This view of the Clyde was a new experience.

'What a wonderful outlook.'

'I was brought up in a fisherman's house built below the high water line. At full tide the water lapped three sides of the house. This is the nearest I can get to that.'

Rhona smiled warmly, pleased by his friendliness. 'My parents were from the Isle of Skye. I spent most summers there, although I was brought up in Glasgow.'

'You speak Gaelic?'

'A little. I watch the Gaelic programmes sometimes to remind myself.'

'I miss Orkney voices the most, but there's always Radio Orkney.'

'God bless the BBC.'

Her small talk exhausted, she locked gazes with him. Magnus took his time about everything. Observing, talking, thinking. It was quite disconcerting in a world where everything and everyone seemed in a rush. His measured delivery almost suggested he was speaking in his second language. Or maybe his brain worked so fast that he deliberately slowed down the articulation of his thoughts.

Magnus indicated the whisky bottle.

'Can I tempt you to a dram?'

'Maybe a small one, with lots of water.'

Magnus placed a cut-glass tumbler on the coffee table in front of her and Rhona handed him the printouts in return. He looked at her curiously, saying nothing, then studied both closely. His intent gaze and the angle of his jawline reminded Rhona of a Greek statue in the Kelvingrove Art Gallery. She was almost surprised when the statue spoke.

'Thank you for bringing me these.'

Rhona hadn't said it was her decision to include him in this development, but she suspected Magnus knew. If he'd queried Bill's attitude, Rhona would have promptly bitten Magnus's head off, so strong was her need to defend her friend and mentor.

'Bill thinks the last one refers to Terri.'

'Maybe.'

His refusal to reach that conclusion irritated Rhona. 'Now we know what the other two look like, it's obvious he picks the same type. And Terri's that type.'

'The looks might be a coincidence.'

'You think so?'

If he noticed the irritation in her voice, he didn't rise to it.

'In the early days of artificial intelligence, the Ministry of Defence developed a neural network designed to identify photographs where enemy tanks were hidden among trees. They thought they'd succeeded until they discovered the program wasn't "seeing" tanks at all. It was picking out the photos that had a certain degree of light. Nothing to do with the hidden tanks.'

'What are you trying to say?'

'We tend to see what we're looking for.'

'What do *you* see?' Rhona struggled to keep the sarcasm from her voice.

'The most recent victim has six stab wounds, the one from a month ago has five, the one before that four.'

Rhona took a closer look. Each body lay in exactly the same position. In fact they must have been posed for the camera. No two bodies fall the same way; our death throes are uniquely our own. Magnus was right. The level of decomposition of the previous victims had made it difficult to determine the presence and number of stab wounds. These photos solved that problem.

'What do you think that means?'

'It could signify his rising level of anger. It could be he's deliberately counting. It might mean nothing.'

'So what happened to one, two and three? When should we expect lucky seven?'

Magnus suddenly looked weary and Rhona wanted to bite her tongue. That was the problem with investigative psychology. There was nothing to get a grip of, nothing to test, no accumulated data on which to base your assumptions. Yet in a case like this, a profiler was seen as an oracle, someone who could supply the answers that tried and tested police procedure and advanced science had failed to find.

'These photographs confirm the ritual aspects of the murders. Serial killers are mercifully rare, so collecting data on them is difficult.' Magnus shrugged apologetically. 'But – there are some things we can hypothesise on. These young women were little more than objects to the killer. The ritualistic nature of their deaths – particularly the insertion of an object into their bodies – suggests this. As far as the murderer is concerned, the body is not a person.'

'And the fundamental nature of the relationship between the body and the person is what makes us human.'

Magnus's nod of approval pleased Rhona, perhaps more than it should have.

'A prostitute is regarded as a commodity, not a human being. And as such they all look alike to the punter,' he said.

'And the majority are in the seventeen to twenty-five age group anyway.'

'They are also the most vulnerable and therefore easiest to kill.'

'And their murderers are seldom caught.'

'But that doesn't mean we can't create a profile for the killer that could help narrow the search.'

Magnus motioned Rhona over to the computer. 'I was going to present this at Monday's meeting.'

'Can I take a look?'

'Be my guest.'

Rhona read through the detailed observations on the appearance, character, social and sexual history of the perpetrator, and hoped Magnus would be able to convince Bill.

She realised he was watching her and, no doubt, working out what she was thinking. Rhona decided to call his bluff and allowed her thoughts to turn to sex. She imagined how many women Magnus had made love to in this room. She imagined him naked – always a good way to demystify academics. Unfortunately the idea backfired. Rhona was suddenly aware from the look in his eyes that Magnus was thinking along the same lines.

There was a moment that lasted an hour, when neither spoke.

'I have to go.' The standard get-out clause. As a put-down, it didn't work. Magnus's keen eye never wavered. Instead Rhona could swear his eyes twinkled. She wanted to laugh. Magnus did laugh.

'Great minds think alike.'

'You are very forward.'

'I try to be honest. We're working together professionally. Otherwise I would have tried my luck.'

'I'm taken.' It sounded like a successful move in chess.

'At the moment.'

How could they be having this conversation? Read one way, it could be a bit of light-hearted banter. But it wasn't. It was a mating dance, with Magnus's mind as the peacock's tail. Rhona thought of Sean – his charisma, the power of his music. Men only choose women who choose them. He'd told her that once. It avoids too many rejections. Their mutual desire was strong, but they never discussed things. A meeting of minds – psychology and science – was an intriguing thought.

After she left, Magnus sat where Rhona had sat, and allowed himself to breathe her in. His body responded to her even more intensely than he thought it would. It had been this strong only once before. In view of the outcome that time, he'd hoped, planned for it never to happen again.

Magnus read the three messages again. There were those who were willing to carry out unspeakable acts, and those who preferred the visceral thrill of watching.

Magnus had no doubt there would be responses to the online auction.

The killer was developing. Now he wanted to be observed while he killed. He wanted to record it, to relive the experience himself through the eyes of others.

The hair on Magnus's forearms rose, as though a draught of cold air had entered the room.

20

THE UNEASY FEELING Rhona had experienced earlier seemed to be following her like a bad smell. The parking below Magnus's flat was close to the river, which Rhona could hear lapping against the concrete barrier. She'd parked in an empty bay, obviously belonging to another resident who had retaliated by blocking her exit with a four-by-four. As she struggled to manoeuvre around the vehicle, she imagined the owner watching, mouthing 'serve you right, bitch'.

Once out of the confined space and back on the road, she felt better. As it was Saturday, she'd promised Sean she would come by the club on her way home. After the session with Magnus, it seemed important to keep her word. Although she would have preferred a quiet night in where she could have contemplated both the case and Magnus's part in it.

Despite all the police warnings, Finnieston red-light district had its usual quota of young women looking for clients. Lights shone from the incident caravan on the corner of Cadogan and Douglas Street. There was a similar set-up in Calton. Hopefully the high police presence would keep the killer away from both areas, but if he'd already picked up his next victim, he wouldn't need to come back.

Work at the incident room would carry on all night, the late shift taking over from the day. The case involved a mountain of work, sifting through interview coverage, CCTV footage, lists of recorded assaults against prostitutes and reports from the general public. At least fifty officers, looking for a needle in a haystack. In reality, they were all just waiting for the next body to be found.

When Rhona reached the jazz club, she found a queue leading to the entrance. Dave the doorman waved her past, eliciting some caustic comments from those left outside.

'Health and Safety'll have our guts for garters if I let any more in,' he growled at them. 'It's like sardines in a tin already.' Hearing the bad news, the waiting group decided to call it a day, heading off down Byres Road to look for fun elsewhere.

Three young women on saxophone and a male guitarist were easy on the eye and the ear. It was no wonder the place was packed. The barman spotted Rhona looking around for Sean and motioned her towards the back office, looking worried. Rhona wondered if it was the three-deep crowd at the bar waiting to be served that was the problem, or something else entirely.

She soon found out.

'Jesus Christ!'

Sean winced as though her raised voice were another blow on his bruised face. He removed an ice pack to reveal a fast-swelling eye.

'Come on. I'll take you to A and E.'

'No thanks.' He shook his head, wincing at the pain that generated. 'It looks worse than it is,' he said through gritted teeth.

'Who . . .' she began before he cut her off.

'Two guys wearing balaclavas. The back door was open because of the heat. They were looking for Sam.'

'Sam?'

'Seemed to think I knew where he was hiding, somewhere in Glasgow.'

'Sam's alive?'

'He won't be if they find him.'

Rhona pulled out her mobile. 'I need to tell Bill.'

'Leave Bill out of this.'

She shot Sean a curious glance.

'We don't want the police looking for Sam too.'

Rhona's joy that Sam was alive was tempered by fear that his life might still be in danger.

'The men who attacked you, they don't know about Chrissy?'

'They knew Sam had worked here. That's all.'

Rhona hoped that was true. If the thugs got hold of Chrissy . . .

'We'd better warn Pastor Achebe.' The Nigerian Church of God in Maryhill had been Sam's second home. Rhona couldn't imagine Sam not making contact with the pastor, if he really was in Glasgow.

'I've called Achebe already. If Sam's meant to be in Glasgow, only God knows where.'

'So what do we do now?'

Sean rose to his feet.

'You take me home and treat me nice.' The smile he attempted gave him the look of a punch-drunk boxer.

'I hope at least one of them looks as bad as you.'

'Difficult to tell under a balaclava.'

They left by the back door, so as not to frighten the customers. The sensation of being watched stayed with Rhona all the way to the flat. Sean kept his good eye on the rear-view mirror. Once or twice he ordered her to turn off the route and double back just in case, but it was obvious no one was interested in them. The Suleimans' men could come to the club any time they wanted, a good reason for asking for a police presence. But Sean wouldn't hear of it.

When they reached the flat, Sean went straight for the whisky bottle and poured a large measure. He knocked it back, grimacing as the alcohol stung his cut lip. Then he poured one for each of them and sank down on the sofa.

'You're sure they don't know about Chrissy?' said Rhona.

'They didn't mention her.'

'But they did say Sam was alive?'

'They seemed pretty sure he was in Glasgow. How, I don't know.'

Sean laid his head back against the cushion and closed his eyes.

'If he's here he's bound to get in touch with Chrissy. I have to warn her,' said Rhona.

This time Sean didn't argue.

Chrissy's mobile rang unanswered, then went to voicemail. Rhona paced up and down, trying at ten-minute intervals. Finally she left a message asking Chrissy to call back as soon as possible.

Sean was stretched out on the sofa with his eyes closed. Rhona hardly dared look at his face, it was such a mess. His knuckles were also skinned and bruised, testament to his attempts to give as good as he'd got. He'd said the voices were definitely Glaswegian, so the Suleiman family must have made contact with the city's criminal underworld. Sean was lucky he'd only got a beating.

Rhona fetched a blanket and covered him, then realised she hadn't seen Tom since they'd got home. They'd confined him to the kitchen, both for his safety and to prevent him scratching every piece of furniture in sight.

He was behind the door as she pushed it open. His mew was plaintive, demanding food and affection. Rhona scooped up the small furry body and hugged it close.

If she hadn't visited Magnus, she would have been at the club when the thugs arrived. Rhona recalled her feeling of being watched in the car park, and later at Magnus's. Experience told her that if she sensed she was being observed, she probably was.

She glanced at her watch again, wondering why Chrissy wasn't answering her phone. Like many women in early pregnancy, Chrissy looked constantly tired as her body adjusted to its new role. Rhona consoled herself with the thought that Chrissy had probably simply gone to bed.

She tried to focus on the fact that Sam was alive. That Chrissy's baby did have a father after all. But she could not forget that Sam was a wanted man, both here and in his homeland; wanted by the authorities and, worse still, by the Suleiman family. If she told Bill about Sean's visitors, he would be obliged to look for Sam. The best outcome would be for Chrissy to see Sam, then for him to disappear again.

The spotlight had come on in the convent garden below Rhona's window, illuminating Madonna and child, their symbolism more poignant now than ever.

Rhona promised herself she would decide the best course of action tomorrow, when she saw Chrissy and Bill. Above all, Chrissy must be kept safe. Chrissy and the baby.

The call came through at 2 a.m. Rhona had placed the mobile on her bedside table and set its ring to loud. Chrissy's voice was thick with emotion.

'Sam's alive. He called me. He's coming here now.'

'Chrissy.' Rhona didn't want to tell her about the thugs, but she had to be warned. 'Two men came to the jazz club tonight, looking for Sam. They know he's in Glasgow.'

But nothing could dampen Chrissy's joy at knowing Sam was alive and she was going to see him.

'Warn Sam,' said Rhona, and hung up.

Rhona heard footsteps behind her and realised the call had woken Sean.

'What's up?'

'Sam contacted Chrissy. He's on his way there now.'

'You told her they were looking for him?'

'I did.'

Sean groaned as he eased himself onto the bed and lay back.

'Do you want me to help you undress?'

'That's the best offer I've had all day.'

Rhona switched on the bedside lamp. The shadows it cast only emphasised the swelling around Sean's eye. Rhona helped him off with his shirt, exposing three large bruises around his ribcage.

'God, you look awful.'

'Thanks very much.' He tried to laugh and groaned instead.

She pulled down his trousers. His legs were the only part of his body that wasn't bruised.

'Do you want something for the pain?'

'Too right I do.' His grin was wickedly suggestive.

'You're joking?'

'I never joke about sex.' He pulled her to sit astride him. 'You'll have to do all the work.'

Rhona lay in the dark, Sean's steady breathing punctuating the silence. She thought of Chrissy lying in Sam's arms. Of Sam's face when Chrissy told him about the baby. If Sam needed a reason to stay alive, he had one right there.

21

LEANNE STEPPED OUT of the shadows as the car slowed.

The Valium was wearing off, allowing fear and despair to surface. The smell of the last punter was still thick in her nostrils; stale beer and a tongue furred by smoking. She'd flinched as he'd shoved her against the wall, the stone scraping her bare back. It was over so quickly she'd been worried he wouldn't pay, but he'd thrown the money in the gutter just to watch her bend and pick it up.

She didn't have enough for Minty yet. She needed one more punter, then she could sleep.

As the car drew up, a hand gestured to her from the open window. Leanne began the walk, telling herself she could still change her mind. She would rather service a drunk in the alley than climb into a car she didn't recognise.

When she reached the vehicle, the door swung open. The inside light came on, illuminating the occupant.

'Oh, it's you,' said Leanne, surprised.

22

MARJE HAD COME looking for Nora at ten o'clock. 'We won't see Leanne now.' Marje didn't add that the girl would be out on the streets, but Nora knew that was what she meant.

In the preceding hours, Nora had drunk endless cups of tea and watched too many young girls buying condoms. Tea and condoms, condoms and tea.

She wondered what David had done when he discovered she wasn't at home. Nora glanced at her phone. There were no messages. David wasn't keen on voicemail anyway. His normal routine in recent months had been to come home to eat, and then go back out. Nora presumed it was because he couldn't bear to be alone with her. Even with the television on, the silence between them was deafening. Nora longed to be held in his arms, to have him kiss her cheek and tell her he loved her.

They'd survived Philip's death because they'd had Terri to think about. When Terri became ill (Nora always thought of her drug-taking as an illness), it was hard not to think that as a couple they produced only grief and disappointment. Nora wondered if they could stay together after this.

Marje had told her that Terri and Leanne were partners. Nora found herself unfazed by the idea that her daughter and this girl had a relationship that was more than just friendship. Picturing Terri in the caring arms of a woman was better than her earlier imaginings.

Nora forced her still-swollen feet into her sandals. Marje asked if she knew her way to the station, and whether she wanted a taxi. Nora's sense of thrift won, and she assured Marje she would walk. It was cooler now.

At the door, Marje gave her a bear hug and told Nora she would give Leanne her number.

'She's a nice girl. Life's just been bad to her.'

Nora knew all about that.

When the catering trolley came down the aisle of the train, Nora ordered a gin and tonic. She should have bought a sandwich, but knew she wouldn't be able to eat it. The drink was warm, but Nora was glad of the gin's kick. She decided she would tell David where she'd been, and explain about Leanne, who she intended to get in touch with. Nora imagined him reacting like the old David, the one who cared.

When she got home, she found the house in darkness, David's car gone from the garage. The effects of the gin were wearing off. Nora stood on the step for a moment, breathing in the scents from the garden, allowing herself to think of happier times.

Later, sitting alone in the dark, she thought about her wee girl alive somewhere. Terri desperately needed her help, and all she'd done was visit a drop-in centre and drink tea. Tears rolled down her cheeks. She was a middle-aged woman, invisible and useless.

How could she blame her daughter for taking heroin, if it dulled the pain? If she'd had some there, Nora could almost imagine wanting to take it herself.

23

'GET IN.'

Father Duffy's face gleamed red with perspiration. Leanne could smell whisky on his breath. Duffy only came looking for her when he was on one of his benders. Leanne hadn't seen him for a month, at least.

She slipped into the passenger seat.

The routine was always the same. If she did what she was told, he remained calm. If she turned him down or argued the toss, his temper got the better of him and he said things he had to apologise for later.

God knows how much whisky he'd consumed, but his hands were steady on the wheel, and they were only minutes away from the chapel house. When they drew in at the back of the building, Leanne saw a light on inside. Father Duffy operated an open door policy. If you didn't have a bed for the night, you could doss down in the church. That's why his parishioners thought him a good man. And he was, in his own way. The drink brought out the other side of him.

He hurried Leanne in through the back door and locked it behind them. She wasn't frightened. Father Duffy had never hurt her, except sometimes with words.

As soon as she was in the bedroom, he ordered her to undress. A bottle of whisky stood on an ancient wooden chest of drawers. He'd already drunk three quarters of it. Above the bottle was a painted plaster moulding of the Virgin Mary, whose eyes seemed to follow you around the room.

The priest gazed at her naked body for a moment, before handing her the loose white shift she'd worn on countless occasions before. It always smelt clean and fresh. Leanne wondered if Father Duffy got his housekeeper, Mrs Hughes, to wash and iron it for him. Did Mrs Hughes know what he used it for?

Leanne slipped the gown over her head. It was too big for her small frame, and hung off one shoulder. The room was warm and stuffy, but she still shivered as though cold, knowing what was about to happen.

Father Duffy poured another glass of whisky and quickly drank it down.

'You're a virgin?'

Leanne bowed her head, as she knew she must. 'Yes, Father.'

'No man has touched you before this?'

'No, Father.'

He set the glass beside the bottle and approached her.

'Kneel before me child.'

Leanne dropped to her knees.

He always wore a cassock at these times, forsaking the usual shirt and collar. She could feel the heat emanating from his body in waves, through the heavy black material.

'You wish to know a man?'

'Yes, Father.'

'You are sure?'

This was the point when his mood could change. Leanne had to sound as though she meant what she said, or he would grow angry, call her names and threaten her with the fires of hell.

'Oh yes, Father.'

Leanne waited, breathless, in the silence that followed. Father Duffy's face was contorted, fighting whatever drove him to do this thing. Then the struggle ended. This time the man, not the priest, had won.

He reached out and raised the shift, exposing her body and covering her face.

Leanne changed out of the white gown and left it in a bundle on the bed. The first time this had happened, she'd felt profound shock and disgust for the sixty-year-old man who now slept soundly on top of the bed. Then she'd learned that this was a regular occurrence. Terri had been here, Lucie, most of the other younger women Leanne knew from the centre.

As far as she was aware, no one had told the police about the priest's nocturnal forays into the red-light district. Leanne wasn't sure why. Maybe it was because they didn't believe he was the killer. Father Duffy was fucked up, but weren't they all? She'd taken drugs to kill the pain, he drank. When he was sober, the priest was kind. He helped people. People no one else cared about.

Leanne made her way through the sleeping inhabitants of the church and found a vacant corner. With her busted door and Minty out there somewhere, it was safer to stay the rest of the night in the chapel. Minty would never come here, not even for her.

Leanne relaxed among the grunts and snores and murmured sleep of her fellow inhabitants. In the red glow of the constantly burning altar light, she closed her eyes and prayed for Terri.

24

MAGNUS CLOSELY STUDIED the calendar of yachting events. It was a long shot, but a geographical profile could be a powerful tool. Serial killers enacted their fantasies within their own world, a world with boundaries. Ted Bundy's 'world' had comprised the university campuses of half of North America, each of his victims resembling the girl who'd spurned him during his college days.

It would be wrong to assume their killer's life was contained within the environs of Glasgow. The notorious Scottish serial killer Robert Black had killed young girls on his lorry route from England into Scotland. The lorry was his home, the route his geographical area. The Clyde was a gateway into Glasgow, much as the road north had been a gateway into Scotland for Black.

A careful examination of approximate times of death provided a reasonable match with the timings of certain yacht races. What would DI Wilson say if he presented such a proposition tomorrow? Probably he'd think it the product of an overripe imagination.

Magnus rubbed the back of his neck. He'd been sitting at the computer for far too long. He glanced over the profile of the killer, as complete as it could be with the evidence he had. He couldn't predict the reaction of the investigative team. Or could he? DI Wilson would regard him as an academic upstart, who thought a fancy degree trumped police officers' power of deduction. Dr Sissons was only interested in the pathological aspects of the case. Dr MacLeod – Rhona – what would she say? Probably nothing, but that wouldn't mean she didn't have an opinion.

Thinking of Rhona, surely at home with her boyfriend right now, enhanced Magnus's feeling of loneliness. Man was a social creature, he thought, a pack animal. Physical or emotional separation from the comfort of others could create a 'rogue male' – someone with no reference points, who took what he wanted. Someone like the man they were searching for.

After Anna, Magnus had vowed that he wouldn't sleep with a woman again unless it meant something more than just sex. He had to feel the relationship might have a future, the way it should have been with Anna. Not just for a few weeks or months, but perhaps an eternity. It was a tall order. Yet his parents had achieved it. Why couldn't he? They'd spent their whole lives together, against the odds. That was what Magnus wanted.

And, against the odds, they would find this killer.

Refocusing on the case, he decided against presenting his profile on the overhead screen. He would present it in words, as the killer's narrative history. The story he lived and breathed. The reason why he killed.

25

RHONA WOKE AT dawn. Sean lay asleep beside her, oblivious for now to his aches and pains. Rousing him would be too cruel. She crept from the bed and headed for the shower.

She sat down to an early breakfast, Tom on her lap and the files she'd requested from records spread over the kitchen table. Some of her work already involved cold cases. Provided evidence was kept, low copy number DNA could now be extracted from victims' clothing, sometimes solving old crimes.

They hadn't succeeded in matching current trace evidence to entries on the database. But what if she looked for some similarities between the old and the new, rather than outright matches? That would throw up any genetic link between the perpetrators of the previous murders and the current crimes. It wasn't the first time a case had been solved this way. Joseph Kappen had been identified as the rapist and murderer of two sixteen-year-old girls in Wales in 1973, by sweeping the national database for entries with a genetic pattern similar to the traces he'd left behind.

There had been no further news on Terri Docherty. Rhona knew Bill was just waiting for her body to turn up. Of course, it might never appear. Given the right time and tide, the river could take it west. If the killer did have access to a boat, he could take it west himself and dump it. But his obsession with burial suggested to Rhona that the body would find its resting place in the earth.

She had a couple of hours before she was due at Craig Minto's apartment. Rhona began to read the long, grim reports.

According to his nearest neighbour, Minty hadn't been home for three days.

'Thank fuck!' was the guy's conclusion. He'd opened his front door as soon as he'd heard their footsteps on the stairs. He was up and dressed, despite it being early on a Sunday. A woman in a dressing gown hovered behind him. 'My wife phoned the council about the smell, but they just came, knocked on the door and went away again.' He shook his head in irritation. 'He doesn't even pay rent.'

Bill explained about the warrant.

'About time too.'

The couple watched from the doorway as the officers positioned themselves. Rhona stood back as Bill knocked, expecting no reply.

It took three slams of the battering ram before the reinforced metal door gave way. Minty took his security seriously, and it soon became obvious why.

A strong chemical smell escaped through the open door. Rhona motioned to Bill not to enter.

'What is it?'

'Whatever it is, it's probably noxious. I think we need to clear the building. Phosphine gas is one of the side products of making methamphetamine. It's extremely toxic when inhaled. He'll also have been using solvents for extraction. We're lucky there hasn't been a fire or explosion. I think we need the fire brigade and some breathing apparatus.' Rhona pulled up her mask.

'Are you sure you want to go inside?'

'The sooner we know what we're dealing with, the better.'

The hall was dark and narrow. Rhona ignored the light switch and used her torch. She had no idea if the electrics worked, and she didn't want a spark igniting any lingering combustible gases.

There were three doors off the hall. One led to a grubby-looking bedroom. Another to a filthy, rubbish-strewn bathroom. The bath was full of something, she wasn't sure what. The final door led to a combined kitchen and sitting room, now a makeshift laboratory.

A number of pots sat on the cooker. Scattered on the counter nearby were matchboxes with the red phosphorus striking panel ripped off. There were rows of empty iodine tincture and solvent bottles, and packets of decongestant tablets. Minty had definitely been trying his hand at making crystal meth.

Rhona opened all the windows and retreated. The fire brigade would have to declare the flat safe before she could properly examine it. She emerged to find a fire engine pulling in below. Small groups of residents had already gathered in a nearby play area. Pulling people out of their beds and homes on a Sunday morning would hardly endear Craig Minto to his already pissed-off neighbours.

Rhona went down to meet the fire officer in charge. When she explained what had been happening in the flat, he wasn't surprised.

'Three call-outs for this kind of thing in a month. In the last one, the guy making the stuff was unconscious from the fumes. One strike of a match and the whole place would have gone up. I'll give you a shout when we've secured the building.'

Bill and Rhona retreated to a nearby café. The coffee was half decent and strong. Bill ordered sliced sausage on a roll to go with it. Rhona resisted, but not for long.

'Sniffing solvents must make you hungry.'

She added tomato ketchup to the thick slab of square sausagemeat and took a bite. They munched together in silence. The café was rapidly filling up with refugees from Minty's building. The neighbour appeared with his wife. He spotted Bill and Rhona in the corner and came across.

'That bastard could have killed us all. What are you going to do about it?'

'He'll be charged, Mr . . .?'

'Jackson.'

'You'll be asked to give a statement. I take it you'll be willing to give evidence in court?'

Mr Jackson looked perturbed. Craig Minto wasn't a man to cross.

After a moment, though, he seemed to master his fear. 'Aye, I will. You cannae let scum like that rule your life. My wee granddaughter comes to stay with us. The bastard could have killed her.'

When they were finally allowed into the flat, the air was a good deal fresher. Rhona insisted Bill wear a mask anyway. The fire team had removed the flammable material, properly logged as evidence.

'Iodine crystals and red phosphorus.' She picked up a sheaf of printouts and glanced through them. 'It's all here. How to source your ingredients. How to mix them.'

'And here's me thinking Minty was stupid.'

They had plenty of evidence with which to charge Minty, if they could find him. Although with a gap of three days between Minty's disappearance from the flat, and the police raid, forensics would have to provide a direct link between the suspect and the apparatus.

Rhona began to take samples from the crude laboratory. Bill hovered nearby, obviously wanting to say something, but having problems coming out with it. Rhona stopped what she was doing to give him an opening.

'You spoke to the professor about the online auction?' he asked.

'I went by his place last night and showed him the photographs.'

'And?'

'He pointed out something I hadn't noticed.'

'What?'

'The most recent victim has six stab wounds, the one from a month ago five, the one before that four.'

'He said nothing about Terri being the same physical type as the others?'

'He suggested all prostitutes fall into a similar type and age range. And level of vulnerability,' she added.

Bill pondered this. 'I hadn't noticed the increase in the number of stab wounds.'

'Neither had I.'

'And he thinks that's significant?'

'He was proving a point. Demonstrating how what's significant may not be the most obvious.'

'Dazzling us with his psychological insight.'

Rhona wanted to reassure Bill she was on his side, that she knew police procedure and forensic evidence provided the best possibility of catching a killer. But in this case, the killer had left traces of himself behind, confident they would lead the police nowhere. Trying to understand him and to anticipate his next move might be the only hope they had.

Rhona switched her mobile to silent while she worked. Bill had departed soon after their conversation about Magnus, declaring his intention of going back to the station. He could have asked McNab or another junior detective to handle the search at Minty's flat, and spent Sunday with his family, but Rhona suspected a day watching Margaret suffer was a prospect Bill didn't relish.

Craig Minto's flat continued to yield interesting results, but nothing obviously linking him to Lucie's murder. Trace samples taken from the bedclothes would probably be a match for the dead girl, but

Lucie's relationship with Minty was already established. Craig Minto might have been Lucie's pimp, but it seemed unlikely he was her killer. When Rhona left the flat, the fingerprint team were still hard at work. No doubt Minty's laboratory would produce a rogue's gallery of prints.

On reaching the car, Rhona checked her mobile and found a message from Chrissy. When she tried to call back, she was switched to the messaging service. She decided to go around to Chrissy's flat in person.

It took three rings on the buzzer before she got an answer.

'It's okay,' Chrissy answered sleepily, when Rhona apologised. 'I was getting up anyway.'

The flat was as messy as usual. Chrissy, though meticulous at work, lived in a pigsty at home. It was a sign of her determination not to end up obsessed with housework like her mum.

'Sam's place was always tidy.' She gave Rhona a rueful grin as she ushered her through. 'God knows what he thinks of this place.'

'How is he?'

A shadow crossed Chrissy's face. 'He's . . . thin.' Her mouth trembled a little. 'I told him about the baby.'

They stood in silence for a moment.

'I'll never forget his face when he felt it move. He says it's a girl.'

They sat in the kitchen, nursing mugs of tea, while Chrissy told Rhona a little of what had happened. Sam had been deliberately vague about his return journey to

Britain. His passport was still valid and no one had questioned his entry. There was no mention of the CD in the story and Rhona didn't ask. If Sean was right and the CD's arrival was the work of the Suleimans, Rhona didn't want to give Chrissy anything more to worry about.

'Is he coming back?' The million dollar question.

'He's going to try.'

Rhona didn't envy Chrissy. Had Sam died she would have mourned, then faced up to a life without him. A halfway house, where Sam, Chrissy and the baby lived in constant danger, might be even worse.

26

MINTY'S FLAT LAY in the criss-cross of streets north of London Road, opposite Glasgow Green. That morning, the Green was sprinkled with family groups enjoying the sunshine, a far cry from its Saturday night clientele. Bill had left the car outside Minty's with a uniformed officer, rather than take a chance and park it near the Barras.

He took a turn into Terri's lane. He had a team looking through the CCTV footage from the entire safe zone. It was remarkable how many punters knew just where to draw up to avoid their number plates being registered on camera.

The alley lay in shadow. No sunlight found its way between the high buildings. The silence was eerie, although not far away he would find the streets near the Barrowland weekend market teeming with people.

A broken pipe trickled water in a continuous stream down a wall green with mould. If Bill half-shut his eyes – the cool shadow, the sound of water, the smell of damp and growing things, the coo of a pigeon – he could imagine himself in what Calton once was. *Coilldum* – Gaelic for 'wood on the hill'.

His eyes sprang open at the clip of heels on the cobbles. A woman in knee-high boots was coming towards him. There was nothing overtly sexual about her approach, merely purposeful. In the shadow, Bill couldn't make out her face.

'Looking for me?' she said softly.

'Who are you?'

'Whoever you want me to be.'

'I'm looking for Terri Docherty.'

She sighed. 'Who the fuck isn't?' Her face emerged from the shadow. She looked him up and down. 'DI Wilson.'

Bill smiled in recognition. 'Cathy McIver. Long time no see.'

They made a right pair, middle-aged policeman and middle-aged hooker drinking tea together in a Barrowland café. None of the other customers gave them a second glance. That was Glasgow for you.

In full daylight, Cathy didn't look too good, although Bill didn't like to pass judgement. He was no spring chicken himself. Not that long ago, a BBC Scotland news report had placed life expectancy in Calton lower than the Gaza Strip or some areas of Iraq. Males were expected to live until they were fifty-eight. Women in Cathy's line of work, especially if they had drug problems, were lucky if they reached thirty. Cathy was a survivor.

Bill had met Cathy through her second husband. Mikey McIver had the Glasgow banter – they said he could sell a crucifix to an Orangeman. His two stalls on the Barras made him a decent living, though most of the money went down his throat. But the days when wide boys ruled the Barras were over. The second-hand goods and banter had been replaced by businesses selling counterfeit DVDs, CDs and smuggled tobacco, run by serious criminal gangs.

Mikey had died in a drunken knife fight. When Cathy came to the mortuary to identify him, she'd cried on Bill's shoulder. He realised later that they were tears of relief.

'Two wasters for husbands – but thank God, no kids,' Cathy toasted that with her tea mug, then asked Bill about his own children. He was surprised she remembered.

'Teenagers now. Robbie's into computers and the cinema. Lisa's . . . she's the same age as the missing girl.' Bill didn't mention Margaret, because the words stuck in his throat.

Cathy gave him an appraising look. 'You're a lucky man.'

Bill didn't feel it.

'Thought you would have retired by now.'

She exposed a row of nicotine-stained teeth. 'Give up sex, you mean?' A laugh set her off coughing. 'I should. But I don't like to let my regulars down.' She sounded as though she meant it. 'I don't do the streets much any more. My flat's safer and I only invite the ones I know.'

'D'you know Brendan Paterson?'

Cathy tilted her head, thought about it for a moment, then said, 'I know Brendan. He's okay.' Coming from Cathy that was high praise. 'Why?'

'He was one of Terri's regulars.'

She nodded, not surprised.

Bill wanted to ask what the word on the street was about the killings, and about Terri, but he didn't want to push it. Cathy had to live there. She'd survived because she didn't piss anyone off.

Cathy fingered the handle of her mug. 'You lot have Terri's handbag, money and bank card. Minty's been around looking for what he's owed.'

'Leanne?'

Cathy nodded. 'She's got to pay him off.'

'When did he show up?'

'Last night. Scared the lassie shitless. That's why I came by the alley – I thought Leanne might still be working. The sun brings the punters out,' she added by way of explanation.

'I'll talk to Leanne,' Bill promised.

'Talking won't help.'

'We'd lift Minty if we could find him.'

Cathy knew what he was asking her. She shot him a shrewd look. 'Streets would be safer without him.'

Bill slipped her a card with his number on it. 'Call me. *Any* time.'

Cathy made no comment, but put the card in her pocket.

A young man came in and glanced their way. Bill deliberately didn't look around, but Cathy did.

'Hey, Brendan, come and meet a friend of mine.'

Brendan placed his mug of coffee next to Cathy's and pulled out a chair. He sat down, avoiding Bill's eye. Cathy did the introductions.

'Cop?'

Cathy nodded. 'He needs to talk about Terri.'

Brendan suddenly looked queasy. 'I don't know anything.' He rose as if to go. Cathy put her hand on his arm.

'Better to talk to the DI here, than at your stall.' She didn't need to add that the stall would be open to prying eyes.

'Or at the station,' added Bill.

Brendan sank back in the seat, a sullen, resigned expression on his face. His eyes darted between Cathy and Bill. Cathy smiled encouragingly. 'You want Terri found, don't you? Otherwise you might end up with an old bird like me on a Wednesday night.' She finished the rest of her tea and stood up purposefully.

'Good luck,' were her parting words to Bill.

Bill gave Brendan a few moments' respite, before he cut to the chase. 'Your number was on Terri's phone. Her partner says you were a regular. She knew your name and that you have two children.'

Brendan assumed a defensive air. 'I never hurt Terri. And I always paid – *and* gave her and her pal freebies.' He stuttered to a halt, realising mentioning the CDs might be a mistake.

'Tell me everything you know about Terri. That's all I'm interested in.'

Bill stood in front of the distinctive neon sign. *Barrowland*. Recently voted by bands as the best venue in the UK, and second best in the world. Not bad for a

Glasgow ballroom with a modest capacity of 1,900 people. Famous for its great acoustics, magic atmosphere, and for the long list of famous musicians who'd graced its stage.

But that wasn't all it was famous for. Bible John, the last serial killer to roam Glasgow's streets, had operated from around there. Three women, all picked up at this ballroom in the late 60s. All strangled and dumped nearby. The last one, Helen Puttock, was seen with a tall, slim, red-haired man, who called himself John, spoke politely and liked to quote from the Bible. The police never found him. No one arrested, no one charged, at the time.

They thought they had him in 1996 and again in 2004. Bible John, for ever Glasgow's bogey man. Already the papers were retelling his story, having noticed the similarities in location and method of these new murders. If Bible John was still alive, he'd be in his fifties. Not too old to kill.

Bill looked up at the famous sign, as the crowds of shoppers divided around him. He was just a teenager when Bible John killed his last victim, and now he remembered his mother's shock and distress as she listened to the news. The whole of Glasgow was talking about Bible John. The tabloids already had a name for their latest city killer, *The Gravedigger*.

Cathy had told him nothing, but he'd got the message. When she knew something, particularly about Minty's whereabouts, she would be in touch. Cathy was willing to put herself in danger to help Leanne.

Brendan hadn't struck Bill as a violent punter, not like Minty. He'd confirmed he'd met Terri every Wednesday night, after his regular darts match at the pub. He'd got a bit stroppy when Bill told him they would require a DNA sample. When Bill had pointed out it was either that, or a constable visiting his home on Monday morning, he had changed his tune.

A general appeal had already been issued for anyone using Terri and Lucie's services to come forward and avoid having the police turn up on their doorstep. So far, the response had been slow.

When Bill returned, two wee girls were cycling on the pavement outside Minty's. The uniform guarding the car was engaging them in conversation, doing his bit for community policing. The lassies only wanted to know if he was carrying a gun, and, if so, could they see it?

'Fingerprint team have left,' he told Bill when the girls had trundled away. 'Someone from the council is resealing the door.'

On the drive back, Bill pondered the dead end the investigation had entered. Everyone working flat out, but no definite line of enquiry, just an endless collection of data. Peter Sutcliffe killed thirteen women before they caught him, in a piss-up of an investigation blamed on too much data, all of it stored on cards, with no proper cross-referencing. The Sutcliffe fiasco had paved the way for HOLMES – the Home Office Large Major Enquiry System, which allowed police forces to store, search and match gathered evidence. Strathclyde force certainly couldn't blame a lack of fast database access, or good forensic facilities, for their failure to identify even one suspect.

Maybe he was wrong and the professor could provide an insight on the killer. Bill had to admit, if only to himself, that he could use all the help he could get.

27

LEANNE HUNG AROUND the church all day on Sunday, keeping well out of sight. She'd explained to the priest about Minty and the money. Father Duffy, suffering from a hangover and the after-effects of mortal sin, offered her enough to pay Minty off.

Leanne stared at him in amazement. 'You'll give me the money?'

'I will.'

Leanne wanted to hug him. 'Oh, thank you, Father.'

He brushed her gratitude aside. 'I'd like you to make your confession before you go.'

Leanne nodded, aware that this was the price of her good fortune. They sat either side of the partition and Leanne went through the usual performance.

'Forgive me, Father, for I have sinned. I let a man have carnal knowledge of me.'

'And who was this man?'

'A priest, Father.'

'And what did this priest ask you to do?'

As she made her act of contrition, there was a grunting noise through the partition. The confession was Father Duffy's dessert, before the whisky wore off. When he finished, he passed the money through the space below the grating. Leanne looked down at the notes, tears streaming down her cheeks.

They had all been there at some time or another, sitting in the confessional, talking dirty. Lucie, Terri, Cathy. Cathy had hilarious stories to tell about Duffy. She never called him Father. Once she swore he stuck his stiff prick through the hole with a crucifix hanging on the end, and told her to kiss it.

'The prick, or the cross?' she'd asked.

They'd all laughed at that.

At least they kept the priest's money for themselves. Minty never knew about Father Duffy's little habit. Even Lucie had managed to keep that from him.

Leanne shut the door behind her and squeezed past the priest's car. She checked the coast was clear, before making her way onto the street. Her relief at getting the money evaporated when she thought about Terri. A sudden hope that she might arrive home and find Terri there quickened her step.

When she reached the flat, she found the door sealed, a new lock in place. Leanne tried her key but it wouldn't work. She longed for something to eat and a hot shower. The Valium she'd taken the night before had worn off, and her nerves were jangling. She could go to the centre, or, better still, find Cathy. Cathy would help, maybe even be the go-between with Minty. Leanne didn't want to face Minty again, even with the money.

Leanne dialled Cathy's number, hoping she wasn't already working. Cathy answered almost immediately.

'Leanne. Are you okay?'

The concern in the older woman's voice brought tears to Leanne's eyes. 'Can I come around?'

'Sure.'

Cathy's flat was in a 70s block on Duke Street. The caretaker let Leanne in, giving the miniskirt and stilettos the once-over, but saying nothing. Cathy and he were pals. In exchange for services, he never questioned Cathy's visitors and fixed anything that went wrong in the flat. 'Better than a fucking husband in all respects,' Cathy always said.

Cathy was waiting at the door. Leanne hadn't realised how bad she must look until she saw Cathy's reaction.

'Jesus, girl, what the hell happened to you?'

Cathy handed her a large glass of vodka.

'The old bugger gave you enough to pay off Minty?' she looked impressed. 'Christian charity, or to keep your mouth shut?'

The priest didn't normally cruise the red-light district. He preferred ordering by phone. A check on his mobile calls could provide *Panorama* with a whole programme on the dissolution of the Catholic clergy.

'Will you pay Minty off for me?'

Cathy understood her fear. 'If I can find him. The police raided his flat. He's gone to ground.'

That changed things. If the police picked up Minty, Leanne might be able to keep the money. Cathy knew what she was thinking.

'Minty's got pals it's better not to cross,' she said, pouring them both another vodka.

Leanne swallowed a mouthful, enjoying the warmth as it slid down her throat. She felt safe with Cathy, just as she had with Terri.

'I'll find Minty and pay him for you.'

'How?'

Cathy shook her head. 'I have my ways.' Despite her light-hearted tone, Leanne knew Cathy had her doubts. The rule was usually to avoid Minty at all costs.

'Thanks.'

Cathy caught her hand and gave it a squeeze. They'd evaded the subject of Terri until now.

'There's something else,' Cathy said. 'A whisper, nothing more, that Terri's still alive.'

Leanne couldn't bear to believe it.

'Don't get your hopes up. I've got to go out later to meet someone. Maybe I'll know more after that.'

Leanne's eyes were closing. A hot shower, food, vodka and the possibility that Terri was alive were all helping her shut down. At Cathy's insistence, Leanne stretched out on the settee and sank into oblivious sleep.

She woke with a start. A full moon shone in through the open curtains, and the flat was completely silent – eerily so. She was used to noise on the stairs, raucous voices. Nine storeys up, there was nothing.

She threw off the blanket Cathy had spread over her, and stood up. Her legs felt shaky and she steadied herself on the arm of the sofa. Was Cathy back?

Leanne listened hard – nothing, not even the tick of a clock. She went looking for the bedroom and found the door lying open, the bed unoccupied. There was a digital alarm on the bedside table. It said 3.30.

Cathy had told her Terri was alive. Leanne had nursed herself to sleep with that thought. Cathy had gone to meet someone. Someone who had news of Terri.

But she hadn't come back.

What if Cathy was wrong and Terri was dead? Leanne sat down on the bed, a small but insidious voice telling her that of course Terri was dead. She was a fucking idiot to think otherwise.

Leanne tried to take a deep breath to quell the panic that seized her. Her chest was so tight the air hurt her lungs as it went in. If she took some more Valium, she would feel better, and be able to think. Leanne opened the bedside drawer. No pill strips. Cathy had given her two Valium with the first vodka, so they had to be somewhere.

Leanne made for the bathroom and checked the cabinet above the sink. When she'd no luck there, she returned to the living room and tried to remember. Cathy had brought her the vodka and pills from the kitchen.

Leanne headed there. A mug of tea sat congealing next to an overflowing ashtray. Nearby, a strip of pills was wedged behind the vodka bottle. Leanne poured a glass and swallowed two pills with the vodka. She felt better almost immediately, although the drug had had no time to work. She contemplated taking a couple more, just to make sure, then decided against it. She wanted to stay awake for Cathy.

A police siren broke the silence. Leanne watched it wail past on Duke Street, her heart pounding. A light flickered on in the derelict building across the road. It moved from window to window on the ground floor, then went out. Someone was using it as a squat, no doubt. Good luck to them.

The moon had disappeared behind thick cloud. Leanne gazed down at the lights of the city spread out beneath her.

'Where are you?' she whispered, not knowing whether she was talking to Cathy or Terri. As though in answer her phone rang out. Leanne stumbled to her bag.

'Yes?'

In the silence that followed, she could make out the sound of someone breathing. Leanne glanced at the screen, but didn't recognise the number. A new punter, or someone who wanted to get off on phoning a prostitute?

'Fuck off,' she said, when she figured she'd waited long enough.

'Leanne?'

'Who the fuck are you?'

'Your friend asked me to call. She wants to see you.'

'Terri?'

28

BILL PULLED INTO the drive. The lights were on, but when he opened the front door the silence suggested no one was at home. He made for the kitchen and heard the chat and laughter coming from out back. God, he'd forgotten about the barbecue. Bill glanced at his watch. Nine o'clock. They must have given up waiting for him.

They were all there. His little family. Robbie playing the man of the house, cooking the meat. Lisa and Margaret talking. Bill stood for a moment at the kitchen window, feeling immensely grateful to have something like this to come home to. Grateful and guilty at the same time. Bill didn't want to disturb them. He felt as if he were bringing a taint of evil into a circle of love. He went upstairs, showered and changed before heading outside.

Lisa spotted him first. 'You're very very late!'

Margaret looked relieved, yet anxious. Bill shook his head, indicating he didn't want to talk about it.

'Any food left?'

Robbie began piling meat onto a plate.

'Wine?' Lisa asked, 'or would you prefer something stronger?'

'Wine's fine.'

Bill tucked into the food while Lisa and Robbie filled him in on the day's events. Margaret sat quietly watching their animated faces. She wore a brightly patterned head-scarf and dangly earrings, in the shape of Celtic crosses. Her face was too thin, but she had some colour today. Bill wanted to sweep her in his arms and crush her tightly. He smiled over, hoping she would get the message.

Bill thought of Cathy, not much younger than they were. A victim of life's great lottery. They said it was about life choices, but what if you didn't have any? Most people would dismiss Cathy's life as useless, but he knew better. Cathy understood humanity – the evil and the good in men. It's easy to be good, when people are good to you. It's easy to be nice, when you're happy.

Margaret brought him a whisky with his coffee. The pale colour told him it was a malt. The sky glowed with the setting sun. Bill loved the long summer light of Scotland. They'd played golf at midnight on that Orkney holiday.

'Remember Orkney?' he said.

'Shipwrecks,' Robbie smiled. 'We played on them on the beach.'

'That funny little Italian chapel made out of a Nissan hut,' Lisa added.

'I have a criminal psychologist working with me.' Bill didn't tell them which case. 'Professor Magnus Pirie. He's an Orcadian.'

He wondered why he'd brought up Magnus. Margaret was looking at him, surprised. He normally never discussed colleagues, or work, in front of the kids.

'He reminds me of that guy in the film you like, *Highlander*. He's kind of . . . rugged.'

'Christopher Lambert?' Robbie said.

Lisa looked impressed. 'When are you inviting him for dinner?'

Bill imagined Magnus there, and realised he would fit right in. Magnus would read Bill's family and act accordingly. They would all like him.

Bill realised his family had fallen silent, and Lisa and her mother were exchanging glances. Lisa had obviously been waiting until he was fed, watered and relaxed before she asked him something.

'Dad, Mum thinks it's okay, but said to ask you.' The words came out in a rush.

Bill was immediately on his guard. 'Ask me what?'

'I've got tickets for a gig at the Barrow . . .'

He didn't give her time to finish. 'No,' said Bill firmly, avoiding Margaret's eye.

'But Dad, I'm going with Susie. We'll stay together. It'll be okay.'

Bill stood up. 'No.'

He walked away, before Lisa's distress could change his mind. Anger bubbled up inside him. Margaret should have realised there was no way he would let his daughter near the Barrowland at night, with a maniac on the loose.

He heard Lisa's wail from the garden as he climbed the stairs.

Later, in bed, Bill held Margaret close, stroking her bare head.

'You can't keep her a wee girl for ever.'

'The area's too dangerous.'

'What if I drop them off and pick them up afterwards?'

Margaret, the voice of reason.

She raised her face to his, and he kissed her. She felt frail in his arms. Bill could feel bones that he hadn't felt before, but he fought the fear that rose in his chest and tried to concentrate on the moment. His mobile buzzed on the bedside table.

Margaret drew away, assuming he would answer.

Bill reached across and switched it off.

29

THE MEETING ROOM was hot and humid. Someone had brought in an electric fan, but its whirring combined with the hum from the overhead projector had made it too difficult to hear. Bill had eventually switched the fan off.

Sissons was currently delivering his report on the third body.

'Unfortunately the usual signs of asphyxiation, petechiae on the eyelids and cyanosis, were all obliterated by decomposition and saponification.'

Sissons caught the Super's puzzled look and put up his first photograph of the corpse. Grave waxing had retained the contours of the face, but it was still difficult to envisage the girl whose photograph they'd found online.

'She was young, mid teens, still carrying what we call puppy fat. Nothing in the remains to identify her, apart from a ring with the initials *AS*. The combination of fatty tissue, damp warm conditions and alkaline soil began the formation of adipocere, a soap-like material. Difficult to say how long she's been in the ground. At a guess, between four and six months. Mode of death assumed to be strangulation, like the others, although this can't be proved. There is, however, evidence of injury to the pelvic area.' He also confirmed that the heel of the victim's shoe had been found inserted into the vagina. 'One more thing. The girl was four months pregnant, with a male child.'

Sissons passed the baton to Rhona, who brought up enhanced images of the knots.

'Skin flakes have been retrieved from all three knots. They have a hundred per cent DNA match.'

'So the same man killed all three women?' Sutherland asked for confirmation.

'The same hands tied all three knots. The chirality, or usual direction of movement, makes it more likely that the person was left-handed. Also, Judy Brown and I sifted through a large quantity of soil from both burial sites. In the case of victim three, I found a single hair in the soil taken from the grave.'

A magnified image of a hair appeared on the screen.

'As you can see, the hair is blond and approximately one inch in length. I can confirm the hair is human and does not belong to the victim. A DNA comparison with the skin cells was again one hundred per cent positive.'

'The killer's blond,' Bill said.

'There was no evidence of chemical colouring.'

Rhona had had the same feeling as Bill, when, after hours of sifting, she'd discovered the hair. This was the first concrete feature they had of the killer. Now they could at least imagine him.

It was Magnus's turn. He pointed the remote at the overhead projector and switched it off. The sudden and complete silence startled them.

'I thought I would just talk this through with you, then if you think it's helpful, you're welcome to a copy of my preliminary profile.'

His manner was modest and unassuming, but with an underlying confidence. Magnus Pirie was passionate about his field and believed he had something to contribute, but he wasn't going to browbeat them into acceptance. Rhona found herself willing Bill to listen.

'Dr MacLeod has given us a partial image of the killer. What I'd like to do is examine his character, and try and make some sense of his world.' Magnus's gaze swept around the expectant faces. Rhona smiled supportively.

'Mercifully, serial killers are rare. Unfortunately, this means data is scarce. Scotland produced four last century, but only Bible John operated within Scotland; rather bizarrely, in the same area as our current killer. He also strangled his victims.' Magnus gave a wry smile. 'I'm not suggesting Bible John has returned. One thing we are reasonably sure of is that killers don't stop killing, not unless they're dead themselves. A gap of thirty-seven years is a long time not to re-offend,' he paused strategically, 'assuming he stayed in the UK.'

Rhona stole a quick glance at Bill and found him leaning forward, listening intently.

Magnus took a sip of water.

'Because Bible John was never caught, we were never able to psychologically examine him. We don't know what happened to him in childhood, or when he began offending. In the mid 70s, in the north of England, Peter Sutcliffe murdered thirteen women and attacked another seven, while living as a married man. Sutcliffe claimed God told him to kill the women. Bible John also referenced God in his dealings with his victims. Sutcliffe's attacks on his victims were particularly violent; one was stabbed twenty-five times.'

Magnus paused again. The atmosphere in the room was electric. They were growing impatient, waiting for him to pronounce on the case.

'I believe that, like Sutcliffe, our man is not a loner. He is confident around women. He can be charming and persuasive and is used to getting what he wants. He does not kill on his own patch, but one he visits for the purpose. He enjoys moving between his norm and what he regards as the degenerate section of humanity. Think Dr Jekyll and Mr Hyde. He's exploring the Mr Hyde in his nature, and is growing increasingly fond of it. He chooses prostitutes because, with them, his power is complete. These women are not people to him, but objects to be manipulated, abused, then dispensed with. He is methodical. He plans and expects the plans to work out. He is confident he can outwit us. The insertion of an object into a victim's body is rare and is sometimes linked to a failure to achieve penetration in the normal way. This may be one factor in his increasing anger and levels of violence.'

Magnus cleared his throat and continued.

'Rapists are usually in their early to mid twenties. Serial killers are more likely to be older. Violent, serious crimes tend to come later in an offender's career. So the question we need to ask is, where has he been? It is possible to slip through the net. Ian Huntley did so successfully for years, being accused but never charged for sexual offences until he finally moved on to murder. Without doubt, our man has been offending. The most likely explanation is that he's been raping and abusing women who haven't reported it, perhaps prostitutes, perhaps a partner.'

He was silent for a moment.

'So our man is mid to late thirties, with blond hair, left-handed. He has a car to transport his victims, which means he has a reasonable income. He is familiar with Glasgow, but doesn't necessarily live here. Dr MacLeod identified sea salt and diesel traces on the ligature used on the last victim, which suggests he is closely connected to boating. We can't be precise on all dates, but on Terri's disappearance and Lucie's death, we are. On those two dates there were a number of yacht races taking place on the Clyde. Competitors in these are not confined to the west of Scotland clubs. I would be interested in seeing a list of members of clubs using the Clyde and also outside competitors.' He paused long enough to take another sip of water. 'I also believe the killer researched the Necropolis well before he chose it, possibly taking one of the guided tours. We need to ask ourselves, why the Necropolis? I understand the place is used by doggers and is a recommended site of theirs. Is that what drew him there in the first place? He chose a secluded spot for the earlier burial. The later ones, a more prominent grave, suggesting a greater confidence. The disturbance of the earlier grave indicates he wanted us to find it, which means he returned despite the police presence.'

There was silence, as they digested the information.

'And this latest development, of a possible online auction?' Sutherland asked.

Magnus took time replying. 'The killer is a sexual sadist. We know his attacks are becoming more frequent and more violent. I think he drew us to the third grave because he is finished with the Necropolis. The question is, where and what next? It's perfectly possible for a website to stay hidden from search engines, with directions given only to a chosen few. If your IT team has found his, then they are either very skilled, very lucky, or – the more likely explanation – the killer intended this to happen.'

'He's challenging us to do something about it,' Bill said.

'It would appear so.'

'And what do you suggest?'

'I suggest I go online and place a bid.'

30

AFTER THE MEETING, Bill disappeared with the Super. Rhona suspected the DI was being grilled on the deployment of personnel, man hours being spent, and of course, the absence of a suspect. Magnus's suggestion that he should make a bid in the online auction had been rejected. Doubtless, the next move was also being discussed behind closed doors.

Bill had been silent after Magnus's performance, though Rhona sensed no antagonism. There was a danger that they would concentrate solely on Magnus's profile, which might be wrong. She, like Bill, was more inclined to deal in hard facts. The murderer was probably blond and sailed in salt water.

Rhona wasn't anxious to hang around with so much to do back at the lab, but it seemed churlish to refuse Magnus's offer of a coffee. They made a mutual decision not to visit the police canteen, and decided to take advantage of Glasgow's famous café society.

A wall of heat met them on their exit from the police station. Car fumes from the busy one-way system choked the already stagnant air. Despite this, Sauchiehall Street was buzzing. There was nothing a Glaswegian liked better than hitting the shops in the sunshine, especially since the sun had been in short supply of late.

Magnus's striking looks and accent caused a bit of a stir among the female staff of the café-bar they chose. The young girl, who came to take their order, lost her tongue in the process. Magnus appeared completely unaware of the effect he was having. It rather endeared him to Rhona.

The coffees arrived quickly and with a smile. Glasgow's citizens had a reputation for friendliness, but in Magnus's company it appeared guaranteed.

'So, what did you think?' Magnus said, when the waitress finally dragged herself away.

'It sounded plausible, but if we're being honest, it doesn't get us any closer to picking up a suspect, or finding Terri.'

Magnus nodded. 'I'm going to see Terri's parents this afternoon. Did you know her father works at the Kip Marina?'

'Why didn't you mention that at the meeting?'

Magnus remained unfazed by her response. 'I discussed my plans with DI Wilson beforehand.'

So that was why Bill's reaction had been more positive than Rhona had expected. One thing was certain, Magnus's next move was never going to be easy to anticipate.

'I wondered if you fancied tagging along in your forensic capacity, to take saline samples and red diesel from the yard?'

Salinity did vary throughout the estuary, so it might prove useful. Red diesel might not be so conclusive.

'Bill's okay with this?'

'It was Bill who suggested it.'

Magnus was silent as Rhona negotiated the city centre traffic and made her way onto the M8. Crossing the Kingston Bridge reminded her of Terri's handbag. It had been retrieved from the westbound carriageway, suggesting the car was heading out of town, although there were plenty of exits that allowed you to double back. Magnus had suggested the killer knew Glasgow well, but didn't necessarily live there. If that was the case, he could have buried Terri's body anywhere in the acres of surrounding countryside, and it might never be found.

Bill had taken Rhona's advice and asked Judy to study aerial photographs of the Necropolis, checking for the telltale colour changes in vegetation caused by recent decomposition. No further graves had been identified from the photos. Maybe Magnus was right and they'd found all the victims who'd met their end in the City of the Dead.

She had called in at the lab first, leaving Magnus to survey the luscious vista of Kelvingrove Park, while she checked on Chrissy, who was attempting to lift prints from Terri's handbag.

'Any luck?'

'Two, but not great and they might turn out to be Terri's. How did the meeting go?'

'The discovery of the hair went down well.'

'And what did our Norse God have to say?'

'He gave us a preliminary profile. It sounded plausible. Also Terri's father works at the Inverkip Marina.'

'Really?'

'Bill wants me to take a water and diesel test, while Magnus talks to Terri's parents.'

'So, a jolly in the sunshine?'

'I won't be away that long.'

Chrissy gave such a deep sigh that Rhona contemplated sending her instead, but she was keen to observe Magnus in action.

As they headed down the M8 towards Greenock, Magnus brought out *A Guide to Clyde Yacht Clubs*. The Firth of Clyde boasted ten sailing clubs, from the centre of Glasgow to Troon on the south-west coast, by way of every loch that fed into the firth. The list included two clubs at the foot of Gare Loch, home to Faslane Naval Base and the Trident nuclear submarine fleet. Looking for a murderous mariner in the sailing world of the Firth of Clyde would be like looking for the proverbial needle in a haystack.

On a day like this with Aegean skies, it would have been difficult to believe they were in Scotland, were it not for the spectacular view across to the Cowal Peninsula and the distant rise of Ben Lomond.

Magnus gazed out of the window, enthralled. 'I've been in Glasgow two years and I've never come this far west. I always go home if I get more than a weekend off.'

'Is Orkney like this?'

Magnus laughed. 'No. The islands are pretty flat. Ward Hill on Hoy is the highest point and it's less than 2,000 feet. Peedie in comparison to those mountains.'

'I take it "peedie" means wee?'

He nodded. 'Although we also say peedie wee.'

Rhona pointed across the water to the village of Kilcreggan. 'I went camping there when I was a Girl Guide. We were eaten alive by midges. Ended up sleeping in the local church.'

'Ah, midges. We're not bothered with them much in Orkney. Probably because of the hundred-mile-an-hour gales.'

They'd relaxed into a camaraderie that made Rhona feel slightly guilty. It wasn't flirting exactly, but it wasn't far off it. She decided to change the subject.

'I understand Terri's mother has already been inter-viewed?'

Magnus took his cue from her and changed tone. 'She said she expected Terri home the weekend after she had disappeared.'

'I thought Terri had cut all contact with her family?'

'According to Bill, one of Terri's regulars main-tained her father told her never to get in touch again.'

'And her mother knew that?'

'That's what I aim to find out.'

31

RHONA HADN'T VISITED Gourock since she was a child. Her father had been fond of the seaside town and had taken her mum and her 'doon the water' whenever the opportunity arose. Rhona suspected that the further west her dad travelled, the more the landscape reminded him of Skye.

Heading to Gourock by train had been one of the pleasures of her childhood. Rhona still remembered disembarking in the Victorian station building, with its glazed canopies; the feeling she'd entered some magical sunlit kingdom. The domed roof was gone, bulldozed in the 80s, the stately ticket office now unbelievably a PortaKabin.

Rhona followed the shore road, noting both the familiar and the new. The outdoor pool she'd swum in as a child was still there, but refurbished and boasting a year-round thirty-degree temperature on the board outside. Years ago, the incoming tide had simply washed over a low concrete wall, covering the base of the pool with sand. Rhona felt a small pang of regret. There had been something exotic about swimming among fronds of seaweed.

Magnus interrupted her reminiscences to give her directions. 'Take the next left going up the hill.'

The Dochertys' house sat alone, high above the town. A post-war bungalow with a large garden, it called to mind children playing on the lawn, or climbing up to the tree house Rhona could see in a large spreading oak. The garden was neat and well kept, but looked empty somehow.

'Mrs Docherty's expecting us.' Magnus glanced at his watch. 'We're a little early.'

The crunch of wheels on gravel brought no response from the house. Later, a flash of colour approached from the direction of the tree house, suggesting their arrival had been observed from there.

The woman who walked towards them wore a blouse and light-coloured slacks, her hair cut short. As her face came into view, Rhona saw her deep worry-lines and under-eye shadows. Here was someone who didn't sleep at night and got no peace in daytime. Worry was as corrosive as any disease.

Magnus held out his hand. 'Magnus Pirie. I'm a criminal psychologist helping look for your daughter.' He indicated Rhona. 'This is Dr MacLeod from Strathclyde forensic department.'

There was silence as the woman regarded Rhona with interest. 'I watch CSI,' she offered, eventually. 'I enjoy seeing them catch the killers.'

Rhona said nothing, not wanting to shatter the woman's illusions.

Mrs Docherty led them into a bright sitting room where the chintz-covered suite matched the curtains, and the carpet was soft and deep beneath their feet. On a polished sideboard stood a row of photographs in silver frames. A couple posed with a little boy and girl very close in age, then there was a selection of the same children growing up. Terri and her brother looked so alike they might have been twins.

Mrs Docherty ushered them to a seat on the couch and offered them tea. When the woman departed to put the kettle on Magnus took the opportunity to wander around the room, looking more closely at the photographs and staring out of the window.

You could tell a great deal about the occupants of a house by the rooms they chose to live in. This had been a bone of contention for Rhona when Sean moved in. He was happy amidst disorder. She wasn't. Gradually they'd adapted enough to rub along together. Still, even now, when Sean went on tour Rhona tidied away his clutter and returned with pleasure to her habitual minimalism.

Rhona couldn't imagine how sad it must be to sit in this room with a photograph of your missing child.

'Please call me Nora,' insisted Mrs Docherty as she poured the tea.

They all drank and Rhona waited for Magnus to start the proceedings.

'Is your husband going to join us?' he finally asked.

A shadow crossed Nora's face, then she mustered herself. 'He has to work today.'

The embarrassed silence extended as a flush blossomed on Nora's cheeks. She sought refuge in handing around a plate of biscuits. Magnus took one. Rhona joined him. The woman looked so uncomfortable she couldn't bear to refuse.

'You expected Terri to arrive on Friday night?' Magnus asked.

'She said she would come down at the weekend.'

'Did your husband know?'

Nora studied her cup. 'We didn't discuss it.'

'Was Mr Docherty here on Friday night?'

Nora threw Magnus a guarded look. 'He went out in the car about eleven. He does that sometimes. Drives about. It keeps his mind off things.'

'What time did he get back?'

'I don't know. I fell asleep.' Nora changed the subject. 'I went to the drop-in centre on Saturday. I wanted to talk to people who knew Terri. I wanted to meet her partner, Leanne,' she added defiantly.

'And did you?'

'She didn't come in, but Marje said she would give Leanne my number and ask her to call. She hasn't yet.' She looked anxiously at Magnus as if he could help with that.

Magnus's next question caught Rhona by surprise.

'Nora, do you believe your daughter is still alive?'

Nora replied instantly. 'I know she is.'

'How do you know?'

Nora took a deep breath, then glanced swiftly at the row of photographs. 'When Terri's brother Philip was sixteen, he collapsed at school and was rushed to hospital. His guidance teacher, Mr Beattie, phoned me. As I drove there, I felt . . .' she stumbled, corrected herself, 'I *sensed* my son die.' Nora was reliving the moment. 'I was right. The time was logged on his chart.' She checked for a dismissive reaction from Magnus and found none.

'And you've felt nothing like that about Terri?'

'I'm very frightened, all the time. But no, I haven't felt that.'

'Tell me about her.'

Nora spoke for an hour; about Terri as a baby, as a little girl who rode ponies with her brother. 'They were so close they were like twins. When Philip died, Terri was distraught. They said she would get over it. She never did.' Nora gave them an apologetic look. 'We weren't much use to her. We were grieving ourselves.' She looked down at her hands, clasping and unclasping them in her lap. 'Terri became clinically depressed. She told me once . . . that she'd lost her soul.' Nora's voice cracked. 'Then she found heroin and that took away the pain.'

Losing one child to illness then losing a second to drugs seemed unbearable. Rhona had avoided all of this by giving her child away for adoption. It was something she tortured herself with every day. Here, in this room, it seemed unforgivable.

'Terri has kept in touch?'

'She said she was coming down this weekend. She told me she was clean. Marje at the centre said it was true,' Nora's tone defied any possible scepticism. She explained about sitting up waiting for a phone call, then seeing the news and calling the helpline.

'Did your husband know she was coming home?'

Over Nora's shoulder Rhona could see the photograph of Mr Docherty with his two young children. She'd heard about this man, through Bill and now

Nora. An elusive figure lurking at the edge of this family tragedy.

Nora looked distressed. 'David won't talk about Terri any more. He says she's as dead to us as Philip.' She threw Magnus an agonised glance. 'Terri lied over and over again. She wasn't Terri any more. She would say anything, do anything to get the drug. It broke David's heart.'

'You mentioned Philip's guidance teacher, Mr Beattie.'

'A kind man. He tried to help Terri after Philip died. He runs the school sailing club. He taught them both to sail.'

By the time they came to leave, Magnus's questioning had revealed much about the Docherty family. How it had operated up until Philip's death, and how they had survived afterwards. Terri had come from a good strong home. It made Rhona sad to think even that hadn't been enough to save her. No wonder her parents were devastated. Rhona wondered how they managed to breathe, let alone function.

Nora didn't look too keen when Magnus asked for directions to Inverkip Marina.

'David won't talk to you,' she said, apologising in advance.

'We'll try anyway.' Magnus clasped Nora's hand. 'I want to thank you, Nora. What you've told me has helped.'

A flicker of a smile crossed her face. Rhona prayed that Magnus wasn't giving the poor woman false hope.

The Kip Marina lay to their west. Rhona was less familiar with this stretch of the road, although she remembered once walking as far as the Cloch Lighthouse. A little past Cloch Point Magnus asked her to draw into a car park next to a picnic area and got out, saying he had to make a call. Five minutes later he was back.

They completed the remaining miles to Inverkip in silence. Rhona had no idea what the call was about or what Magnus was thinking, and he didn't seem in the mood to share it with her.

The area around the marina was a hive of activity in the sunshine. Sailing the west coast of Scotland was a popular pastime. A sign near the gate informed them that any visitors should make themselves known at reception. The woman in the small office gave them a sharp look and asked for identification, which she examined closely.

'You're not from the press then?'

'We're definitely not from the press,' Magnus assured her.

'I don't want folk hounding David. God knows how he manages to get out of bed in the morning, let alone turn up for work.'

Docherty was in the servicing yard, a sleek motor yacht hoisted above him. He must have heard their approach, but didn't look around from his work painting the keel.

'Mr Docherty.'

'Aye.'

'May I speak to you?'

The muscles on the man's shoulders bunched as he slowly turned around to face them.

Rhona saw the likeness immediately. Of the two children, Terri looked most like her father. Rhona wondered if they were alike in temperament.

Docherty's expression remained blank while Magnus explained who they were. 'We'd like to ask you a few questions about your daughter, Mr Docherty, if that's all right.'

Docherty turned his back on them and went back to painting the keel. 'My daughter's dead.'

'Mr Docherty . . .' Rhona began.

'I said my daughter is dead.' The words came out in an angry staccato.

'We don't think Terri is dead,' said Magnus.

At this, Docherty's head jerked around. The brush remained poised in the air, red paint dribbling down the handle onto his hand. A flicker of something like suspicion lit his eyes.

'You've been meeting Terri without telling your wife, haven't you, Mr Docherty?'

Docherty turned swiftly away.

'When did you last see Terri?' Magnus's voice had changed tone. His jaw was set, his stare steely.

The tension between the two men was palpable. Still Docherty didn't look at Magnus or answer him.

'We have reason to believe you met with Terri the night she disappeared.'

A police car swung into the yard, Bill in the driving seat, McNab at his side. Now Rhona knew who Magnus had been talking to on the phone.

The car drew alongside and Docherty caught sight of it. Rhona watched as the paintbrush slid from his hand and rattled down the side of the keel, splattering paint like sprayed blood.

'Mr Docherty,' Bill said. 'I'd like you to accompany me to the police station to be interviewed in connection with the disappearance of your daughter Terri.'

32

DOCHERTY WAS SLUMPED in the back seat next to
McNab. It looked as though he was on standby. Bill
had tried suggesting he call his wife, tell her where he
was going, but had got nothing back but a blank look.

After his initial shock at their request to accompany
them to the station, Docherty had come quietly. Bill
wondered if Docherty cared much about anything any
more. According to Beattie, Terri's father had forbidden her ever to contact the family again. That's why
she'd called Beattie for help. Bill wasn't impressed with
the former student counsellor, nor his account of
events. Leanne, on the other hand, he did believe.
She said Terri and her father had always been at odds.
It had just got worse after her brother died. 'Terri said
Philip was her dad's favourite. She'd got it into her
head he'd rather she'd died.'

Leanne claimed Docherty had come to the flat,
furious that his wife had been putting money into
Terri's account and accusing Terri of spending it on
drugs. 'He lost it. Told Terri as far as he was concerned, she might as well be dead.' A week later, a
distressed Terri had seen her father's car cruising her
patch, watching her pick up punters.

There but for the grace of God, thought Bill, as he glanced at the man in the rear-view mirror. Illness and death had torn this man's family apart, maybe even tipped him over the edge. Then Terri, the black sheep, had taken them down an addict's route, little more than a living death.

On the way back to the station, Janice called to tell Bill that Gary Forbes had been brought in. She'd also managed to contact Posh Guy, whose real name was Ray Irvine. He'd agreed to come along too, after asking that his name be kept out of the papers. Gary was a motor mechanic, Ray an investment banker. It seemed visiting prostitutes was a habit shared by all sections of Scottish society.

Bill instructed Janice to contact Beattie as well.

'According to Magnus, Beattie taught the Docherty kids to sail, which meant he knew them both well. He managed to forget that little piece of information during his earlier interview, conveniently.'

'What about Geordie?'

'Him too. And put them all in the same room to wait.'

Let them sweat it out together. Old Geordie would be the one to suffer least. 'And make sure Geordie gets a chocolate biscuit with his tea,' Bill had added.

They hadn't had any luck putting together Lucie's client base. There had been no handbag or mobile with the body, and Minty wasn't likely to reveal who used Lucie's services, even if they found him. Despite numerous appeals for her clients to get in touch, the response had been almost nonexistent. No one wanted to be linked to a murder, especially the murder of a prostitute.

They were stuck in a tailback on the Kingston Bridge when the call came through. A 'hidden Glasgow' enthusiast, trying to follow the underground course of the Molendinar Burn, had spotted what looked like a body. The burn surfaced briefly just south of Duke Street, close to the spot Terri had disappeared.

'He says it looks like a woman,' Janice told Bill.

'Contact Dr MacLeod. Tell her to get there as soon as she can.'

Bill kept his reply to a minimum. He didn't want Docherty to realise what the call was about. Bill glanced in the mirror again, but Docherty appeared as impassive as ever.

Maybe the online auction had already taken place. Maybe the body Rhona was about to view was all that remained of Docherty's daughter. Bill would have to wait until he'd offloaded Docherty before finding out for himself.

33

THE MOLENDINAR BURN emerged from a culvert under Duke Street and disappeared a few yards later, beneath a deserted goods yard. It was overgrown and inaccessible and only the sound of running water warned you of the burn's presence. Above the southern culvert, the ground rose in a perpendicular wall topped by a high wooden fence. To the west lay the car park of a business centre, surrounded by an eight-foot high metal barrier.

It would take a determined man to get into a position to see the burn at all, and Mr White was just such a man. He was currently standing in the car park, earnestly clutching a digital camera, his face pale and shocked.

'I went to the goods yard and got a shot over that fence. It was more difficult from here,' he told McNab. 'You can't see much because of the undergrowth. I stuck the camera through the railings, clicked and hoped for the best.'

McNab had downloaded the photographs from Mr White's camera to his laptop and was flicking through them, with Mr White giving a running commentary.

'That's the outfall at Hogganfield Loch, where the burn starts. It flows under Wishart Street on the western flank of the Necropolis. Then Duke Street. Then here.'

McNab stopped at the photograph that had started the panic. The lower culvert was in deep shadow, but the object lodged in its entrance was definitely a body.

Bill couldn't believe where he was standing. The building in front of him had been part of his school, St Kentigern's. At that time, a high stone wall had run alongside the burn. To peek over, you had to ask for a backie off a mate.

The Molendinar might look like just a wee burn, but any self-respecting Glaswegian knew that St Kentigern, or St Mungo as he became better known, had established Glasgow by building a monastery on its banks. A monastery that became Glasgow Cathedral.

Bill swung his gaze across the stream to the back of the now derelict Great Eastern Hotel, once Glasgow's largest hostel for homeless men. At school, they'd called it Heartbreak Hotel. He'd never realised then, how apt the name was. Over a hundred men, each living in a seven-foot-square cubicle.

It wouldn't be allowed now, a junior school next door to a doss house. He'd heard the building was going to be converted into luxury flats, but there were problems with the structure. Back then, it was famous for the number of lice crawling up its walls.

The mountain rescue crew had set up shop in the goods yard. McNab had sectioned off an area between the fence and several piles of rubble and bricks, the demolished remains of a nearby railway building.

The brick piles were already causing Bill concern. If the murderer liked burying bodies in this area, the dump offered an ideal opportunity. Bill had ordered in the dog handlers to have a sniff around, just in case.

Mr White's photograph only showed the lower half of the corpse. Until a team got down to the culvert they wouldn't know if it was Terri or not. Bill was also worried about Leanne. He'd sent a uniform around to her flat, but she was nowhere to be found. He'd promised Cathy he would help the girl, but it looked as though Minty had got to her first.

Rhona, McNab and Sissons stood kitted up and ready to go down, Magnus watching from nearby. A portion of the wooden fence had already been removed to ease their descent. This wasn't the first time Bill had had to use climbing experts to retrieve a body. A few years before, a young woman's corpse had been spotted lying at the bottom of a gorge used for illegal dumping. It had been a nightmare of a crime scene from a forensic point of view. But not as bad as the body they'd found in the sewage treatment plant. Forensically examining tons of sewage demanded a stomach stronger than Bill's.

Fortunately, the Molendinar Burn was fresh water from the nearby Hogganfield Loch. How fresh it was remained to be seen. Bill glanced up anxiously as an ominous cloud moved to obscure the sun. They'd been lucky up to now. Another dose of stair rods would dump gallons of water in this waterway, resulting in a crime scene washed clean of evidence.

The first item to be lowered was the tent. It would keep the rain off the personnel and the exposed part of the body, but could do nothing to prevent a rise in the water level. A few spits of rain hit Bill's head as Rhona followed Sissons over the edge. Once all three were safely down, Bill headed for Magnus. He wanted to hear what the professor had to say about the Docherty family, and Terri's father in particular.

34

RHONA KNEW IT wasn't Terri as soon as she was close enough to get a better view of the legs. Terri was young and slim, and these thighs above black boots, suggested an older woman.

The body was wedged on a shallow ledge at the entrance to the lower culvert. A few feet further in, and she would have been hidden from view even for Mr White.

Her mouth had been roughly taped, her hands tied tightly behind her back. There was a hole on the left side of her head.

'She was shot?'

'At close range,' Sissons said.

Shootings were rare in Scotland, unlike in many southern cities where gun culture was rife, especially in areas associated with crack cocaine.

'Any sign of a bullet?'

'Not so far.'

Rhona came to crouch beside the pathologist. At first glance, this looked nothing like the work of their killer. The only similarity lay in the outfit the victim wore; the tight skirt, the skimpy top that exposed rolls of flesh, and the fake leather knee-high boots.

Abrasions and lacerations covered the exposed parts of the body.

'What about the scratches?'

'At a guess, the water carried her over rough ground. I'll know better when I've examined her properly.' Sissons rose to his feet. 'Okay, I'll leave you to it. Let's hope the rain keeps off.'

Bill arrived ten minutes after Sissons was pulled up. In the meantime McNab had raised the tent, having secured it on either bank. Rhona was inside sampling when Bill's white-suited body appeared, his feet encased in regulation wellingtons.

'Not Terri, I hear?' Bill's relief was short-lived. As he peered at the sprawled corpse, half out of the gurgling water, his eyes widened in shock. 'Jesus, it's Cathy!'

'You know her?'

Bill was finding it difficult to contain his emotions. 'I spoke to her yesterday. She told me Minty was threatening Leanne. I said I would help the girl.' His lips thinned in anger. 'I bet that bastard Minty had something to do with this.' He glanced into the culvert. 'How the hell did he get her down here?'

The patter of drops on the tent heralded the arrival of the rain proper. Somewhere above them, thunder rumbled.

'We'd better get the body out as soon as possible,' Rhona said. 'There must be scores of drains using this waterway for runoff.'

Bill went to give the fire crew the thumbs up. Shortly afterwards, Rhona heard a grinder blast into action. A two-hour minimum forensic study *in situ* was the norm, but in the present circumstances, impossible. If the water rose abruptly they could lose more than they gained.

Rhona swiftly bagged the hands, noting the broken bloodied nails. Cathy had put up a good fight before she was killed. The rough tape used to silence her was wet, but with luck they might still pick up a print. Rhona was wrapping the head, when McNab arrived with a body bag.

'They've taken a section of the metal fence down. We can get her out that way.'

Once the body had been removed, Rhona concentrated on the nearby undergrowth, taking specimens of the variety of bushes, plants and grasses that clustered around the culvert opening. Then she headed back inside.

Under the arc light, the varied colours and textures of the moss formed a patchwork on the curved wall. The rule was to miss nothing, otherwise your omission came back to haunt you. If the killer had been there, he would have traces on his clothes.

When she emerged she was confronted by Magnus, his height and the white suit making him look like an abominable snowman.

'A shooting,' Rhona told him. 'Bill knows the victim. It doesn't look like the work of our killer.'

Magnus went past her into the tunnel, the beam from his torch playing across the brick arch. When Rhona followed, she found him sitting on the narrow ledge, head bowed, one hand trailing in the water.

If she imagined Magnus was in some deep contemplation of life's mysteries, Rhona was wrong. There was a swift movement, a splash, then he held out his hand to reveal a silvery-flanked tiddler, about two inches long.

Magnus observed the panting fish for a moment, then put it gently back in the water, where it flicked itself into the current and headed for the Clyde. It was a strange thing to observe in what had moments before been a grave.

Something else had caught Magnus's eye. He dipped his hand in again.

'What is it?'

Magnus showed Rhona a small silver charm, in the shape of a half-moon. He turned it over in his hand.

'There was a carving of a moon and a fish on the gravestone, where he left Lucie's body.'

'You think that's significant?'

Magnus looked thoughtful. 'This stream runs underground west of the Necropolis. Which means we're a stone's throw from his hunting ground.' He glanced between the high flats on the opposite side of Duke Street, as though he could see the City of the Dead in the distance.

'And?'

'And nothing.' Magnus looked annoyed, as though his brain had let him down. He handed Rhona the charm and she slipped it into an evidence bag. 'What did you think of Terri's father?'

Rhona remembered the strained face, the hand that gripped the paintbrush. 'He was frightened.'

'Do you think he wanted his daughter dead?'

It was a chilling thought. 'The parents of a drug addict live in their own special kind of hell. Death might seem like the only way out. But few, if any, kill their child. The drugs do that for them.'

Magnus nodded, as though he approved of her answer.

'You're still convinced Terri's alive?' she asked.

'Until Nora calls to tell me otherwise.'

It sounded like a case of positive thinking to Rhona, and she'd never known that to bring the dead back to life.

35

RHONA WATCHED AS the search team, heads bent, moved slowly across the wasteland towards the derelict hostel. It would need a keen eye to spot anything in the tall mix of grass and weeds, made abundant by a long wet summer.

The back of the building rose seven storeys high, the ground-floor windows boarded up. On the upper levels, splashes of tattered blue plastic escaped through broken glass, fluttering like pennants in the breeze. A few folk had gathered on the nearby bridge to gawp, but incident tape didn't excite much interest in this part of Glasgow.

The only other possible access to the stream was by a metal ladder attached to a concrete wall on the wasteland side, close to the bridge. The bank there was high, but it might have provided an entry point for the body.

Rhona dipped under the yellow tape and used the treads to reach the water's edge. There was no sign of footprints in the wet ground, nor any broken foliage nearby. It didn't look as though Cathy had been dumped from this spot.

McNab came and stood outside the tape. 'Any luck?'

Rhona shook her head. 'You?'

'Nothing so far. Land Services are organising a search of the culvert.'

He was trying too hard to look casual, which immediately put Rhona on her guard. She knew Michael McNab too well.

'How's the Prof doing?'

'Bill seems happy enough,' Rhona said in a neutral fashion.

'What about *you?*'

'What about me?'

'You know – a woman's intuition.'

Her woman's intuition told her McNab was winding her up. 'Why don't you ask Judy?' she suggested, her smile as sweet as McNab's.

He laughed. 'You want to be on my tunnel expedition?'

'Of course.'

'Tomorrow morning probably. I'll give you a shout.'

McNab moved off towards the search party, as Rhona hunkered down for a closer look at the embankment.

By the time she returned to the car park, most of the service vehicles had left. Rhona called Chrissy and brought her up to date.

'And I thought you were still on a jolly with the handsome Viking,' Chrissy said, placated.

'Talking of Magnus, he guddled a fish in the Molendinar Burn.'

'No kidding?' Chrissy whistled through her teeth. 'Is there no end to the man's talents?'

There was a short silence while each waited for the other to speak. Finally Rhona broke it. 'Any word from Sam?'

It was the question Chrissy had been waiting for. 'A text. He's coming to see me tonight.' She sounded excited.

Rhona wanted desperately to tell her to watch her step.

'We'll be careful,' said Chrissy, reading her mind.

Rhona rang off then, not wanting to labour the point. The Suleiman family wouldn't give up on Sam, not if they believed he was still alive. If they got the slightest inkling there was a connection between Sam and Chrissy, they wouldn't hesitate to use her. After the attack on Sean, the jazz club staff had been warned not to discuss Sam with anyone, and to report any suspicious enquiries. It wasn't enough to stop Rhona worrying.

Chrissy had left the lab by the time Rhona made her way through the evening rush hour. She stored her samples and sat down with a coffee to read through the notes Chrissy had written up in the log book.

Cathy's clothes had been delivered from the mortuary. One thing caught Rhona's eye in particular. The plastic boots had trapped some interesting material that might give them a lead on where Cathy entered the water.

Rhona glanced at the clock. She should be on her way home by now, but anything that could help with tomorrow's search of the culvert would be useful. Rhona settled down to examine the mix of soil, water and vegetable material.

36

DOCHERTY WAS STUDYING his hands, where the red paint had hardened on his skin.

'You were watching your daughter?'

A bluebottle buzzed around them. Bill wanted to swat it but knew he'd miss.

'Leanne told us Terri saw you.'

Docherty switched his attention to the fly, as though Bill wasn't there.

'We're trying to save Terri, Mr Docherty.'

The insect settled on the table between them. Docherty approached it from behind, palm open. Caught it in expert fashion.

'Where is she? Where is Terri, Mr Docherty?'

The fly buzzed frantically in Docherty's closed fist. Then his hand slammed onto the table and silence fell.

Bill was in danger of losing his temper. Everything about this man set his teeth on edge. After the flash of fear in the boat yard, Docherty had shut down. If he wouldn't talk, there was nothing they could do to make him.

'If you were kerb crawling you must have seen Lucie. She worked near Terri. Small girl, half starved, crack addict. Did you watch her too? Someone strangled her with her own bra. That man had salt on his hands. Sea salt.'

Quick as a flash, Docherty's eyes came up to meet Bill's. 'What did you say?'

This was a different Docherty. Alert, interested and calculating.

Bill had silently questioned his decision to mention the salt. It wasn't common knowledge to anyone outside the investigation. They had kept it from the press releases so as not to alert the killer. Why had he told Docherty? Because he wanted to see his reaction. And to convince himself Docherty wasn't involved in the murders.

'There was salt and diesel on the killer's hands.'

Realisation dawned. 'That's why I'm here. You think I did it. You think I killed those lassies.' Fury erupted on Docherty's face. 'You bastards. You pathetic bastards. Some maniac's got my daughter and the best you can do is blame me!' Spittle sprayed the table.

'What have you done with Terri?'

'You make me sick.'

'You forbid your daughter to come home. You threaten her. When she walks the streets you follow her. I think you'd had enough. I think you wanted it all to end.'

The anger drained out of Docherty as quickly as it had arrived.

'We've got to keep hoping. That's what Nora says. Hope. Another fucking word for torture.' He looked at

Bill with haunted eyes. 'If you had to watch your daughter sell herself. What would you do? Eh?'

Bill couldn't answer.

By the time Bill let Docherty leave, he knew the man had gone to Glasgow late on Friday night to look for his daughter, intending to take her home. Docherty maintained, despite driving around for an hour, he'd never found Terri.

Geordie had said in his statement that he'd seen Terri get into a black car around ten thirty. He'd waited, but she never came back. The two stories matched, but Bill didn't see either man as a reliable witness. He still had a vision of Docherty trying to take Terri home and her refusing. What would he have done then?

37

MAGNUS TOOK THE only vacant seat in the room, which was next to Geordie. The strong odour emanating from the old man hit his senses like a sledgehammer. Magnus concentrated on analysing it to weaken its power.

It reminded him of the first sealskin he'd attempted to cure. He'd worked on it in the old smoking shed, but even the lingering scent of salted fish had failed to disguise the mess he'd made of the skin. Eventually, on his mother's orders, he'd buried it far from the house, watched by the circling seagulls that had followed him to the burial site.

The other men in the room were suffering more than Magnus. Only Geordie looked unconcerned, munching on a chocolate biscuit and slurping a mug of tea. They'd all looked up when Magnus entered, then had returned to studying their hands or the floor between their feet.

Geordie savoured every last taste of chocolate, then held out his hand to Magnus. The skin was wrinkled and grimy but the handshake was warm and firm.

'Geordie Wilkins.'

'Magnus Pirie.'

Geordie contemplated the name. 'Had a mate in the army called Pirie. He was from Orkney. Talked like you.' Geordie's eyes grew vague as his mind moved into the past.

Magnus surveyed the other occupants. Brendan Paterson had been there that morning to give his mouth swab. That left Beattie, Ray Irvine and Gary Forbes. A faint scent of motor oil helped him identify Gary as the mechanic who'd travelled up from Dumfries and Galloway. He was young, barely early twenties, looking shocked to be there. His furtive sideways glances indicated his discomfort at being in the presence of Terri's other clients. When in fantasyland you could kid yourself you were the best she ever had. Sitting in a room with men who'd been there before and after him was causing Gary some problems.

Beattie, Magnus had picked out right away. His face was a study in anger. Terri's former guidance teacher and sailing instructor, who was trying to stay aloof. He, of course, had told Bill he'd only talked to Terri by phone.

Magnus suspected Ray Irvine, with his expensive clothes and well tended hands, fancied himself more than any woman. Magnus wondered why Ray chose to slum it in the red-light district. He read him more as a sauna man. Sex in the comfort zone. Bought and paid for, like his manicure.

Magnus tried to imagine each of the four men with Lucie, luring her to the Necropolis, strangling and stabbing her, raping her with a stiletto. It was difficult, because they looked so normal. But then most serial killers looked ordinary. The only thing recorded as common among them was the emptiness of their eyes. Magnus didn't accept that. He'd seen photographs of Ted Bundy. Not only did the serial killer look charming and friendly, his eyes sparkled with laughter and life. That's why the girls went with him in the first place. If the eyes were the mirror of the soul, Bundy had managed to fake a soul pretty well.

When Bill opened the door they all raised their heads expectantly, apart from Geordie, who went on mumbling and humming to himself. Bill nodded at Magnus and he stood up. Beattie immediately complained.

'He's only just arrived. The rest of us have been here for hours.'

Bill ignored him and ushered Magnus out. Once they were in the side room, Bill asked him what he thought.

'Beattie's hiding more than just the sailing lessons. The Gary character smells of oil. There's no chance he works on boat engines, as well as cars?'

'We'll check that out.'

'I take it they've all given samples?'

'On arrival.'

The one-way glass gave a clear view of the interview room. Gary Forbes, his face drained of colour, was brought in first to sit at a table opposite DC Clark.

'I let Geordie go,' Bill said. 'He's done his bit.'

'I wrote that stuff on the web about Glasgow pussy.'

Gary had barely waited for the tape to start before he began his confession. Magnus, observing through the one-way glass, saw how taken aback Bill was. But Bill couldn't have stopped Gary's verbal diarrhoea, even if he wanted to.

'It was a joke. Blokes travelling to Glasgow for sex. A blog to tell them what to expect.'

Anger suffused Bill's face. 'Mangy crackheads?' There was a moment's silence, then Bill's fist came down hard on the table. 'Still *fresh*?'

Gary's face flushed, then went white.

'That's a joke?' The sneer in Bill's voice sliced through Gary's remaining veneer like a knife.

'I copied it from something else I read online, I swear.'

Bill read from a sheet. 'If you fancy beating up a whore, this class is for you. Nobody gives a shit what happens to them, including the police.'

If Gary had thought confession was good for the soul, he was fast changing his mind. 'I didn't mean it.'

Bill's tone was pure ice. 'You didn't mean it? Well I mean this, so listen carefully. I'm going to book you for incitement to violence and conspiracy to commit murder.'

Bill wasn't faking his anger. Magnus could almost feel it radiating through the glass.

Gary was near blubbering. Bill let him stew for a bit while he sat back in his chair and waited. Finally he said, 'Did you set up the online auction?'

Gary's head came up, his face puzzled. 'Auction?'

Magnus watched Gary intently. Bill's voice was calm now, circumspect.

'A murder auction. Highest bidder gets to watch Terri being killed, any way they like.'

Gary's confusion gave way to horror. 'I wouldn't do that. Terri was . . .'

'Was what?'

He forced the words out. 'She helped me.'

'How?'

Magnus thought about Gary's expression in the waiting room, the furtive embarrassed glances at the other men.

Gary indicated Janice's presence. No way was he going to say anything more in front of her.

'Let me get this clear,' Bill said. 'You don't mind publishing web pages that refer to women as mangy crackheads, but you won't talk sexually in front of my constable.'

Gary's jaw tensed stubbornly. Magnus wondered if Bill realised the younger man had reached his limit and was about to clam up.

Bill motioned to Janice to leave and stared directly at the glass, indicating he wanted Magnus in there.

Magnus could smell Gary as soon as he entered the room. A mix of perspiration, fear and adrenalin. Gary was like a cornered animal, his eyes darting, his muscles twitching, ready to run, except there was nowhere to go. Magnus could imagine the man's brain twisting itself into knots. Gary had decided to admit to the blog, only to find himself in even deeper shit.

Bill introduced Magnus as a criminal psychologist assigned to the case. Whatever Gary expected, it wasn't that. Magnus took his seat next to Bill and offered Gary his hand. After a moment Gary accepted it, his glance moving between Bill and Magnus, trying to read the scenario.

'It is imperative we find Terri,' Magnus said. 'Can you help us with that?'

'I wouldn't hurt her.'

'I believe you.'

Gary kept his eyes on Magnus now, like a lifeline.

'She helped you?' Magnus prompted.

The shifty look was back in Gary's eye. He was planning a lie or a retraction, then changed his mind.

'I couldn't get it up,' he said flatly. 'Terri made it work.'

'You tried others before Terri?'

A spasm of pain crossed Gary's face. 'That's why I wrote that stuff. Who wants to fuck a zombie?'

Bill made a noise between his teeth. Magnus covered it with his next question. 'How many times did you meet Terri?'

'Twice a month over the last six months.'

'What about the night she disappeared?'

'I came looking for her. She wasn't there.'

'What time was that?'

'Early on. Ten o'clock maybe. I hung around for a bit, then left.'

'You didn't go with anyone else?'

Gary shifted almost imperceptibly in his seat. Magnus had been conscious of his scent all through the interview. There was a change now, a subtle one; but to Magnus's keen nose it was unmistakable.

'Lucie worked near Terri. You didn't see her?'

Gary shook his head.

'When people engage in sexual activity they exchange fluids, skin flakes, even human scent.'

The change in body odour was more distinct now. Gary was sexually aroused. Talking about sex obviously turned him on.

'You had sex with Lucie Webster?'

'No.'

The 'no' was emphatic and probably true, but there was something that linked Gary to Lucie. Magnus took a shot in the dark.

'You watched someone have sex with Lucie.' Gary's eye twitched and Magnus knew he was right. Bill was itching to interrupt. Magnus begged him silently to say nothing. Gary's swab would not link him to Lucie, but he had been there that night.

'I *paid* to watch her,' Gary emphasised the 'paid' as though that made it all right.

'And?'

'She showed me where to stand so the punters wouldn't notice. After a couple of times, she asked me for more money.' He sounded peeved. 'I said no. We argued for a bit. A big guy turned up. She called him Minty. He told me to fuck off. I left.'

Bill came in. 'What time was that?'

'I don't know, before midnight.'

'You fix boat engines as well as cars?'

Gary wasn't happy with the change in interviewer. He threw Magnus a pleading look. Magnus didn't respond.

'I don't know anything about boats.'

There was a knock at the door. DC Clark's expression was grim – bad news. Bill terminated the interview.

'Can I go home now?' Gary's wail followed them out.

'It's Geordie,' Janice said, once Bill closed the door behind them.

The old man lay under a white sheet, wires leading from his chest to a monitor that bleeped steadily.

'The car hit him full force from behind,' the doctor said.

'Will he live?'

'The internal injuries are extensive. A younger, healthier man might survive them but . . .'

'Geordie isn't a young healthy man.'

Bill felt a rush of pity. If he hadn't let the old man leave the station, Geordie might be there now, eating chocolate biscuits, drinking tea and stinking everyone out.

'Did you keep the clothes?'

The doctor pointed to a white, sealed plastic bag. 'They smell pretty bad.'

'Forensic will need to examine them.'

Bill sat for a bit beside the bed, knowing he was wasting his time, but staying anyway. The PC attending the scene was convinced Geordie had been knocked down on purpose. 'You don't drive that fast down a narrow lane with an old man in full view.'

Geordie had told Bill he'd seen a fancy black car take Terri away, but couldn't recall the number plate.

It wasn't worth killing for.

Of course it could have been a kid driving a stolen vehicle, accelerating through a lane where Geordie just happened to be, but that would have been coincidence. Bill didn't hold with coincidence.

If Geordie had seen the car that lifted Terri, then the driver had probably seen him.

38

CATHY'S KILLER SHOULD have removed her boots before he disposed of the body. Sand gets everywhere. You don't have to be a beach lover to know that.

Rhona peered through the microscope at the mix of sand and water. Sand particles ranged in diameter from 0.0625mm to 2mm, their shape and composition dependent on age and origin. But that wasn't all. The watery cushion that surrounded sand was a natural habitat for bacteria, algae and tiny animals. Cathy had brought a microscopic world back in her boots. A world that could tell Rhona where she first entered the water.

According to Judy, horned wrack was found only in brackish water. In the Clyde estuary, it grew on the northern shore, notably at the village of Cardross. The village itself didn't have a sailing club, but there was a marina at nearby Rhu. The MO might be different, but Cathy's death looked suspiciously linked to the watery world of their killer.

Rhona tried Bill's mobile. When it rang unanswered, she called the main desk and asked if he was still about. The sergeant told her the DI was at the hospital. Rhona immediately thought something had happened to Margaret, but the sergeant put her right.

'An old guy, pulled in for questioning on the Necropolis case, was knocked down near Duke Street.'

'Geordie Wilkins?'

'That's the one.'

'Is he alive?'

The sergeant didn't know. Rhona had to be content with his promise to tell the DI she'd called.

A smell of cooking greeted Rhona's entrance to the flat, lifting her spirits. Then she heard voices, and realised Sean had a visitor. Rhona wasn't in the mood for small talk. Sean was easy if she didn't want to chat, and there were plenty of other ways to take your mind off the job. Rhona had been thinking of one in particular as she climbed the stairs.

She listened in the hall, wondering if she could head for the shower in the hope that the visitor would have left by the time she'd finished. The voices were low, but quite intense, and for a frightening moment Rhona thought it might be something to do with Sam. She opened the kitchen door to find Sean and his visitor at the table. They were drinking red wine.

Sean spotted her, and both men stood up together. When the other man turned, Rhona's heart leapt in recognition.

'Liam!'

Rhona's eyes ranged over her son. He seemed taller, or thinner, or both. His skin was burnt brown, his hair bleached by the sun. Africa had changed him, just as it had changed her the first time she'd gone there. He had an air of confidence she didn't remember from their last meeting.

Neither seemed sure what to do next. At last Liam stepped forward. He smiled, but made no move to embrace her. Rhona would have given anything to put her arms around her son, but felt that wasn't possible – not yet.

'I tried calling you,' Sean said.

'Sorry, I switched the mobile off while I was in the lab.'

'I've asked Liam to join us for dinner.' A forced smile turned Sean's bruised face into that of a circus clown. 'I told Liam about falling into the cellar in the jazz club. How it spoiled my good looks.'

Rhona nodded, glad Sean had warned her. No point freaking Liam out with tales of the Suleimans. She asked if Liam minded if she went for a shower before eating, deciding they could both do with a few moments' grace. Now her son was here, Rhona had no idea what to say to him, how to treat him. She only wished she could be as relaxed as Sean obviously was.

Standing in the shower, the water beating down on her head, Rhona shut her eyes and allowed herself to acknowledge a feeling of intense happiness. Her son had sought her out. He was sitting in her kitchen, talking to Sean. She would share a meal with him, hear about his time with the VSO in Nigeria.

Rhona stepped out of the shower and took a mouthful of wine. Already nerves had begun flickering in her stomach, thoughts of how she might screw up. How Liam might never return after tonight. Rhona fought her growing anxiety as she dressed. Part of her wished that Sean wasn't there, and that she could have Liam all to herself. Another part was relieved he was, so she and Liam might avoid long empty silences where they realised they were strangers to one another.

She couldn't help but think of Nora Docherty, sitting in an empty house with the ghosts of her children. Nora deserved to get her daughter back. Rhona didn't deserve her son. Sean would dismiss such ideas as fanciful, and not worth talking about. But then again, he hadn't given away a son. Rhona took herself through to the kitchen, before her moment of happiness was completely extinguished by guilt.

Liam was setting the table. Sean had put on some jazz, something Rhona recognised for once. A second bottle of wine was open and taking the air. Rhona suspected Sean had raided his 'cellar' and brought out the best. She felt a rush of affection for his thoughtfulness.

They ate in comfortable semi-silence. Rhona realised Sean's laid-back attitude had put Liam at ease. Sean peppered the intermittent silences with Irish charm and craic, while Rhona spent her time surreptitiously studying Liam's face, as though he were a painting.

She imagined she saw Edward in the young man's jaw line, herself in his eyes. She'd been Liam's age, no, younger, when he was born. Edward was only a few years older. The years flowed backwards and Rhona saw herself then, burdened by a desperate desire to hang on to Edward. Confused, frightened and guilt-ridden.

Liam looked up, sensing her eyes on him, and Rhona rose from the table, ostensibly to fetch a glass of water. Behind her Liam muttered something about having to go soon, and Rhona was seized by a panic that she would never see him again. Then she heard Sean urging him to stay for coffee, as there was a tune he wanted to play for him. By the time she sat back down, Sean had gone to fetch his saxophone.

'I'm glad you came,' Rhona managed to say.

Liam smiled. 'So am I.'

It was enough to be going on with.

They finished with coffee and an Afro-jazz number. Then it was time for Liam to leave. Watching the two men shake hands, Rhona silently acknowledged that Sean would make a good father, better than Edward could ever be.

Sean busied himself clearing the table, leaving Rhona to take Liam to the door. They were only there a moment. Liam struggled between offering his hand or giving her a hug. Rhona wondered what happened between her son and his adoptive mother, at such a time. If he usually hugged her, doing the same to Rhona might feel like betrayal. She solved his dilemma by putting her hand lightly on his arm and telling him he was welcome any time. Liam nodded, an awkward teenager again.

Rhona stood listening to his footfalls on the stairs, then the sound of the outside door clicking closed behind him. When she eventually turned to go inside, Sean was waiting in the hall.

'He's a great kid.'

'All the better for having been brought up by some-one other than me.'

Sean didn't rise to her challenge.

'Maybe it's in the genes. My mother gave me away. I gave Liam away.'

Rhona was spoiling for an argument and Sean knew it. His face was wary. He was trying to read her and failing. Probably because she herself had no idea what she would say or do next.

They stood trapped in time, each waiting for the other to dictate the next step in the dance. The evening had gone well. Why did she have to spoil it? What would that prove? That she wasn't cut out to be a mother?

Her mobile broke the spell.

It was Magnus. Rhona stepped out of earshot, hoping Sean would use the excuse to move out of harm's way.

'You heard about Geordie?'

'The desk sergeant told me.'

'He's in a coma, not expected to last the night. Bill suspects it was no accident.'

The thought had crossed her mind too. Geordie was a witness to Terri's abduction. Perhaps her abductor had spotted the old man?

'There's something else I need to talk to you about,' Magnus went on cautiously. 'Before the meeting to-morrow.'

Rhona waited for him to continue.

'Can you meet me?'

She contemplated suggesting he came there, but decided against it. Instead she gave him directions to a nearby bar that stayed open late.

Sean was in the shower, a CD playing above the rush of water. Rhona opened the cubicle door.

He was rinsing lather from his hair, sending water cascading down tautly muscled arms.

'Coming in?' he offered.

It was stupid leaving like this. She should call Magnus, tell him it could keep until tomorrow.

'There's been a development in the Necropolis case. I have to go out.'

39

'THE MOON?'

Rhona looked up at the evening sky, where drifting clouds partially obscured the moon and stars. Magnus had met her outside the bar, but had declined her invitation to enter. Instead he'd led her to the outskirts of nearby Kelvingrove Park, lovely by day but not the safest place for a midnight stroll. When questioned, Magnus had merely said 'the moon'.

Rhona was waiting for him to expand on this. She could feel Magnus's underlying excitement, but whatever was causing it, he was finding it difficult to put into words.

'You're aware that the moon affects people's behaviour?' he began.

'Folklore that's never been scientifically proven.'

'Sussex police force put extra men on the beat for the days surrounding a full moon, because there are more aggressive incidents recorded during that time.'

'I can't see Strathclyde falling for the lunar effect.'

Her scepticism wasn't putting Magnus off.

'I checked. Lucie was killed two days before a full moon. The other girl in the grave, a month before. The earlier victim . . .'

'What are you trying to say?'

'The symbol on the grave was made up of a fish and a full moon.'

A terrible thought struck Rhona. 'You're not planning to bring this up at tomorrow's meeting?'

'If he has killed Terri, don't you think it strange we haven't found her body, when he made sure we found the others?'

'Why are you changing the subject?'

'I'm not. The moon has an affinity with water. It rules the domain of the night, the unconscious mind, the world of dreams and fantasies. *His* fantasies.'

Rhona was at a loss for words, so Magnus continued. 'The lunar effect describes behaviour over the days surrounding the full moon. Lucie died in the early hours of Thursday morning. The full moon was Sunday.'

It was like being told a story. Enticing, alluring, compelling – but, ultimately, fiction.

'Remember our killer is working to a plan in the world he has created for himself. We have to try to understand that world, however bizarre it might appear to the rational mind.'

'I don't see how any of this helps.'

'If I'm right about the lunar effect, he'll kill Terri within the next forty-eight hours.' Seeing that Rhona was unimpressed, he carried on. 'We questioned Gary Forbes today. He confessed to running the blog, but claimed he knew nothing about the auction.'

'And you believed him?'

'I don't think Gary originally wrote those words.'

Suspicion rooted itself in Rhona's mind. 'You were ordered to do nothing about that auction, Magnus.'

He continued as though he hadn't heard her. 'Remember the Vancouver serial killer, Robert Pickton?'

She did. Pickton, a pig farmer, had murdered upwards of fifty drug addicts and prostitutes, burying them in slurry on his farm or feeding them to the pigs.

'The police suspected Pickton was running online auctions for snuff videos. Subscribers could bid to determine how the next woman should die. We were assuming our man was doing the same. But I don't think he is. I think he's offering up his victim. To anyone who wants to rape, torture or kill her.' Magnus left his bombshell until the end. 'So I went online and made my bid.'

40

MAGNUS SAT OUT on the balcony. It was neither dark nor light. The broad expanse of river lay silvery grey under a full moon. This was the time he liked best. In Orkney, during the summer months, there was virtually no night, only a delicate twilight zone before dawn. He'd played football once at 3 a.m. They'd sailed to Sanday from Kirkwall after work, spent most of the time on the crossing drinking home brew and still managed to win the match.

He realised he could never live where the summer days ended in early darkness. Visits to London only served to emphasise the difference a few degrees of latitude made to the length of a summer's day.

Magnus breathed in the scent of the river. He was calm enough now to contemplate his meeting with Rhona. Her anger when he'd revealed what he'd done had caught him off guard. He should have read the signs better, but he found his ability impaired when with her. He was too busy controlling his other emotions.

Since the night she'd visited the flat he'd tried to maintain a distance, although he enjoyed the intensity of their exchanges. Rhona, he'd noted, was adept at changing the subject if she believed they were becoming too familiar, like in the car en route to Inverkip. Her voice then had said one thing, while her body language told a different story. Few people can hide their true emotions, even when they try.

The faint scent of soap or shower gel had intrigued him when he'd met her outside the bar earlier that evening. Had she been in the shower when he called? The scent, however, seemed masculine.

He and Anna had often showered together. Before, during and after making love. He could never forgive himself for what happened to his last lover, but neither could he turn back the clock. It was at moments like these, Magnus realised how deep the wound still was.

He'd left the computer on, the mail program open and waiting. The ping of an incoming message ended his contemplative mood. As he approached the laptop, the landline rang. Magnus hesitated between the two, then answered the phone. No one spoke. Magnus heard a sharp click, then a moment's silence, followed by the sound of a female weeping. Every hair on his body stood on end.

The terrible sound stopped as suddenly as it had begun. The silence that followed seemed to breathe even more horror. Then a man's hoarse voice spoke.

'She's waiting for you – but you'll have to find her.'

'How?'

The line went dead.

Magnus quickly checked the incoming email. At first glance the title looked like typical spam, but he opened it anyway. Disappointment rose like bile as his eyes scanned an advert for Cialis and Viagra at a special low price. He'd thought, arriving as it did with the phone call, it would contain a clue about how he might find Terri. Magnus double-checked the paragraph at the bottom. It was a typical string of nonsense inserted for the search engines. The email wasn't remotely relevant.

He'd been set up. The killer had challenged him, knowing full well he had no chance of finding Terri. Frustration and anger drove him back onto the balcony. He gripped the rail, steeling himself to admit he'd failed. He should call DI Wilson, but he would have to admit he'd done exactly what he'd been told not to do. And with nothing to show for it. The only crumb of comfort he could offer was the possibility that the crying he'd heard had really been Terri, which meant she was still alive.

Magnus had a hunch he was missing something. He'd had a similar feeling in the culvert, when he'd told Rhona about the symbol on the grave.

He went inside and laid out all the crime scene photos on the dining table. He'd looked at them a million times already. What had he said to Rhona about studying images and missing the obvious?

An hour later Magnus was none the wiser and infinitely more frustrated. He made up his mind to go out. He cycled slowly eastwards through the slumbering city centre, his only companions taxis and night delivery vans. As he approached Glasgow Cross, he was aware a white van had been sitting close on his tail for some time. Magnus was used to drivers who saw harassing cyclists as a sport, and kept well in. The van finally overtook as he swerved right into London Road, and Magnus allowed himself the pleasure of swearing at its rear end.

He cut up through the network of streets that led to the Gallowgate, with no clear objective, except he wanted to be in the killer's hunting ground. He located Terri's alley and walked the bike in. Terri's spot had been taken over by another teenage girl. Magnus could smell her on approach, cheap scent masking perspiration and the stink of sex. A few discarded condoms lay nearby.

The girl regarded him with clouded eyes. An attempt had been made to cover a bruise on her cheek with make-up, and there was an angry scab at the corner of her mouth. She opened a short jacket to expose her breasts, and offered him whatever he wanted. Magnus asked if she knew Terri.

Her expression grew sullen. 'Are you the polis?'

'I'm a friend of Terri's.'

'A friend,' she sneered. 'Is that right? Well, friend, Terri's gone, disappeared. That's why I'm here. If you're not interested then fuck off.'

'What if I pay you for information?'

'About what?'

'Anything you can tell me about Terri.'

She thought about it. 'Same price as a blow job?'

Magnus asked how much and handed over the money. The girl, who said her name was Nikki, counted it and stuffed it in her pocket.

'Terri disappeared from this very spot. Got in a car and never came back. Cathy says she's still alive.'

'Cathy McIver?'

She nodded. 'Cathy met a punter she knew from way back, who said he'd seen Terri some place outside Glasgow. Cathy went with him for a look.'

From the way Nikki was talking, she didn't know Cathy was dead.

'Cathy's a friend of yours?'

'Aye.'

'Nikki. There's something you should know.'

'What?'

'The police found Cathy's body today. She'd been shot through the head.'

Fear and shock broke through the drugged haze. 'Who the fuck are you?' She stepped away from Magnus.

'I'm a psychologist working with the police.'

Her eyes narrowed angrily. 'You fucking liar!' Nikki took a swipe at him. Magnus stepped back, but she came at him, fists flying. He tried to catch her arms, conscious of what this must look like on nearby CCTV, and tried to reason with her.

'Nikki, if you know anything about the man Cathy met, you have to tell the police.'

She spat at him and he caught it full in the face.

Just at that moment a car entered the alley, its headlights blinding them. Nikki broke away and ran towards it. She had the passenger door open and was inside before Magnus got moving.

The black car revved hard and Magnus realised it was headed for him. He flattened himself against the wall as the car screeched past, inches from his chest.

41

BILL PLAYED THEM the mobile message. Cathy's voice was upbeat but cautious. *I think Terri's alive. I'll call when I know more.*

'Cathy McIver phoned me late Sunday night,' he explained. 'I didn't take the call. I only discovered the message later.'

'*After* you found her body.' Superintendent Sutherland's tone could be interpreted as accusatory.

Bill's demeanour suggested he was already beating himself up about this and didn't need any help.

'What time did she call?' Rhona asked.

'Ten past eleven.'

'Sometime between then and when we found her, Cathy was submerged in salt water.' Rhona's announcement caused a ripple of surprise. 'There were traces of sand and seaweed inside her boots. A particular type of seaweed called horned wrack. It's only found in special conditions in the Clyde estuary, such as the brackish water around Cardross.'

'Cardross,' repeated McNab, amazed.

'On the northern shore, fifteen or so miles west of Glasgow,' Rhona expanded.

'Bloody hell!'

'Cathy rarely sets foot outside Calton, let alone Glasgow,' Bill said.

'And she's got no way to get to *Cardross*,' mused McNab. 'Not without help.'

'It's got to be something to do with Terri,' Bill said. 'That's why she tried to speak to me.'

Rhona knew he was torturing himself about not taking the call. She would have been the same.

'So who took her there and brought her back?' McNab said.

'I bet that bastard Minty has something to do with this,' Bill muttered.

'Has Dr Sissons confirmed she died of a bullet to the head?' asked Rhona.

'I've still to get the full report, but yes,' replied Bill.

'No mention of salt water in her lungs?' The thought had crossed Rhona's mind the shooting might have been a way to cover up the real manner of death.

'No.'

A moment's silence as they all pondered the latest piece in the jigsaw. Then came the question Rhona dreaded.

'Where's Magnus?' asked Bill. 'We could do with his take on this.'

When Magnus hadn't appeared at the meeting, Rhona had convinced herself he would at least have told Bill what he'd been up to. By Bill's expression, she knew that wasn't the case. It looked as if she would have to do the honours.

'I met Magnus late last night.' Rhona avoided McNab's eye. 'He was convinced Terri was alive and the online auction referred to her.' She stole a look at Bill, wondering if he had any idea what was coming next. 'He explained about the lunar effect, how he thought the killer was working within the full moon window.'

'Full moon window? What's he on about?' interrupted McNab.

'He thinks the killer commits his violent acts during a full moon,' Bill answered. 'Go on.'

She outlined what Magnus had said about the Pickton murders, the suggestion of snuff material on-line. 'Magnus believes our killer has changed his MO.' Rhona paused. 'He thinks the auction is a direct challenge to us. That we have very little time left before Terri dies.'

Superintendent Sutherland's voice was icy. 'What exactly are you saying, Dr MacLeod?'

'Magnus made a bid in the auction.'

42

THE STUNNED SILENCE following Rhona's revelation was short-lived. Sutherland's barked orders sent McNab to the Tech department, then demanded Bill locate Professor Pirie immediately and bring him to Sutherland's office. The fact it was he who'd set Magnus loose on the investigation, without prior consultation with the officer in charge, had been conveniently forgotten.

Bill protested. 'Magnus is no fool. If he's right, then playing the killer at his own game might be the only way to find Terri.'

Sutherland didn't look convinced. 'Send someone to Cardross. Find out what the hell is going on there.'

Bill waited until Sutherland had banged the door behind him.

'What exactly did Magnus say?'

Rhona repeated the conversation in as much detail as she could recall.

'Was there a response to his bid?'

'No. Or if there was, he didn't tell me. We had a few words, then he clammed up – so he could have got a reply and not told me.'

'Okay. Leave it with me. I need you to go to Cardross and check out your seaweed theory.'

Rhona called and left a message for Chrissy, telling her she would be in later. The lab book would bring Chrissy up to date with what an examination on the boots had produced. Rhona made a point of relaying Bill's final request. If there was anything in the trace examinations that might link Terri to Cathy's killer, he wanted to know right away.

Bill had organised transport but failed to tell Rhona the identity of her allotted driver. McNab hooted the horn as she entered the garage.

'I thought you were off to IT?'

'The boss issued his own orders, as is his prerogative.'

As far as Bill was aware, any 'relationship difficulties' between Rhona and McNab had been resolved. Since their Nigerian trip together, things had certainly changed, but McNab was always a man to watch.

'So you and the Prof get on well?' he probed as he steered them through the city-centre traffic.

Rhona didn't answer. McNab was fond of digging, particularly in her relationships. As a man scorned, he felt entitled. It was best not to encourage him.

McNab eventually gave up on his attempts to wind her up and concentrated on the road. Meanwhile, Rhona tried calling Magnus's home and mobile numbers. When there was no response to either, she left a message and a text. Finally she called the Psychology Department at Strathclyde University. When she asked to be put through to Professor Pirie, Rhona was told what she already knew, Magnus was currently on secondment to Strathclyde Police.

McNab listened to her flurry of messages, gauging her concern by the tone of her voice.

'The Green River murders,' he said, when she finally put the mobile away.

'What?'

'The American equivalent of the Canadian case. Gary Leon Ridgeway killed forty-eight prostitutes and threw them in Green River, Washington State, or buried them nearby. When they finally got him on DNA evidence, twenty years after he started killing, he took the police on a tour of the graves. He'd visited them regularly over the years apparently. Gave him a kick remembering what he had done to his victims.'

'You've been doing your homework.'

'I've been looking at past cases that sound similar. The Prof said he thought the killer had been back at the Necropolis even when we were there – exhibiting similar behaviour to Ridgeway. In his statement, Ridgeway said he killed prostitutes because he hated them, he didn't want to pay for sex, and because he knew nobody cared when they went missing. He could kill as many as he wanted without getting caught.'

'We care,' Rhona said firmly, 'and DNA caught Ridgeway in the end.'

'There's something else.'

'What?'

'Atlantic City USA last year. Three bodies of prostitutes found under the boardwalk. A month apart.

And no I haven't checked if they died on a full moon,' he gave her one of his winning smiles. 'But similar MO, probably strangled, and with their own bras. That's not all. Only one per cent of serial killers insert something into the body after death.'

'And?'

'Each of the women had the heel of their right stiletto inserted in their vaginal cavity.'

Rhona's voice betrayed her excitement at the possible connection. 'Can you get a copy of the case notes?'

McNab looked pleased with himself. 'My colleague stateside emailed me the material last night.'

Magnus had reiterated what they all knew – the killer must have a history building up to the first kill. The world was a small place. New York to Prestwick by plane in seven hours.

'Are the forensic results included?'

'Should be in there. I've forwarded the whole thing to Bill and Janice, but why don't we take a look together after we finish at Cardross?'

Rhona tried to read McNab's expression – difficult as he kept his eyes firmly on the road.

'Okay.'

They were entering Dumbarton. The massive volcanic crag with its rooftop castle dominated the horizon. From school history Rhona knew this had once been the capital of the Kingdom of Strathclyde. Dumbarton castle was a Scottish Royal Fortress as were Edinburgh and Stirling. If Prince Charles ever took over as king, he'd have to come to Dumbarton Castle to accept the keys. A sudden downpour greeted their arrival on the main street. The wipers had no chance against the deluge of water, so McNab pulled over.

'Good job we weren't in the culvert,' McNab said.

'What happened about that?'

'This was forecast so they put it on hold. I'm waiting for a plan of the entire culvert and access manholes. A team is up at the loch taking a look at the outfall.'

They watched the curtain of water descend on the windscreen, obscuring everything.

'Just like Nigeria,' McNab reminded her.

When the rain subsided, he drew out again. Minutes later they were in Cardross.

43

'NO HARBOUR, THEN,' Rhona concluded.

They'd been up and down the main street, found a church, a pub, and a sign pointing the way to the local golf course, but no indication of a harbour.

'Let's see if we can get closer to the water.'

McNab took the next left, which led through a small housing development then over a railway crossing, finally reaching the water's edge. The road continued as a single track, skirted the shore and ended a few yards further on, at the closed gate of a lumber yard.

'Looks like this is it,' McNab said.

At first glance it was obvious why the nearest harbour was further west at Rhu. The tide was out, exposing a blanket of seaweed that stretched into the distance, suggesting shallow water.

On the other side of the river, Rhona could see the two cream-coloured towers of the new flats on the Greenock foreshore. The older Gibshill housing scheme, known locally as the Gibbie, climbed the hill behind. The view was definitely more impressive from the opposite side.

Rhona got out and extracted her wellies and forensic case from the boot.

McNab joined her, sniffing the air. 'Pongs a bit.'

'*Fucus ceranoides*, smelly seaweed to you.'

'I'll check out the lumber yard and railway station, then do a bit of house-to-house.' McNab glanced at the threatening sky. 'I'll leave you the car, just in case.'

Rhona decided to start in front of the lumber yard and walk eastwards towards the railway station, taking samples on her way. For the first half-hour she was alone apart from the circling seagulls. No vehicles approached the yard using the nearby track and she assumed there must be a bigger entrance on the other side. She saw a couple of cars arrive to meet an incoming train, but no one out walking their dogs along the grey grit beach scattered with broken concrete.

There was still no sign of McNab when she came level with the station. A train pulled in and a few passengers disembarked and headed towards the main street, leaving her alone again. As she retraced her steps, Rhona was struck by how secluded the spot was. A car parked here at night would be hidden, its lights shielded by the ten-foot privet hedge bordering the nearest garden.

By the time McNab reappeared, Rhona had taken refuge in the car and called in to check how things were at the lab. Chrissy had sounded excited.

'The remainder of the soil you gave me to sieve? I found something else.'

'Another hair?'

'A paint flake.'

Paint was very specific, in the case of cars even down to make, model and year. As evidence of association, it could prove invaluable. They chatted on for a few minutes, Rhona promising to be back soon, then she spotted McNab approaching in the driver's mirror and rang off.

McNab threw open the door with gusto.

'You found out something?'

'The privet hedge owner, Mr Evans, reports a car down here on Sunday night. He suspected late-night drinking by local youths and took down the registration number.'

'Thank God for good citizens.'

McNab rang in and asked Janice to check the number. She gave him an update on his request for train services.

'Cathy could have got here by train,' he told Rhona. 'They run every half an hour until 11.24 p.m., even on a Sunday.'

Rhona was working out a possible scenario in her head. Cathy arriving here by train, meeting a car by the shore.

'Did Mr Evans hear anything?'

'Apparently the stereo was very loud, which is what alerted him to the car being here in the first place.'

If Cathy tried to get away in the dark, maybe she stumbled into the water. That would account for the boots. Maybe she was shot right here on this beach?

'I think we should take another look at the shoreline,' Rhona said.

They concentrated on the area above the high-water mark, walking it side by side. An hour later they gave up.

'Too much rain.'

McNab was right. It was useless.

'Okay, let's head for Rhu,' he suggested. 'According to Mr Evans, lots of Glasgow sailors berth there. Members of the cruising club apparently sail all over the globe, not only in Scottish waters.'

The marina lay just west of the town of Helensburgh. It followed the same pattern as Inverkip, all facilities available on site, including boat and engine repair. They checked in at reception, causing a flurry of interest. Visits from the police appeared to be rare in Rhu. Rhona wondered how soon it would be before the whole marina and village knew of their arrival, despite McNab's request that it be kept low-key.

They split up again, Rhona to sample and McNab to ask questions. He sought her out a short while later to deliver Commodore Lang's offer of coffee in his office overlooking the harbour. Lang turned out to be a surgeon who'd spent most of his career in Glasgow and was now retired and living in Rhu.

'A reasonable proportion of our members are Glasgow based,' he said, answering a question from McNab. 'Or work in the city. This is the only marina on the north of the estuary, which makes it quite popular.'

McNab's request for members' contact details caused Lang some concern. 'Of course, if you think it's necessary.'

'Just one of our many lines of enquiry,' McNab reassured him. 'Does the information include photographs?'

Lang nodded. 'Everyone is issued with an ID card. Goes with the times, I'm afraid.'

'You don't happen to have any Americans on your books?'

Commodore Lang looked surprised. 'In the days of Polaris in the Holy Loch we had quite a few,' he smiled in fond memory. 'The submarines have moved up Gare Loch to Faslane, but the Americans have gone, I'm afraid. Apart from an occasional sailing visitor.'

The commodore promised to email them a copy of the members' database, to include ID photos. McNab asked Lang to keep the request confidential until he heard from them again, keeping his expression neutral so as not to alarm him.

The commodore looked relieved. 'We're a law-abiding bunch here.'

'You don't happen to know a Charles Beattie who runs a sailing club for kids across at the Kip Marina?' McNab's parting shot brought a smile to the commodore's face.

'I certainly do. Charlie often brings his juniors over to compete in our dinghy section.'

44

BILL ESCAPED TO his office and shut the door. He needed time to think. That was the problem with a murder hunt, all effort and activity and no time for contemplation. He sat in the old leather swivel seat that had been his predecessor's. DI Jock Martin had taken him under his wing when he'd entered CID. Jock had died of a heart attack at sixty, shortly after his retirement. When Bill visited him in hospital, Jocky told him his heart had beat too long and fast when he was in the job. He'd worn it out.

Bill's own heart had raced a few times recently. Both at home and at work. Like most people, he paid little attention to the muscle that beat in his chest. Never noticed it until the rhythm changed, which had been happening a lot recently, like this morning when he'd listened to Cathy's call from beyond the grave.

The thought crossed his mind that someone had seen him with Cathy at the Barras. And that someone had told Minty. Until now, he hadn't associated Minty with the Necropolis murders. Had Lucie been the only one to die, Minty would have been centre frame. But Bill's gut told him Minty was involved somehow in

Cathy's death. How Cardross fitted into the picture, he had no idea.

His run in with the Super after the morning's meeting hadn't helped Bill's mood. Sutherland didn't voice it outright, but it was clear he thought the DI wasn't on top of the job. Choosing not to argue his case seemed to make matters worse. The notion he should excuse himself because of worry over Margaret was anathema to Bill. His wife had never failed to do her job, despite worrying about him for twenty years.

The superintendent wanted a breakthrough, if not an immediate result. He had people on his back, not least the media. It wasn't Bill who had to face the daily press briefing. Terri's story, from nice girl to heroin addict to prostitute, had grabbed their attention, fuelled by the fact she might be alive and in the hands of the killer. Add in a criminal psychologist with Magnus's looks and personality and it was a heady brew. No doubt the media would soon be aware of the 'moon' angle. It was common practice for moles in the force and among hospital and mortuary staff to alert the press with a good story. In the case of the lower paid, any supplement to their wages was welcome.

Having to let both Beattie and Irvine go had added to the fallout. Beattie was hiding something, but Bill had a feeling it was something other than Terri's disappearance. Perhaps he made a habit of hooking up with his female pupils – that wouldn't make him a murderer. They were probing a bit deeper into Beattie's sailing club connections, checking if there had been any complaints made against him. It wouldn't be the first time warning signs had gone unnoticed.

Irvine was a different but equally unpleasant character. A high earner, he'd professed to frequenting the red-light district when he'd made, as he put it, a *killing* on the stock market. According to Irvine, slumming it with street prostitutes added to his high. Both he and Beattie had alibis for the night in question. If the alibis checked out and neither man's DNA was a match, then both were out of the picture.

Magnus had shown his worth in both interviews, describing afterwards the subtle changes in body movement suggesting truth, evasion or lies. Things Bill had sensed intuitively, or learned over two decades, now apparently had a scientific name – kinesics. Thinking of Magnus now, Bill wondered where he was.

Repeated calls to his mobile and home numbers had yielded nothing. Neither had a check on his flat. Magnus, like the online auction, had simply disappeared. Bill reminded himself Magnus was not his responsibility, but it didn't prevent him from worrying that the professor had done something stupid and possibly dangerous.

Bill checked his watch. He had a meeting in half an hour with ballistics. He decided the time in between would be best spent in the incident room.

Information overload was the impression he got on entry. That was the problem with modern-day detective work. Everything had to be checked, double-checked and cross-referenced. For most of the incident team, that meant sitting all day in front of a screen, interrogating a database.

For the team trawling CCTV footage of the red-light district, it meant hour after hour of grainy images of shadowy cars. Geordie had given them a time for Terri's departure, but bearing in mind the old man had shown signs of memory loss and confusion, it probably wasn't reliable. DC Mark Geddes showed him footage of a dark car arriving around the allotted time.

'That looks like a towbar to me,' he suggested.

Bill peered at the screen, trying to reshape the blob Mark was indicating into a towbar. It wasn't easy.

'No registration number?'

Geddes shook his head. 'I've played around with what I think the figures might be. I'm running that through now.'

Cathy's photograph had been added to the wall display of victims, although at the moment they had no forensics to link her to their killer. It was just too much of a coincidence that hours after discussing Terri's disappearance with him, Cathy was dead.

Janice, like the rest of the team, was hunched over a computer. She had a train timetable from Glasgow to Cardross on the screen.

'McNab called in. Said there was a train station close to the shore. Asked me to check the schedule. Trains run every half an hour. The last one on a Sunday night leaves Queen Street for Helensburgh via Cardross at 11.24 p.m.'

'Bus?'

'Not at that time on a Sunday.'

So Cathy could have got there without a car.

'Okay, let's see if we can get a sighting of her at Queen Street. Do we have an address for her yet?'

'Just in. She lived in a block of flats off Duke Street, near where her body was found.'

'Right. See what you can find out there. I'm off to ballistics. I take it there's no word on Magnus?'

Janice shook her head.

DC Tweedie showed Bill a photograph of the bullet wound. 'The wound suggests a handgun with a rifled barrel, used at close range. A small, clean, circular wound with bruising, singed skin and a muzzle imprint. I checked the inside of the culvert but I'd say she was shot elsewhere. It's likely to be a reactivated gun because there's plenty of them about. A father and son team from Manchester have just been charged with reactivating 4,000 handguns and selling them on, so no problem getting hold of one. Land Services have okayed a culvert trip, now the water level's down. Maybe we'll find the weapon.' He didn't sound hopeful. Why dispose of a gun you'd want to use again?

Guns and crack cocaine went together. Ask colleagues in Manchester or London. Glasgow was still the home of heroin but, as Craig Minto's recent business venture suggested, what happened south of the border made its way north sooner or later.

45

BILL STOOD IN the centre of Cathy's small sitting room and looked about him. A blanket spread out on the sofa suggested someone had been sleeping there. An empty vodka bottle and two glasses stood on a nearby coffee table. He took a closer look but didn't touch. Each rim was smeared with lipstick. It seemed Cathy had had a female visitor before she went out.

On his way to the kitchen, he took a look out of Cathy's window. Nine storeys high, facing south, it provided a clear view of the Great Eastern, with the goods yard behind, his old school playground and of course the foliage around the Molendinar, where Cathy's body had been found. Cathy hadn't had far to go between home and grave. So why the round trip to Cardross?

A tiny kitchen led off the sitting room. The only item of interest in there was a packet of Valium, the prostitutes' standby, lying next to a filled ashtray.

The bedroom was an altogether different matter. It could have won a prize in a bordello competition. Cathy had done her clients proud. The walls were painted a deep red, the king-sized bed spread with scarlet satin sheets and covered by a tiger-patterned throw. Behind and above hung large mirrors. A fluffy bag next to the dressing table revealed an assortment of sex toys, including a large blue dildo that looked like it had been modelled on King Kong.

Bill heard a knock on the open front door. The caretaker, Jimmy Fairlie, stood in the doorway looking worried.

'I was told you wanted to speak to me.'

Bill and Jimmy went back twenty years. As far as Bill was aware Jimmy had kept his nose clean for the last five years, since he got this job. Door to door interviews in the block of flats had given the impression Jimmy was well liked, and probably just as law-abiding as the rest of its inhabitants.

Bill stepped out onto the landing to question him.

'Cathy had a visitor Sunday night?'

'Aye. A lassie, about eight o'clock. Cathy was expecting her. She rang down and told me to let her in.'

'What did she look like?'

Jimmy gave a reasonable description of what sounded like Leanne. 'She was in a bit of a mess. Like she'd been out all night.'

'Did Cathy say the name Leanne?'

'She might have.' Jimmy looked cagey. He didn't want to point the finger at anyone.

'And what happened after that?'

'Nothing.'

'No one else came to see Cathy?'

'Nope.'

'Did you see Cathy leave?'

Jimmy shook his head. 'I knock off at eleven. She must have gone out after that.'

'What about the girl?'

'She never came down before I left.'

Jimmy was avoiding looking over Bill's shoulder at the open bedroom door.

'How well did you know Cathy?'

Jimmy cleared his throat. 'Eh. We were pals.'

'How pally, exactly?'

Jimmy was considering his reply. One look at Bill's face convinced him that honesty was the best policy.

'I helped her out with anything that needed fixing in the flat – she was nice to me.'

'When was she last nice to you?' Bill kept his voice level.

'A week ago Saturday, when I knocked off work.'

The pathology report suggested Cathy had had sex in the hours before her death. Jimmy might be telling the truth, but they had to be sure.

'We'll have to check your DNA.'

Jimmy shrugged his shoulders. 'You've got it already.' He didn't look bothered, which suggested he might be telling the truth. The man had been a small-time crook, not known for violence. Breaking and entering and trading in stolen goods was his business. He hadn't jumped on the drugs bandwagon when it arrived either. Bill had no doubt Jimmy was still operating in a low-key way. Why pay Inland Revenue your hard-earned money when the really rich never did?

'Any idea who would shoot Cathy?'

Jimmy shook his head. 'Fucking terrible.' He looked genuinely sorry.

'Did Cathy say anything to you about Terri Docherty?'

'Only that she thought the missing lassie wasn't dead.'

'When did Cathy tell you that?'

Jimmy looked scared, as if he'd said too much. 'I don't remember.'

'Try.'

'Okay. It was Sunday. She had a cup of tea with me in the booth.'

'Did she tell you why she thought that?'

'No, but she sounded pretty sure.'

They were back at that telephone message. Bill cursed himself again for not answering the bloody phone when it rang.

46

CHRISSY HELD UP a paint chip as big as her little fingernail.

'That was in the soil?'

'On Geordie's clothes.'

Rhona took a closer look. The shape was black and irregular, which was good for matching. Under a microscope the layers would be obvious, the chemical analysis of them straightforward. Every model, make and year of car had its own distinct colour mix. Paint was a forensic scientist's dream trace evidence.

'And this,' Chrissy gestured to the microscope, 'is what I found in the soil.'

The flake was much smaller and the colour of wood.

'I haven't gone any further than just admire it,' Chrissy said. 'But the thought did cross my mind it might be varnish.'

Rhona had done work on spar or marine varnish before. It resembled regular varnish except for the higher oil content, making it more flexible and better in humidity. UV inhibitors were often incorporated, because of exposure to the sun. It would be more difficult to match a yacht varnish to an actual yacht than a flake of paint to a make and model of car.

They took some time out to discuss progress in general.

'What happened about the partial print on the gag?' Rhona asked.

'Livescan have it, and the one lifted from Terri's handbag. So we'll see if they find a match in the DNA database. The partial isn't good, but I did rescue some skin cells from the tape. I'm waiting for results on those too.'

Rhona related her tale of the Cardross trip.

'You and McNab getting cosy again?'

'Chrissy,' Rhona warned.

'McNab's good at pretending to be good.'

'He's seeing Judy at GUARD.'

'Really?' Chrissy pulled a face. 'It was Janice Clark last I heard.'

That's what McNab had told Rhona on the Nigerian trip, but she'd seen no evidence of it on her return.

'Funny he never fancied me.' Chrissy pondered, mock-affronted.

'He'll get around to it.'

Chrissy patted her belly. 'Not when he finds out about this.' She dug in the pocket of her lab coat and extracted a small photo. 'I know it looks like a blob.'

Rhona sought the shape of a baby in the blur. Chrissy helped by pointing to the curve of the backbone. Recognition sent a shiver up Rhona's own spine.

'Boy or girl?'

'I prefer surprises.'

There was a moment's silence, while they both

digested the enormity of what the image actually meant, then Chrissy changed the subject.

'How's the Viking doing?'

'He's disappeared.'

'What?'

'Magnus didn't come to the meeting and is non-contactable.'

'You're worried,' Chrissy said, stating the obvious.

'He'll turn up,' said Rhona, hoping her conviction would make it true.

On the way back from Cardross, McNab had repeated his suggestion that they study the Atlantic City file together. Rhona's request that he fax her the forensic details had been stonewalled – poring over them together seemed to be his preferred option.

He'd finally given in. 'You'll let me know if you find anything interesting?'

'Of course.'

McNab had been as good as his word. The documents were with her an hour later. Rhona put them with the unsolved cases for later study and set about examining the flake sieved from the grave soil.

Chemical analysis established it as spar or marine varnish, as Chrissy had said. Matching it to a particular company took longer. She eventually located a family firm called Realpaints, specialising in paints and varnishes that incorporated only traditional ingredients and production methods. Their spar was based on tung oil, similar to her analysis. The man Rhona needed to talk to wasn't there, but his assistant

promised he would get back to her. Her call did
establish that their varnish was designed for use on
the masts and wooden hulls of older yachts. Useful
once they had a suspect who owned or worked on such
a yacht, but as yet just another piece in an increasingly
complex puzzle.

Magnus had seemed pretty certain on two things –
the importance of both the killer's geographical profile,
and his signature. Rhona had already marked up a city
map with the various crime scenes, like the one Bill had
on display in the incident room. She drew a line
through the various locations. The Necropolis to Duke
Street, to the emergence of the Molendinar, and finally
to Calton, where Terri and Lucie had been picked up.

The line formed the shape of a wide crescent,
bizarrely like the shape of a half-moon. Apart from
a possible link with Cardross, the killer had operated
within this boundary. Magnus had suggested the perpetrator would have a base not far from where he
killed. He would retreat there as soon as possible
afterwards, like a lion returning to its lair.

Rhona pondered the map. Glasgow's inner city
renewal project meant the reinvigorated Merchant
City, with its designer shops and café society, was
within walking distance of the poverty of Calton.
Expensive riverside flats like Magnus's, lay just west
of the red-light district of Glasgow Green. It would be
easy to move swiftly between the two worlds. If the
killer was holding Terri, where would that be? In the
world he killed in, or in the safety of his lair, wherever
that was?

Burial was important to the killer, but his original hunting ground, the Necropolis, offered no opportunity to hide Terri alive. The Molendinar culvert was underground, but, according to those responsible for its upkeep, was largely inaccessible and liable to flooding.

Rhona traced a line down to the goods yard south of Duke Street, halfway between the Necropolis and the point Terri had disappeared. She recalled standing among the heaps of old bricks. Bill had set the police dogs loose on the piles, worried he might find another body there, but the dogs hadn't picked up a scent. The back boundary of the yard dropped steeply to the car park. To the left was a massive hole, all that was left of a former railway building and its maze of brick cellars; to the right, the rear of the Great Eastern. Rhona remembered the broken windows on the upper levels of the once-impressive building, blue plastic flapping in the rain.

Bill had had the empty shell searched and drawn a blank. The old hotel held nothing but the forgotten hopes and dreams of the hundreds of men who'd lived there.

Rhona gave up on the map and turned to the Atlantic City notes. McNab had sent the complete set, rather than just the forensic results. They proved to be interesting reading. McNab was correct in thinking there were similarities in the investigations.

Decomposition in his first two cases had made it impossible to determine cause of death, but the most recent victim, killed just before Christmas, had been strangled with her bra. No mention was made of a slipknot. Karil Heidner, their criminal profiler, seemed to agree with Magnus that the insertion of a stiletto heel in the vaginal cavity of all three victims was symbolic of a penis and could suggest that the killer did not – or could not – have sex with his victims.

Unlike the Glasgow case, all three Atlantic City victims had eventually been identified. All were working as prostitutes at the time of their death. Two were in their teens, one in her early twenties. The youngest, eighteen-year-old Aurora Catania, was a known crack addict. She'd been the first to be found but the most recently killed. Rhona took a look at the forensic evidence.

Because of its proximity to salt water and the weather at that time of year, the scene of the earlier crimes had been washed clean as far as forensics was concerned. In Aurora's case, luck had brought an interested dog under the boardwalk. Some attempt had been made to bury the body in sand, but the dog had unearthed it. The girl had been dead less than a week.

An earlier photo of Aurora showed her with long blonde hair pulled back from a pretty face. It reminded Rhona of the family photos of Terri she'd seen at the Docherty's. Aurora's story was similar, driven to Atlantic City by an addiction to heroin and crack cocaine after a series of family traumas. She'd worked Pacific Avenue as a prostitute to feed her addiction. Atlantic City had 40,000 permanent residents and thirty million gambling visitors a year. Among such a fluctuating population, prostitutes arrived and left with frightening regularity, so no one noticed if they went missing, unless they turned up dead.

The forensic report on Aurora stated traces of semen had been collected from her vagina. It hadn't matched the DNA of their prime suspect and he hadn't been charged. His name was Ryan Williams, he was forty-five years old and he worked in one of the casinos on the boardwalk. He also owned a small yacht in the nearby marina. He'd left town after his release. An accompanying photograph showed a clean-shaven, smartly dressed man.

Rhona fished out the DNA profile. Since the year 2000, most USA labs had begun testing for the same STR points, storing the results in CODIS, the Combined DNA Index system, so that results could be shared. This side of the Atlantic, the Scottish DNA Database regularly uploaded to the National Database, looking for matches. A submission to NDNAD would hopefully be quick but not immediate. It was worth running a comparison, because of the stiletto connection.

Rhona started on the unsolved cases.

Forensic methods had improved considerably over the last decade, but however meticulous they were at keeping evidence, however successful they were at extracting DNA, they still relied on a match with current records.

Seven murders in six years and not one conviction. In two cases, the men accused were acquitted, Scotland's Not Proven verdict providing a get-out clause for the jury. Suspects in a further two cases weren't brought to trial, and there had been no arrests in the last three murders.

If these women had been 'ordinary' as opposed to prostitutes, there would have been a public outcry. The notes made depressing reading. Beaten, strangled, stabbed, and in one case possibly drowned, only the 1993 case had a vague similarity to the current murders. Karen McGregor had been found near the Scottish Exhibition Centre, battered and throttled. The forensic report suggested an object had been forced into her vagina. Her husband was charged, but witnesses retracted their statements and Charles McGregor walked free after a Not Proven verdict.

The unsolved prostitute murders in Glasgow were a disturbing tale of lost lives and drug addiction, a haunting replica of the story told by Lieutenant Blum. The hell these women lived was the same on both sides of the Atlantic.

Chrissy came looking for her at six o'clock.

'You won't find anything in there you haven't read before,' she reminded Rhona.

'McNab wanted me to take a look at a similar case in Atlantic City.'

'Across the pond?' Chrissy looked intrigued.

'Similar MO and signature, strangulation and the insertion of a stiletto heel. The criminal profiler on the case voiced the same opinion as Magnus, that the stiletto served as a penis. The killer didn't or couldn't have sex with his victim.'

'Any word on Magnus?'

'No.' Rhona had checked her mobile at regular

intervals all afternoon. She'd also tried to call him but got voicemail.

'Maybe he's out of range?'

'All day?'

As if on cue, Rhona's mobile rang. It was McNab.

'Ryan Williams was formerly known as Peter Henderson. He changed his name legally online for £14.99.'

'Is Ryan Williams British?'

'Born in Glasgow in 1962.'

'You're sure it's the same man?'

'I talked to Lieutenant Blum. He said the guy had an American passport, but a funny accent. It reminded him of Shrek.' McNab paused, then went on. 'That's not all. Henderson was briefly detained in Edinburgh in 1977 during the World's End murder enquiry, but released without charge.'

The police had eventually charged sixty-year-old Angus Sinclair for the murder of the two teenage girls, last seen at The World's End pub in the Royal Mile in Edinburgh thirty years before. Despite forensic evidence linking Sinclair with the girls, the case wasn't presented to a jury.

'Why was Henderson a suspect?'

'He said he was in the pub, saw the girls leave, generally made himself available.'

Even back then, before psychological profiling, thrusting yourself in the spotlight always brought suspicion. It was a well-known feature of the behaviour of certain types of killer, Ian Huntley in Soham being a prime example.

'Have we any proof he's been back here?'

'I'm working on it.'

Maybe McNab's lead was really going somewhere.

Magnus's text, asking to meet at her flat, arrived as she departed the lab. She had been praying for this for so long, Rhona almost cried out in relief. She texted back to say yes, then left a message on Bill's phone to let him know Magnus had been in touch.

On the drive home, her sense of relief was swiftly replaced by anger at Magnus for causing so much worry. Rhona spent the drive rehearsing out loud exactly what she planned to say to Magnus Pirie when she got there.

47

MAGNUS OPENED HIS eyes to suffocating darkness and an overpowering scent of damp and decay. Since he could see nothing, he focused on the smell, identifying it as both organic and cement-based, like a building being reclaimed by nature. At a guess, he was in a cellar. Magnus listened. He could hear water, both trickling nearby and running more freely elsewhere.

Concentrating on water brought on a sudden and devastating desire to urinate. Only then did Magnus become fully aware of the wire that gripped his hands painfully behind his back, digging into the tender skin of his wrists. He tried to persuade himself that he didn't need to go, but his body eventually took charge and emptied his bladder regardless. Magnus felt a rush of heat inside his trousers, then the dampening of the ground below him.

Through a thudding head, he tried to work out how he'd got there. He remembered the girl, Nikki, running from him in the alley; then the discovery that the black car had trashed his bike, rendering it unusable. How he'd decided to leave it propped against the wall, accepting he was never likely to see it again.

He should have turned homewards then, but hadn't. Instead he'd walked through Calton towards the Necropolis. He'd been crossing a strip of waste ground when he'd suspected someone was following him. He'd caught a scent at first, then heard a soft crunch as a foot met gravel.

At that point he'd upped his pace, heading for a distant street light that marked the main road. The last thing Magnus remembered was a rush of air as something came down heavily on his head.

As his eyes grew accustomed to the darkness, Magnus began to distinguish the shape of the space he was in. Low-ceilinged, a brick archway to one side. He had no idea how long he'd been trussed up there, but judged by his biting hunger and thirst, it might have been up to twelve hours.

He'd no doubt his abduction had been prompted by his online bid, and railed at himself for not calling Bill immediately. Magnus winced at the bitter memory of Anna losing her life because of his stupidity and arrogance. What if he'd hastened Terri's death too?

A rush of anger engulfed him. He'd thought himself clever. So clever he could catch the killer by psychological insight. What a fool he'd been. The killer was smarter than him. The killer had read his weakness, and played it to perfection.

The cramps in his arms had worked their way up to his neck. Magnus twisted his hands in an effort to free them, then stopped when he felt the wire draw blood.

There was a growl in his guts and he realised his bowels would move soon of their own accord, despite his efforts to prevent them. Magnus didn't care about pissing his pants, but he was damned if he would soil them too.

He rolled onto his front, then rose to his knees and with a huge effort climbed to his feet. His ankles were tied, but more loosely, with cord. Magnus worked at one shoe. Once one foot was out, the other was easy. Then he began to twist his wrists in ever expanding circles, spitting a litany of curses, as the wire stretched and loosened. The release, when it finally came, made him stagger in agony. Magnus realised in that moment that he had never experienced real pain before. He'd merely observed and analysed it, kidding himself he understood.

When he'd regained control of his body, he dipped his head and exited through the archway. This space gave immediately onto another. Magnus paced its perimeter until he found a matching archway on the opposite side.

He stood for a moment and listened. The sound of water seemed louder now. Magnus took a deep breath, expecting to smell an underground stream, but it was the faint smell of sweat that met his nostrils. At the same time he was conscious he was on the outskirts of a source of light.

As Magnus crept forward, the human scent grew more intense. More than one person was or had been close by. Magnus looked through the archway.

A harsh arc light held her full in its gaze, like a stark camera shot in some horror movie. Crouched and rigid with fear, Terri Docherty watched Magnus emerge from the shadows.

48

'I'M NOT GOING to hurt you.'

Terri pressed herself to the wall, mewing like a kitten.

'It's okay, I'm here to help you.' Even to himself, it sounded weak and pathetic. A man who could barely walk, was here to help her. He tried again. 'My name is Magnus. I'm a profiler with the police. I've been looking for you.'

'And now you've found her.'

Magnus swivelled around, looking for the voice's owner, finding no one.

'You bid for her and now she's yours.'

'I'm here to help her.'

The shot, when it came, was unbelievably loud in the confined space, ricocheting from wall to wall. Magnus flung himself to the ground. Eventually the bullet buried itself somewhere and died.

'Next time I shoot her through the head, just like Cathy.'

Magnus had never felt so cold.

'You're here to fuck her. Get on with it.'

The place went eerily silent. All Magnus could hear was the rush of water. For the first time in his life his brain had ceased to function. It offered him nothing. No thoughts, no ideas, no possible solutions.

'Fuck her, or I kill her.'

Terri's naked body glistened with sweat and blood. Magnus realised she'd already been wounded. Something – a bullet? – had scored her neck, and her left breast had an oozing wound. Her terrified eyes sought his and Magnus read the truth of her anguished request. Terri would rather submit than die. Magnus crawled slowly towards her, running various scenarios in his head.

'I won't hurt her,' he shouted into the blinding light. He moved to cover Terri's body with his own, trying to judge where the last shot had come from.

Suddenly the arc light snapped off and they were plunged into darkness. Somewhere behind him, Magnus heard a footfall, then something sharp jabbed his neck.

Magnus knew he was in darkness, yet his mind insisted on pretending otherwise, swooping him through a kaleidoscope of images that exhilarated and nauseated him at the same time. The realisation he had no control over any of his senses terrified Magnus. He'd been drugged. With what, he had no idea. His tortured brain tried to remember what Rhona had said in the lab about crystal meth and its effects on the nervous system.

He'd no idea how long he lay in this semi-hallucinatory state, but eventually reason reasserted itself and he opened his eyes to the glare of the arc light.

The first thing to hit him was his smell. He reeked of sweat, blood and fear.

Magnus rolled off Terri's inert body with an intense feeling of guilt and remorse. Then the memories came in a rush. The crack as the bullet hit the brickwork near his head. His dive to the ground. Crawling towards Terri and covering her body with his. Then darkness. After the jab in his neck, a rush of heat and light. A throbbing sensation as the drug entered his blood-stream. Every sense suddenly alive and drowning in heat and pleasure.

Shame burned at him now as he recalled his attacker's order. Could he have done something in his altered state? The idea repulsed him.

Magnus crawled towards the stream, expecting any moment to hear the whine of a bullet or hear a warning shout. When none came, he ducked his head under and lay there for a moment, letting the sharp chill of the water clear his brain.

On his return, he found Terri curled in a foetal position, her eyes closed. Magnus checked her pulse and sniffed at her mouth, picking up a faint chemical smell he couldn't identify. He examined her bonds. Her manacled neck and wrists were attached by what looked like an anchor chain to a large ring embedded in the wall.

'Terri,' he said softly. 'I have to go for help.'

She stirred and gave a small moan.

'Can you tell me who brought you here?'

Her eyes flickered open. Magnus was horrified to think the fear he saw there might be directed at him.

'What does he look like?'

Terri shook her head as though she didn't want to remember.

'Please try, Terri.'

Spittle trickled from her mouth and her eyes rolled in her head. She was still tripping on something.

Magnus felt for her pulse again and found it faint and skipping. He got to his feet. Terri's only hope was for him to get out of there and bring help.

49

THERE WAS NO sign of Magnus or his bike outside her flat. Rhona propped open the front door and went upstairs.

Tom was alone and pleased to see her, greeting her arrival with much purring and ankle-twining. She picked him up and gave him a hug. Her meal sat ready to re-heat. Rhona felt momentarily guilty – she hadn't even thought to call Sean to tell him when she'd be home. She poured a glass of wine and settled on the window seat to wait. Magnus had said he would be there in twenty minutes.

Half an hour later there was no sign of him. Irritated, Rhona decided to have her meal. She ate in silence, the kitten having ceased its sound effects and retreated to its basket to sleep. Afterwards, Rhona went through the motions of clearing up, her temper shortening with each passing minute. Her vocal rehearsal of what she planned to say to Magnus when he finally arrived made Tom prick up his ears warily.

Rhona eventually deserted the kitchen for her study, trying to ignore the gnawing feeling that something wasn't right. She texted Magnus's number asking where the hell he was. Seconds later a text message arrived, containing an image.

The bodies were bleached by a strong white light, but Rhona immediately recognised Magnus and the missing girl. Terri was naked, her manacles visible, her face contorted like a cat hissing in fear. Magnus lay on top, eyes closed, his face turned to the camera, as though caught in the act.

Shock sent Rhona sliding into a chair. She stared at the screen in disbelief, but however she tried to explain the image, it looked like a rape scene. She used the landline to call Bill, unable to contemplate using the mobile. Bill answered almost immediately and Rhona blurted out what had just happened.

'Okay, stay there, McNab and I are on our way.'

Rhona waited in her study, her mind reeling, her gut churning, the mobile with the offending image beside her on the desk. Was Magnus capable of such an act? Did she know him at all?

When Bill and McNab arrived, McNab took the phone and downloaded the image to his laptop. The larger version that now filled the screen was even more damning.

'Terri was definitely alive when this was taken.' It was the only positive thing that could be said. McNab threw Rhona a sympathetic look, which didn't help.

'Can we find out when it was taken?' Bill said.

'Not unless we have the phone.'

'When exactly did you last see Magnus?'

'Midnight on Monday night.'

'Almost twenty-four hours ago.' Plenty of time for both Terri and Magnus to be dead.

'Was Magnus swabbed and fingerprinted when he joined the team?'

It was standard practice that the DNA and fingerprints of all police personnel were stored on the Scottish National Database.

Rhona shrugged helplessly. She had no idea. McNab looked uncomfortable. As crime scene manager, that's something he should have checked. Rhona wondered where this was leading. 'What are you saying? That Magnus is complicit in this?'

The words were out in the open now.

'He could have been forced to have sexual intercourse with her,' McNab offered.

'We don't know that's what's happening. Not for certain.' Rhona looked to Bill, willing him to agree.

Bill's troubled expression didn't change. 'Okay, let's see if we've got anything more from the mobile company on the whereabouts of Magnus's phone,' he told McNab.

'You've been tracking him?' Rhona didn't know why that surprised her.

'The only activity on this phone in the last twenty-four hours are the text he sent Rhona before, and this photo.'

'Magnus didn't send it,' said Rhona, firmly. 'The killer did.'

50

AFTER BILL AND McNab left, Rhona went to bed. She lay wide awake, staring at the ceiling, unable to banish the image of Magnus and Terri from her mind.

The online auction had been an invitation to torture, rape and murder the girl. If Magnus *had* been coerced into having sex with Terri, what else had he been forced to do?

Rhona ran through every exchange she'd ever had with Magnus, back to the first strategy meeting. She was a reasonable judge of character, but not as astute as Chrissy, whose judgement Rhona would stake her life on. Chrissy had openly declared her liking for Magnus.

Magnus could be arrogant, determined to go his own way regardless of orders or advice. But a rapist? No. She couldn't believe that of him. But what if his life were in danger? Or Terri's? What then?

The red light of her mobile blinked at her from the bedside table. If a call came in from Magnus's phone, Bill wanted to know, whatever the hour. Rhona had turned up the volume in case she dozed off, although at the moment it didn't look likely.

Eventually she did, drifting into a fitful sleep punctured by nightmarish images of Magnus looming over her, his hands holding her down, his mouth hot on hers.

She wakened suddenly, to find Sean next to her.

'I was having a nightmare.'

'Sounded like a different kind of dream to me.' Sean's expression was inscrutable.

Had she talked in her sleep? Rhona knew she should say something, but couldn't. A flash of something like pain crossed Sean's face. Rhona reached for the mobile and brought up the image. 'Take a look at this. *That's* what I was dreaming about.'

Sean stared dumbstruck at the photograph. 'What the fuck's going on?'

Rhona told him the minimum. The girl in the image was Terri Docherty. Magnus had gone missing, having been, they believed, in contact with the killer. She'd received a text to meet him earlier at the flat. He hadn't turned up, but the image had been sent as soon as she contacted him.

Sean listened in silence. When she finished he said, 'The sex looks real to me.'

'Yes, but . . . it can't be. Magnus wouldn't . . .' she stumbled to a halt.

'The girl was terrified.'

'I know,' Rhona's voice faltered.

Sean drew her into his arms.

'I don't want you involved in this,' Sean said angrily.

'It's my job.'

'Fuck the job.'

'I'm not in any danger.'

'Yeah right. You've been hanging out with a nutter I just saw rape someone, but you're not in any danger.'

She shouldn't have shown Sean the photo. She should have made an excuse, a joke about rude dreams.

'This is police business. It has nothing to do with you.'

Rhona felt Sean's body go rigid.

'If that bastard comes near you again, I'll kill him.'

Rhona waited until she was sure Sean was asleep, then slipped out of bed and headed for the kitchen. Tom, curled up in his basket, didn't open an eye. Rhona left him in peace and took her seat in the moonlit room. She thought of Nora, who'd sensed her daughter was still alive. She remembered how Magnus had taken the woman's hand and told her he believed her. What would Bill do now? Tell Nora she was right, her daughter was alive? At least she was twenty-four hours before, because he had a photograph to prove it. The thought of Nora viewing that image of Magnus with her daughter was almost too much to bear.

51

THE ROOM REMINDED him of the alleyway; the hot stink of damp, piss and stale sex. Only the movement of air over water made it bearable. Magnus had paced the perimeter twice, but the only way out seemed to be the way he'd come in.

He'd decided at that point that the stream must provide an exit and had waded in, bent over, walking with the current, the swift flow of water reaching his knees. Darkness had quickly swallowed him and his pace had slowed as he'd tried to avoid cracking his head on the low roof. After what he'd estimated as sixty feet, the perfectly formed round brick tunnel had lost its shape to stalactites and thick reddish deposits of what looked like iron oxide, leeching in from above. Eventually it had become impossible to go on, the jagged ceiling brushing the surface of the water.

Magnus had returned to the cellar to find Terri still unconscious, her face pale. She wasn't losing any blood and her pulse was steady, but her skin felt cold and clammy despite the humid heat. Magnus took off his shirt and covered her as best he could.

His venture upstream ended in the same way as his earlier jaunt. This time his hopes were raised by the length of time it took to reach the encrustation. More like a hundred feet than sixty. But the result was the same. Water could filter through, but a human being would have to lie flat and wriggle their way out.

Disappointed, Magnus returned to Terri and checked her pulse again, grateful to find it still steady. He sat close to her for a bit, hoping his body heat would help raise hers, and turned his mind to working out where the killer had shot from. He replayed the scenario, trying to place himself in the same position, careful not to disturb Terri in case she woke and thought he was moving in on her again.

Magnus examined the wall above the girl and saw the track of the bullet he'd dived to avoid. He turned his gaze to where he thought it originated and met the arc light full on. The killer had to be positioned up there, where the dazzling beam made it impossible to see him.

The wall under the arc light was brick built, supported by a cast-iron frame, rising to a vaulted roof. The lamp was mounted high on an arch, with no visible means of reaching it from there, suggesting it'd been lowered through from above. The gunman must have shot from there.

Magnus went to glance at his watch, forgetting again that it and his mobile had been taken from him or lost somewhere between the waste ground and the cellar. It troubled him greatly that he had no idea how long it had been since the gunman left, nor how soon he would return.

If he was right about the lunar effect, Terri's death was imminent. If he stayed there, Magnus had no doubt he would be made complicit in it. The thought horrified him, as did the alternative, which was to leave her to face her fate alone.

He had to find a way through the vaults, and quickly.

He checked Terri one more time before he left. He knew she was seventeen, but lying curled in a ball she looked little more than a child. Nora had been right, her little girl was still alive. It was his job to make sure she stayed that way.

After the harsh light, the darkness of the neighbouring room blinded him. Magnus waited for his eyes to adjust, trying to imagine the layout. He'd crossed three spaces before finding Terri. If the killer was operating alone, he'd managed to transport Magnus down there somehow. Which suggested the stairs weren't too far from where he'd first regained consciousness.

The further he moved from Terri's prison the thicker the darkness became, and Magnus began to rely on his sense of smell. The overriding scent was damp and disuse, but there were subtle differences from room to room. Access upwards would involve the movement of air, and moving air smelt noticeably different.

Magnus was beginning to believe he was going around in circles, when he finally caught a whiff of fresher air. He stood perfectly still and breathed in, praying he was right. The touch of it on his cheek nearly made him whoop for joy.

He followed the scent until his right foot hit concrete, then knelt to feel with his hands. Definitely stairs. Magnus raised his eyes, searching for some subtle change in light that might indicate a door, but could distinguish none.

He dropped to his knees, conscious that the stairway might not be complete, and began to crawl upwards. He'd counted six steps before he reached for the next and found emptiness. Magnus felt left, then right, trying to interpret what lay under his hand, eventually establishing the concrete had crumbled, leaving behind the metal reinforcing rods. The following step, as far as he could tell, was more or less intact.

Magnus resumed his crawl, keeping as close to the right-hand wall as possible. He knew he'd reached the top when he found an open stretch of concrete. He dragged himself up and sat for a moment to regain his composure, then ran his hand along until he found the outline of a door.

52

MAGNUS WAS TRYING to prise the door open with one of the steel rods when he heard Terri scream. The shock sent him reeling backwards, and he momentarily lost his balance, almost slipping over the edge of the staircase. The deathly silence that followed horrified him even more, propelling him downwards. At the bottom, he broke into a blind run.

He found himself trusting instinct, as he had on the islands as a child during the long dark northern winters. Then it had been field and dyke, river and road. Here, intuition swerved him from walls towards openings, as he mentally counted the spaces he'd crossed. In all the time he ran, there was no sound, bar the crashing of his heart. He prayed for a distant moan or whimper.

As Magnus ducked under the archway into the full glare of the lamp, the metallic scent of fresh blood hit his nostrils, and he understood why Terri had made no further sound. Magnus ran to the spot he'd left her, as though by his presence Terri would miraculously reappear. The shackles hung empty, his dirt-streaked and bloody shirt discarded. When he had left Terri, he would have said things couldn't get any worse. How wrong could he have been? Magnus raged at himself, impotent in his fury. He'd deserted Terri when he should have tried to protect her.

Eventually he stopped his useless pacing. Castigating himself would achieve nothing. It was self-indulgent and despicable. His job now was to find Terri. Magnus examined the ground below the shackles. There was fresh blood, but not much. He tried to read its pattern, wishing he had Rhona beside him. Blood, she'd told him, was a storybook. Every drop a word, the resulting pattern a complete narrative of what had happened to make it spill. His natural optimism won. Terri had been alive when she was taken away. But for how long?

Magnus made for the wall below the arc light. The cement between the bricks was crumbling in places, offering the chance of a foot or handhold, much like the red sandstone cliffs and stacks of Orkney.

He felt for the first available grip and began to pull himself up. His fingertips were already bloodied and bruised from his earlier attempts to open the door, but they sought the space between the bricks and clung there like limpets. The action of climbing brought vivid memories of scrabbling up the cliffs of Yesnaby. Gulls screaming, angry waters surging below, the scent and taste of salt and sandstone.

The heat from the lamp streamed sweat down his neck and chest. It ran freely now that he'd given up his shirt for Terri. The memory of draping it over her cold body drove him on. Eventually he came level with the metal arm of the arc light and hung there, trying to make out what was above him.

He made a grab with his right hand and swung forward on the metal support. Above was the opening he sought. A perfect viewing platform and ideal location to take pot shots at the room below, and more importantly, big enough to climb through. The muscles in his upper arms screamed as Magnus made the final thrust upwards, to roll panting and groaning into the upper level.

When he could breathe freely again, he manoeuvred the arc light so part of its glare now illuminated the upper room. He was fed up rooting around in the dark. He wanted to see where he was, and what he was dealing with.

The room was small and low-ceilinged, with a table and chair against the wall. Lying next to a laptop was his watch and mobile. Magnus couldn't believe his luck. He grabbed for the mobile and turned it on. It fired up for a few moments, raising his hopes, then died, the battery flat.

Magnus tried to console himself, as he strapped the watch to his wrist. It was an old psychological trick to deprive people of time. With no sense of it passing, of when it was day and when night, people lost their grip on reality. Magnus checked the time and date. Now he knew how long it'd been since he'd walked the waste ground in Calton.

Magnus focused next on the laptop. A selection of pictures filled the screen. Grotesque images of Terri and her injuries. The killer needed broken skin and blood to turn him on. Magnus scrolled through a dozen, his stomach contracting with each new image.

He'd been right about one thing. Their ritualistic nature suggested the killer saw Terri as an object, not a person.

The final picture confirmed Magnus's worst fears. Now he saw what had happened after the drug entered his bloodstream. Now he knew what he'd done. He was no better than the killer, who'd manipulated and out-matched him at every turn.

53

'OKAY, WHAT HAVE we got?'

Bill looked as though he'd had the minimum of sleep, much like herself. Rhona had grabbed a couple of hours before dawn and then headed back to the lab. There had been no further messages from Magnus's mobile.

'The registration number of the car parked on the foreshore at Cardross has been identified as stolen, last seen by its owner in the car park under his flat three days ago.' McNab read out the address. It wasn't far from Magnus's apartment on the banks of the Clyde. 'The car has turned up on waste ground in Calton. It was reported on fire in the early hours of Tuesday morning. The fire brigade were there promptly and the damage is superficial. The flake of paint found in Geordie's clothes matches damage to the front of the car.'

'So we've got the vehicle that killed Geordie but not the driver?'

Rhona interrupted. 'Chrissy also reports the finger-print on Terri's bag matched fingerprints lifted from the car.'

'And the partial on the gag?'

She shook her head. 'Inconclusive.'

'If the car only went missing three days ago, it can't have been the one that picked up Terri,' said Bill.

McNab brought up the CCTV footage on the screen.

'This is the car we think took Terri just after midnight. It's a black Mondeo, registration number unclear, obscured, we think, by mud. However it does have a towbar attached.' He flicked forward. 'This looks like the same car crossing the Kingstown Bridge going west, close to where we picked up Terri's handbag.' He changed images. 'The same car leaving the M8 at Junction 21. Next sighting twenty minutes later, back at Glasgow Cross, and the final one is Duke Street.'

All roads led to Duke Street and the nearby Necropolis.

'Okay. We assume he's got her and Magnus somewhere in that triangle,' Bill said. 'So we concentrate all our efforts there. Anything from the Cardross connection?'

'We're awaiting the database of members of the sailing club. I've called the commodore to remind him. Should arrive soon.'

Collecting and sifting through material took time. Time they didn't have.

'And the forensics?' Bill asked Rhona.

'None of the DNA profiles of Terri's regulars match the skin flakes on Lucie's bra. However two of the men – Beattie and Brendan Paterson – had unprotected sex with Lucie in the days before her murder.'

'But not Gary Forbes?'

Rhona shook her head. That would fit with Gary's story about watching rather than doing.

They kept coming back to the same three men. But that was always the case in prostitute murders. The same cars, the same drivers, the same punters.

'And we have nothing to link any of these men directly to Lucie that night?'

McNab shook his head. 'Alibis check out and none of them drive a car like the one caught on camera.'

'Nothing more from Terri's phone?'

'We've been through the entire history and every number. She spent more time calling Leanne than anyone else.' McNab fell silent at that. Leanne was a source of worry. No one had seen her since she'd visited Cathy's flat. The press had got hold of that story, too. Bill had begun to suspect they had a mole at the station feeding newspaper and online speculation. As far as the press and the general public were concerned, Terri and Leanne were already victims of the killer, their bodies still to be discovered. The fact the two young women had also been lovers hadn't gone unreported either. How the Dochertys were surviving the licentious coverage of Terri's life, Rhona couldn't imagine.

McNab moved on to a discussion of the possible American connection.

'So this Ryan Williams began life as Peter Henderson?' Bill said.

'He changed his name by UK deed poll to Ryan Williams four years ago.'

'How did he get an American passport?'

McNab shook his head. 'No idea. But Lieutenant Blum said he'd no reason to suspect it wasn't genuine. According to their records a Ryan Williams was born in Atlantic City in 1962.'

'He could have stolen an identity,' Rhona suggested.

'So where is our Ryan Williams now?'

'He dropped off the radar in the States after his release. Then his British namesake popped up here to change his name to Mark Gordon and applied for a new UK passport and driving licence in January this year.'

'It's that easy?' Bill looked incredulous.

'You can apply online and have a certificate emailed to you in ten minutes. You use that for the passport application. The Home Office says the Criminal Records bureau keep track of those who change names if they are under suspicion of anything,' McNab didn't look convinced. 'It also says on the form that those who have a criminal record are required to let the police know.'

'But our guy, as far as we know, hasn't been convicted of anything.'

'That about sums it up.'

Rhona spoke again. 'We have a record of Ryan Williams's DNA profile taken in Atlantic City. We're checking it against what we have. I also traced the varnish flake to a specialist manufacturer based down south called Realpaints. They're sending up a customer list.'

So many threads in the complicated web. What they needed now was luck to connect them. Bill hadn't mentioned the mobile image in the meeting. He'd told them earlier that he wanted it to stay strictly between Rhona, himself and McNab, at least until he showed it to the Super. The existence of the photograph probably spelt the end of Magnus's career.

'The last time I spoke to Magnus he said the gravestone had a carved symbol made up of a moon and a fish. He said the moon has an affinity with water. It rules the domain of the night, the unconscious mind, the world of dreams and fantasies. The killer's fantasies. If we think Cathy's death is linked to the killer, isn't the fact she was found in the Molendinar significant?'

McNab looked at Rhona askance. This was way too fanciful for him. But Bill didn't dismiss her so readily. Talking about Cathy had reminded him of something.

'Fairlie thought it was an old punter of Cathy's told her Terri was alive. Someone from way back.'

They exchanged looks.

'Maybe Cathy recognised someone from her past. Someone who didn't want to be recognised?' Rhona suggested.

'Right, we need to check records again. Cathy's on file. Have we anyone linked to her? Anything significant at all? Check for any further connection between Henderson and the World's End case. Talk to Lothian and Borders. And find out exactly when Henderson, or Williams, left these shores.'

DC Clark caught Bill on the way out.

'There's a Father Duffy in reception. He wants to talk to you about Leanne Quinn.'

54

BILL COULD SMELL the drink before he saw Father Duffy. The priest looked wrecked, his face a highball of colour. He was in a worse state than Bill. Maybe there were more stressful jobs than being in charge of a murder enquiry.

The priest stood up, a little shakily.

'Father Duffy, I'm Detective Inspector Wilson. I believe you wanted to speak to me about Leanne Quinn?'

'I saw her face on the screen in the Central Station.' His voice was a soft burr, a perfect mixture of Irish and west coast Scottish. 'They said she was missing.' He looked distressed.

'You have some information about Leanne?'

Father Duffy nodded.

Bill took him through to his office, avoiding the incident room. The man looked bad enough without subjecting him to what was on display in there. He ushered the priest to a seat and offered him a mug of tea. Father Duffy shook his head. Bill suspected nothing but whisky had passed his lips for some time. Bill waited for the priest to begin.

'I know Leanne. She comes to the chapel sometimes. I open the doors for those who have nowhere to sleep.

Leanne slept there on Saturday night.' He shifted in his seat.

It didn't take a knowledge of kinesics for Bill to tell Father Duffy had just delivered a partial truth. He decided to stay silent and see what emerged next.

Eventually Duffy went on. 'Leanne was worried about some debt she had to pay.' He ran his tongue nervously over his lips. 'I gave her money for it.'

Bill wanted to ask what he'd got in return, seeing the guilt on Duffy's face. Instead, he asked how much.

'Two hundred pounds.'

The money had to be for Minty. Leanne was running scared from him because the police were holding on to Terri's handbag, including her bank card.

'Did Leanne tell you who the money was for?'

The priest looked relieved. That question he could handle.

'A man called . . . Craig Minto.'

He said it as though he didn't know who Minty was. Bill didn't believe that either.

'And that's the last time you saw Leanne?'

'She took confession in the morning,' he stumbled a little over the words, 'then left.'

He's lying, Bill thought. The bastard's lying.

'And you haven't seen her since?'

The priest shook his head and looked down into his lap.

'What about Cathy McIver?'

The priest's head snapped back up.

'You must have known Cathy. She was a friend of Leanne's. Her body was found in the Molendinar with a bullet through her head.'

Duffy attempted to look as though he'd just recalled the name.

'Oh Cathy. Of course. She comes, came, into the church sometimes.'

'And Terri Docherty. And Lucie Webster. Did they come to *confession* too? What about the poor wee pregnant lassie we have no name for yet?'

The priest's hands were trembling. A bubble of spit had formed in the corner of his mouth. The man needed a drink. Bill was tempted to take out the bottle he kept in the filing cabinet for emergencies. But not before he got what he wanted.

The priest's hand rose and fluttered in front of him, as though making the sign of the cross.

'I swear I did not hurt any of those women.'

'But you paid them for sex?'

Duffy's face collapsed like a dam breaking.

'When I drink . . .' his voice faltered. 'I do things I'm ashamed of.' He drew himself up in his seat. 'But I never harmed them.'

'So you want to be eliminated from our enquiries?'

'I want to help.'

'How?'

Duffy cleared his throat. 'A man saw me with Leanne. He asked me for her mobile number.'

'Who was he?'

'I hadn't seen him for years.' Father Duffy shook his head in amazement that the past should come back to haunt him like this. His eyes moved to Bill. He was calculating just how much he had to reveal. 'Back then, he and I had an arrangement.'

'What kind of arrangement?'

'He brought women to me.'

You couldn't make it up. A priest with a pimp.

'He reminded me of that, so I gave him Leanne's number. I didn't think he meant her any harm.'

'You handed over Leanne's number to save your own skin?' Bill tried to control his temper. 'What's this man's name?'

'I never knew.'

This time Bill did believe him.

'What does he look like?

The only word Bill fastened on in the rambling description was blond.

'Okay. Here's what's going to happen. First you're going to give us a sample of your DNA. Then you're going to talk to a police artist and give him a description of this man. Then you're going to look at photographs.'

Father Duffy had shrunk inside his black suit. When all this got out he was finished as a priest, and he knew it. Bill wondered if that might not be a blessing. Working for God was screwing him up. Bill went to the cabinet and pulled out the whisky bottle and poured a large one.

The man was shaking so hard he needed two hands to hold the glass. He drank the whisky and Bill poured him a second, then put the bottle away. He wanted the priest functioning and lucid.

God worked in mysterious ways. Father Duffy's confession seemed to have provided a catharsis for the man. It might also turn out to be the stroke of luck Bill needed.

55

THE FORENSIC REPORT from Hogganfield Loch stated that neither the metal mesh on the outfall nor the three manholes in the vicinity had been disturbed, which meant the killer had access to another entry point to the burn. Glasgow City Council were in the process of having the Molendinar surveyed by a professional company. According to their CCTV survey report, there were portions they hadn't managed to access, as no manholes had yet been found. If the killer had discovered such an entrance, it would be an ideal disposal point.

Rhona had tried to keep Magnus and the photograph from her thoughts, but it had proved impossible. The image of him with Terri kept punching its way back into her consciousness, leaving her with a sick feeling in her stomach.

Bill had made it clear he was operating on the principle Magnus was alive and innocent until proven otherwise. She'd respected Bill's wishes and told no one but Sean about the image. Chrissy already smelt a rat. Rhona's assistant would make an excellent psychological profiler. She could read people, especially Rhona, like a book. Chrissy knew something had happened that she hadn't been told about, but hadn't pressed Rhona for the details. It had been amusing to watch. Chrissy McInsh trying not to ask questions. Rhona had changed the subject to Sam and discovered he was accompanying Chrissy to her pre-natal appointment that afternoon.

'I thought he was keeping a low profile?' Rhona had asked.

Chrissy had tried to sound nonchalant. 'I told him it wasn't a good idea, but you know Sam . . .'

Wherever Sam was hiding, he'd managed to avoid Suleiman's men. Sean had tried to convince his hunters Sam had returned south. Rhona hoped they'd believed him.

When Chrissy left for her appointment, Rhona got down to some work. A second call to Realpaints put her through to the owner and director, a Mr Hollister, who apologised for not getting back sooner.

'Computer was on the blink. We have a customer list now, I can email it.'

'How many in Scotland?'

'The Clyde estuary's a big sailing location. We supply a few marinas there, although most yachts are modern now, with fibreglass hulls.'

'What about individuals? In particular I'm looking for a Henderson, Williams or Gordon.'

There was a moment's delay while he scanned.

'Nobody with those names as far as I can see.'

Rhona's heart sank. That was the problem with anticipation. It didn't always produce the goods.

'I'll send it now, shall I?'

She thanked him and rang off.

The ping of incoming mail heralded Hollister's list and the long-awaited report from NDNAD. Rhona took a deep breath before she opened the report. This time anticipation did result in a pay off.

Williams' profile matched one Peter Henderson who had been lifted and swabbed during an investigation into the rape of a prostitute in Bradford in 2003. The charges were dropped and Henderson walked. It must have been shortly after that Henderson changed his name and headed for the States. Details suggested he had been implicated in at least one other violent assault against a prostitute in Bradford, but was never charged. It looked like Henderson Williams had been getting some practice for what would come later.

Rhona opened the results on the other search. The profile of the skin flakes left on Lucie's bra was a match for Lieutenant Blum's chief suspect in the Atlantic City killings. He might have avoided leaving his mark on the three women there, but not here. This was the man they were looking for, whatever he chose to call himself now.

She immediately phoned Bill, who listened to her without interrupting.

'I've got the local priest at the station giving a description – I think it might be our man. I've still to show him the Williams' mug shot, but I'm hoping he'll ID him.' Bill filled Rhona in on the Leanne connection.

And all the time they'd hoped Leanne had simply gone to ground to avoid Minty. The darker alternative was that Minty had found her. What Bill hinted at now was much worse than even the latter.

'Bill, the Molendinar . . .'

'I know. McNab's going ahead with a search of the culvert.'

'I said I would go with him.'

'The forecast's heavy rain again. The water board aren't keen. I had to tell them it was urgent we take a look.'

'There should be someone from forensics with McNab.'

Bill went silent for a bit. 'You'll have an official with you, someone familiar with the route. If he's concerned about the water level, you get out, whatever happens, understand?'

Rhona glanced out at the threatening sky. It had been hot, overcast and humid all day, the air crackling with unspent energy. A perfect atmosphere for a thunderstorm. In the new climatic conditions, the rain tended to be localised. Hopefully when the downpour came, it wouldn't be over Glasgow City Centre.

Rhona called McNab on his mobile and set up a rendezvous point.

'It'll be easier to walk with the water, so we'll enter upstream and work our way down. This won't be pleasant,' he warned her.

'So when did you or I choose a career that was pleasant?'

Before she got her gear together, Rhona took a look at the list from Realpaints. Mr Hollister had sorted his customers into regions. He had about a dozen in

Scotland, mostly dotted up the west coast. The Kip Marina was listed as a customer, as was Rhu. Individual sales didn't include the name Henderson, Williams or Gordon.

The varnish trace was important evidence to link their killer to the scene of crime. To carry such a trace, the killer had to have been working on or near a boat that shed the varnish. They just had to find the actual boat. Rhona forwarded the list to Bill.

A few drops of rain greeted her as she carried her gear to the car, but never materialised as anything more sinister on her drive across the city. She parked in the cathedral car park alongside McNab's car and a van with 'CCTV Survey' on the side. Judging by the crowds around the cathedral and the constant stream of people crossing the Bridge of Sighs, visitor numbers were on the increase thanks to the Necropolis murders.

McNab introduced the two men with him. Kenny was young and keen and dressed for a walk through water. The other man was Andy Crawford from the City Council, who looked far less confident.

Crawford reiterated his concerns about the weather and issues of health and safety as they got kitted up. McNab did his best to reassure him. 'Dr MacLeod and I both have previous experience of sewers so we know the drill.'

Crawford looked relieved at that and reminded them once more of the forecast, before he finally left them to it.

Kenny gave them a grin as Crawford's car departed the car park.

'You're safe with me,' he told them, winking at Rhona.

Behind her, McNab gave a cynical grunt.

The manhole lay buried in greenery just south of the Bridge of Sighs, hidden from view, like many of the graves tucked away in this part of the cemetery. Steam rose from the surrounding damp foliage and grass, swathing the Necropolis in a mist reminiscent of the morning they'd discovered the bodies.

'Apart from this one, the manholes in the section run down the middle of Wishart Street, so we would have to stop the traffic to gain access,' Kenny said. 'We can walk the culvert from here to Duke Street no problem. North of here, there's a lot of encrustation, particularly the section along Alexandra Parade. Anything could be hidden up there. It's like something out of *Alien*.' Kenny looked impressed. 'Magic.'

Kenny climbed down the step irons first, lighting their way. The powerful beam gave the culvert an iridescent glow that reminded Rhona of standing under a street lamp at night in the rain. Once they were down safely, Kenny radioed the surface where his mate stood guard. 'When we go deeper, he won't be able to pick us up. Sonar's no use then either.'

Kenny gave them a moment to admire the seven-foot diameter circular brick structure, which was in perfect condition. 'Wouldn't think this was well over a hundred years old, would you? Couldn't find a brickie that could build this now.'

He led the way downstream, his camera recording as they went. 'Always wondered why we never found a body down here. My mate found a machete once, in the Camlachie culvert,' he said proudly. 'He said it belonged to the murderer Jimmy Boyle, had his name carved on the wooden handle.'

The culvert continued the same for some time. Clean walls and low running water. Torchlight settled on frogspawn in a deeper pool and gave them a quick glimpse of the red eyes of rats, but no gun.

'Where are we now?' Rhona asked.

'Under the brewery car park.'

Some yards further on, they met an egg-shaped confluence on the western side. 'A CSO,' Kenny said in answer to her question. 'Combined sewer overflow. The Molendinar isn't classed as a sewer, but when there's been a lot of rain, like this summer, the real sewer overflows into it, which doesn't please SEPA or the locals when the Duke Street section smells. Trouble is we don't know where a lot of the stuff comes from. Last time I was down here, we had a sudden rush of hot water and steam. We think it might have come from the Royal Infirmary, just north of the cathedral. They have a big laundry at the back.'

'We should check the CSO,' Rhona said.

The two men eyed one another. Kenny didn't look quite so keen now. 'The roof level dips quickly because of sagging. After that, there's a lot of encrustation.'

Rhona wasn't sure whether her insistence was driven by their expressions, or a real professional need. McNab finally conceded, rolling his eyes at Kenny, which pissed Rhona off. They backed up as far as the CSO. Kenny was right. There was no way the men could walk upright. Rhona offered to go alone, which resulted in troubled looks from the two men.

'How far before it dips?' she asked.

Kenny consulted his map. 'About forty feet.'

McNab wasn't happy. 'I'll come with you.'

'No point in us both breaking our backs. It's not far. I'll call you if I find anything.'

It was a compromise of sorts. McNab wrestled with his conscience briefly, then agreed.

Rhona dipped her head and moved in. The CSO was two thirds the size of the main culvert and even more claustrophobic. She tried not to think about the confined space and how much earth was above her. A tidal line more than halfway up the wall indicated how high the level could rise. Eventually the high-powered torch Kenny had given her picked out a dip in the roof.

The flow in the CSO was slower than in the main chamber, suggesting it was restricted. Rhona shone the torch under the dip and saw what Kenny had described as encrustation. A cluster of stalactites hanging from the roof and red deposits of iron oxide streaking the walls. Gone was the beautiful brickwork of the main culvert. Kenny was right. It did resemble a scene from *Alien*. If Cathy had been dumped further up the CSO, could the body have made it through?

Rhona called out to tell them she was on her way back, her voice reverberating through the tunnel. As she emerged, McNab quickly masked his anxiety. Rhona hammed it up for Kenny's sake.

'You weren't worried about me, were you?'

McNab assumed a nonchalant air. 'If I let you drown, the boss'll kill me.'

Rhona decided to get Kenny's opinion on how Cathy's body had got into the burn. He looked pleased to be awarded temporary detective status.

'A lot of the manholes are in the middle of a road, so he couldn't use them. The section that runs parallel to Alexandra Parade is like you described the CSO. We can't find the access points. The Victorians avoided building over the culvert to protect it and give access. You can see that from the old maps. More recently they didn't care. If I was dumping a body, that's where I'd do it.' Kenny said it through gritted teeth, as though he had someone in mind.

'And the body could have been washed down from there?' Rhona said.

Kenny pointed to a line on the wall above them. 'That's where the water can rise to. Anything and everything gets washed down, if the water's high enough.'

'Any grilles?'

Kenny shook his head. 'Grilles cause blockages.' He gave Rhona a winning smile, as though he'd just solved the case for them.

They'd been walking slowly on as they talked. Rhona spotted a circle of daylight in the near distance.

'Not far to Duke Street now,' Kenny sounded genuinely disappointed. He'd expected more excitement on his guided tour.

56

'WE'VE MISSED SOMETHING,' Rhona told McNab.

'There's nothing there. You said so yourself.'

Cathy's body had been badly scratched and bruised. They'd had no explanation as to why, but seeing the encrustation on the tunnels she thought that might be a possibility. Rhona stood in the culvert, under the lee of the wall fronting the goods yard. In the neighbouring car park folk were dashing from the building to their cars, trying to avoid the pelting rain.

The heavy shower had begun as they emerged from the culvert. The plan had been to keep going. According to Kenny, the next section under the railway yard was built with blue engineering brick and was even more remarkable. Rhona didn't like to point out this wasn't a sightseeing tour.

Kenny hadn't refused her request to backtrack, but he kept glancing at the thick grey clouds, as the rain pinged off his yellow macintosh.

'This is on for a while,' McNab informed them gloomily.

'How long before the water level rises?' Rhona asked Kenny.

'Half an hour.'

'We can't go back in. Not unless this goes off.'
McNab was adamant.

A deep roll of thunder sounded almost directly
above them. Rhona counted to seven before lightning
cracked the sky. The effect was spectacular.

'I think we should,' she repeated stubbornly.

'Why?' asked McNab.

'Because Cathy had post-mortem injuries which
might be consistent with hitting the encrustation in
the CSO.'

Rhona glanced across the car park to the large hole
in the ground and the distant brick arches of the old
railway building. Judging by the depth of excavation,
the railway cellars had gone deep down, perhaps to the
level of the burn. She asked Kenny if that was the case.

He shook his head. 'Sorry, no idea.'

McNab, looking pissed off and miserable, had taken
refuge beside her in the culvert. Finally he decided he'd
humoured Rhona long enough.

'Okay, we're out of here, before the water tops my
waders.'

They made their way back to the cathedral car park
through the teeming rain. The crowds of visitors had
taken refuge in the cathedral or in their cars. Those
caught by the downpour in the Necropolis had had to
make do with sheltering under trees, or in the lee of a
gravestone. The cemetery's steep downward paths had
already been transformed into streams. The monsoon
rains had come to Glasgow.

When they reached the vehicles, Kenny pronounced
himself happy to continue as soon as the weather

improved. Disappointment bit deep at Rhona, but she didn't voice it. They'd done their best and found nothing. She declined McNab's suggestion that she go back with him to the station, saying she was headed for the lab. In truth, she wanted time alone to think.

She drove down Castle Street and took a left into Duke Street. She'd been in this area so often recently, she felt she lived there. The creeping gentrification of the Merchant City would get here eventually. Already inner city regeneration had created a sleek curve of pink and cream flats, just south of the goods yard. Looking at future plans online, she had seen more such architectural wonders in store. Rhona felt quite proud of the planners' vision. You couldn't beat Glasgow for big ideas.

She drew in at the lorry entrance to the demolished railway building. From there she had a good view down Duke Street. On her left was the seventies-style block of flats Cathy had called home. Further along on her right was the imposing Victorian frontage of the Great Eastern.

She got out of the car and went to stand over the culvert and watch the water emerge below. McNab had been right to cancel the search. The level was visibly higher now, rushing from one opening to another as sheets of rain moved in from the west. Scenes like these must have driven Noah to build the Ark.

Rhona turned and walked back to the car. She was wasting her time when she could be doing something more useful. She started up the engine and switched the windscreen wipers on full. As she indicated to pull out, a figure darted across the road in front of her, taking shelter under the portico of the Great Eastern.

Rhona cancelled her signal and peered through the swishing wipers, trying to get a better view. The man took a swift look around before disappearing from sight. Rhona waited, puzzled, expecting him to reappear from behind one of the two central pillars. When he didn't, she looked up and down Duke Street. There were no cars besides hers. The guy had either vanished into thin air or gone inside the building.

Bells began to go off in Rhona's head. She locked the car and went for a look. The heavy front door was closed and locked. If the man had gone inside, he'd locked the door behind him. In the redevelopment plans for the area, the Great Eastern was due to be converted into flats, with a nursery built on the waste ground behind. Maybe the man had been an official from Glasgow City Council here on a visit?

Rhona walked the length of the building. There were no lights on inside, despite the gloom caused by the rainstorm. If a councillor was taking a tour, he was doing it in the dark. When she reached the end of the building she decided on impulse to take a quick look around the back.

A mess of outbuildings littered the rear, including a couple of corrugated iron sheds. On the Duke Street side, the hotel was five storeys high. Here it was seven. Rhona had never really noticed how close the basement was to the level of the burn. If there were cellars, they would be at water level or even lower. The Great Eastern had been built as a Victorian cotton mill. No doubt the works had used water from the burn in some capacity.

Rhona checked each of the back entrances, but the majority of them were firmly sealed. Only one gave her some hope, its padlock hanging loose from the rotten wood of the door. She stood for a moment, working out whether to take a look herself or give Bill a call. Then she saw a light flicker past a broken shutter on a basement window.

Rhona gently pulled the padlock free and slipped silently inside. In the dim light she made out a row of deep sinks and surmised this had been a laundry. She passed through swing doors into a long narrow corridor and turned west in the direction she'd seen the light.

What had been built as a workshop for cotton machinery had been divided by wooden partitions into numbered cubicles for homeless men. The effect was like a prison, apart from light filtering through the lattice work atop each partition wall.

The corridor ended in a set of stairs going downwards. Rhona decided to go no further until she told someone where she was, then cursed herself when she realised she would have to go outside to get a decent signal. Curiosity finally won over caution. The staircase grew darker the lower she went. Assuming the man she was following had come down here, whatever source of light he carried was well out of sight by now.

Rhona was already working out her position in relation to the burn, and decided she must be nearly level with it. The police had searched this building and found nothing, but Rhona couldn't shake off the feeling that if there was access to the culvert from here, it would be an ideal location to lose a body.

The foot of the stairs gave onto another dark corridor. Rhona cursed herself for not thinking of bringing the torch from the boot of the car. It was pointless going on without light. She might as well sit in the car and wait for the mystery man to emerge.

Standing in the semi-darkness, her senses on high alert, Rhona heard a faint female cry. For a moment she thought she'd imagined it. Then she heard it again. If she were hearing a ghost, it was the wrong sex. Any troubled spirits here would surely be those of lonely men.

57

RHONA STOOD STOCK still, the hairs on the back of her neck lifting. The faint cry came again, from somewhere below her. Her first instinct was to run. She stood poised for flight, adrenalin coursing through her veins, but didn't move or call out. Whoever was in the building had no idea she was there. Until she knew what was going on, Rhona wanted to keep it that way.

She edged along the lower corridor, seeking a way down, wondering whether Terri was in the hostel and had been all along. When she reached the end, she found nothing but a brick wall. Rhona felt her way around one more time, in case she'd missed an opening in the dark, but it was definitely a dead end. If a lower level did exist, she couldn't get to it from there. She grimaced in frustration and disappointment. There had been no repeat of the muffled cry in the last ten minutes and she was beginning to wonder if she'd simply fashioned it from the dead whisperings of an empty building. Rhona gave up and began to retrace her steps.

The return journey caused her more unease than the trip out. Then, she'd been intent on following the sound. Now she sensed that she was being followed, and it was making her uneasy. Rhona stopped and glanced behind her for the umpteenth time, finding nothing but darkness.

As she approached cubicle eleven, a low rustling brought her to a halt.

'Terri?' Rhona tried the handle.

When there was no response, she put her weight against the door. On the second push the lock gave way and the door swung open. Grey light filtered into an empty room and a torn curtain flapping at a broken window was revealed as the source of the sound.

The cubicle smelt strongly of decay, the walls spotted with damp. Rhona pulled the curtain aside and let daylight stream in. In the light the marks on the wall looked more like smears of old blood, but without her kit to test she couldn't be sure. Anyone could have dossed down in the derelict building. Finding blood on a wall might have nothing to do with the current investigation. Rhona checked out the rest of the small cubicle, but apart from a metal bed frame and a broken chair there was nothing.

Intent on her examination, she almost forgot about the man she'd followed until she heard the heavy slam of the front door. Rhona made for the stairs, but by the time she got to a window, whoever had left by the main entrance was long gone.

Irritated, she retraced her steps to the laundry room. She would contact Bill, tell him what had happened. He could check with the council and find out who might have been visiting the building. Whatever the outcome, she would urge another search of the hostel, particularly the lower levels.

When she pushed open the swing doors, the shadowy space of the old laundry echoed to the drumming of heavy rain on its corrugated roof. If she ventured outside, she would be soaked in seconds. Rhona decided to try and call Bill from where she was, despite the poor reception.

As she selected his number, she was suddenly aware that someone had stepped up behind her. Before she could cry out or turn, the muzzle of a gun jabbed the left-hand side of her head.

'Drop the phone.'

Rhona released the mobile and it clattered to the stone floor. A kick from her hidden assailant sent it spinning into the shadows.

'I'm . . .' she began.

'I know who you are.'

He pulled her backwards towards the swing doors.

'I've called the police,' Rhona tried to disguise the panic in her voice.

'You'll be dead by the time they arrive.'

58

'WE'VE BROUGHT IN Craig Minto,' Janice said. 'Liz Paterson from the food van reported him going into a pub in the Gallowgate. We have him in an interview room, if you want to speak to him.'

Bill couldn't think of anything he wanted to do more.

Minty's cheek tattoo said 'No Surrender', and he had one to match across his left hand. Bill assumed it was a religious war cry and not a message for the police. Minty was a big guy, more so in the confines of the interview room. Not the definitive wee Glasgow hard man, but his expression of malevolent defiance was the same as every other drug dealer and gangland member Bill had ever brought in. His baldness was made up for by thick eyebrows meeting in the middle of a jutting forehead. Minty was a perfect illustration of the missing link. Glasgow's answer to Neanderthal man.

Forensic had found Minty's prints all over the equipment in the flat, so there was no way he could get out of that one. What interested Bill was any link with the deaths of Lucie, Cathy and the disappearance of Leanne.

'Lucie Webster,' Bill said.

Minty cocked his head to one side, like a dog that doesn't understand a command.

'We found your semen in her body.'

A storm gathered between the big man's brows.

'Mine and who the fuck else? Wee bitch was doing it more than she told me.'

'So you killed her.'

Minty looked offended. 'I don't kill my bitches.'

'You just knock them about.'

'I teach them what's mine.'

'What about Leanne Quinn?'

'She wasn't mine.'

'She owed you money.'

'Half of fucking Calton owes me money. If I killed them, how would I get it?'

'Cathy McIver.'

'Too old for my stable.'

'Not a junkie, you mean?'

Minty gave Bill a withering look. 'You're fucked. You know that? You've no fucking idea who killed Lucie or Cathy, so you bring me in to look fucking good.'

There was an element of truth in what Minty was saying. Picking him up looked like a success. Against constant failure that was a plus.

'What if we do a deal? You give us what you know, we'll tell the judge you helped.'

Bill's suggestion was met with a blank look. He tried another tack.

'Father Duffy gave Leanne money to pay you off.'

Minty looked surprised. 'So that's where the wee bitch got it.'

'Leanne brought you the money?'

Minty shook his head.

Leanne had been terrified of Minty, what if she'd asked someone else to deliver? Bill went for it.

'Cathy brought you the money, didn't she?'

Minty's expression was a picture of wounded innocence.

'She pissed you off, so you shot her.'

'I don't have a gun.'

'There was a print on the gag used to shut her up.'

'A gag? Not surprised. Cathy always was mouthy.'

Minty knew it wasn't his print on the gag. But he had met Cathy the night she died. Bill was sure of it.

'Cathy contacted you and you met her to pick up Leanne's money.'

Minty's piggy eyes narrowed calculatingly.

'What if I did?'

'Any help finding Cathy's killer will be noted in your file.'

Minty digested that, decided he had nothing to lose.

'Cathy got word to me she had the money. We met. She handed it over. I left.'

'When?'

'Sunday night. Near her flat in Duke Street.'

'And?'

'And nothing.'

'Where was she when you left?'

'Standing outside the Great Eastern.'

Waiting for her killer.

'Did she say anything about meeting someone?'

Minty thought about that. He was smart enough to know he'd given Bill nothing worth writing in a file.

'She was headed for High Street Station.'

High Street was on the North Clyde Line. Cathy hadn't gone to Queen Street to catch a train for Cardross. She'd left from the High Street.

Bill left the pimp to stew. The incident room was a buzz of noise. Bringing in Minty had been good for morale. Bill tried to check on McNab, see how he was getting on in the culvert. When he couldn't reach him, he assumed they were still below ground. No doubt McNab would call in if they found anything of significance.

Bill was reading the emails from Rhona when Janice came in.

'Sir, Ray Irvine has a lock-up not far from the Necropolis, off Alexandra Parade.'

Irvine was the type to have an expensive flat in Merchant City. Why did he need a lock-up in Denniston?

'The CCU picked up the address via a porn distribution network,' Janice told him. 'When they checked who owned it, they discovered it was Irvine.'

Bill remembered Irvine's arrogant smile. The man who could afford to buy anything.

'Okay, go down there. Take someone from CCU with you. If Irvine's involved in a distribution racket, we'll get him on that.' Bill would dearly love to see the smirk wiped of Ray Irvine's face.

Bill got onto the latest from forensic. Rhona had noted in her email that no individuals called Henderson, Williams or Gordon were on the list from

Realpaints, but both Rhu and Kip Marinas were customers of the specialised varnish. Bill gave Rhu a call and asked for the repair department. They put him through to Daniel Bradley.

'We do stock that varnish, although it's fairly specialised. Wooden-hulled yachts may make the heart beat faster, but they can also be a world of trouble. They need regular maintenance or they rot.'

Bill asked if they'd had a yacht like that in the yard recently.

'Matter of fact we have one now. It's still standing in the stocks. The guy working on it hasn't been around this week.'

'His name?'

'Gordon. Mark Gordon.' Bradley sounded worried. 'Has something happened to him?'

Bill kept his voice steady. 'Do you have an address or contact number?'

There was a moment's silence.

'I'll need to look it out. Can I call you back?'

Bill agreed and rang off. Throw enough darts at the board and you hit the bull's-eye eventually. He allowed himself to feel hopeful for the first time since they'd found the bodies in the Necropolis.

He called the incident room together, went to the whiteboard and circled Mark Gordon's name with a flourish. This was the bastard and they were going to get him.

Ray's lock-up was located at the end of a block of small business premises off Millbank Street. Standing out front, Bill could see the rise of the north flank of the Necropolis, an easy cruising distance from there.

The room looked as though it was serving as a storage and distribution point, packaging and boxes piled everywhere. The boxes were filled with a variety of hardcore porn magazines and DVDs. A technical guy from the Computer Crime Unit was busy dismantling the computer system.

Janice indicated a manhole-size opening and a steep set of steps leading down to a basement, or dunny. As a kid Bill remembered being frightened of the dunny under his tenement home, its dank smell and darkness. He descended into familiar smelly territory, but here a long fluorescent bulb lit the shadowy recesses.

Bill looked about him. If he'd wanted a nightmare, here it was. Janice had followed him down, her expression mirroring his own. This was why she'd asked him to come right away.

An Aladdin's cave of filth and depravity, it was a picture gallery of what Gary Forbes had written about in his blog. Countless photographs of countless women formed a gruesome collage on the walls. Lucie was there, the pregnant girl they had no name for, and the second victim in the Necropolis. All were being made to do things no human being should be subjected to.

Ray Irvine featured in many of the photographs. He'd said he went slumming when he made a killing in the financial markets. He'd taken photographs to prove it.

Bill sought Terri's image in the gallery of horrors, and was grateful not to find her. But he did see the three murder victims whose photos they'd found on the internet.

'He could have downloaded those, like we did,' said Janice, echoing his own thoughts. 'The rest could have been taken any time.'

Ray Irvine had been quite open about his relationships with prostitutes. They were a service he paid for. No doubt he paid to take photographs too. Just like Gary Forbes had paid to watch Lucie in action. Bought and paid for. No laws broken.

'Forbes and Irvine. There's no chance they know one another?' suggested Janice.

Forbes wrote a blog on 'Glasgow pussy'. Irvine ran a business distributing obscene photographs of local prostitutes. A connection between the two men seemed more than likely.

Janice drew his attention to another section.

'Take a look at these, sir. Remember the doggers using the Necropolis? Looks like Irvine was their official photographer.'

The sequence of photographs Janice indicated had definitely been taken in the Necropolis. John Knox must be turning in his grave at the fornication going on in full view of his monument.

'I want Forbes and Irvine back in. See what they have to say.'

Magnus had predicted that the killer worked alone, but there were always sick-minded disciples lurking in the shadows of killers they admired. If Forbes and Irvine were hanging about the same playground, maybe they knew more than they'd said.

When his mobile rang Bill thought it was McNab with an update from the culvert, but it was Daniel Bradley, sounding flustered.

'I'm sorry. I don't seem to have contact details for Mr Gordon. As far as I recall he was a member of the yachting club. You could try the commodore. He might be able to help.'

Bill thanked him and rang off. He knew McNab and Rhona had visited the Rhu yard and requested a membership list from the commodore. Bill tried McNab's mobile again. This time he answered.

'We're out of the culvert. Water level's too high to check any further.'

Bill heard the disappointment in McNab's voice. They'd obviously found nothing. Bill told him the latest news on Mark Gordon. 'He should be on the membership list the commodore emailed through.'

McNab perked up. 'I'll be with you in five minutes.'

'There's no Mark Gordon on this.' McNab threw the hard copy on his desk and went back to the screen. He made sure the list was in alphabetical order and checked again. 'Bastard!'

'He's on to us,' Bill said.

'Maybe he got a whiff of our visit to the marina. Or saw us there.'

Bradley had seemed nervous during Bill's phone call. He'd put it down to a natural fear of the police.

'I'll go down. Check this out,' McNab offered.

'Take the mug shot of Williams. See if Bradley recognises him.'

'I can feel him. We're close. So close.'

'If he thinks we're near, he could run.'

'Leave the country?'

McNab was right. If Williams, Henderson and Gordon were the same man, he might even now be on his way across the Atlantic on his American passport.

'Take Rhona with you. Get her to look at the yacht Bradley mentioned. If we can match the flake found in the grave . . .'

'I'll pick her up on my way.'

Bill took a look at Williams's photograph. The quality was so poor he could have been any middle-aged man. Stopping people at airports wasn't as simple as it sounded. Williams could be travelling on one of three different passports. And he didn't necessarily look like this in any of them. He only needed to have his hair cut differently, or change the way he dressed. Passport photographs were notoriously unreliable. They could be ten years out of date for a start, hence the move to a biometric version.

Bill stared at the photograph. Just like McNab, his sense of being near the killer was strong. The puzzle was coming together. The myriad of tiny threads weaving the web with which they'd catch him. And Father Duffy was one thread.

The priest was in an interview room, a full mug of tea cooling in front of him. His face shone with perspiration.

'When can I go?' He licked cracked lips.

'Just a few more questions.'

Bill produced the whisky and a glass. Drying out the priest wasn't his job. A sudden absence of alcohol could kill an alcoholic. Bill didn't want Duffy collapsing while in custody. He handed him the glass. The priest looked at it and shook his head.

'You'll need help to dry out.'

'I've managed in the past. God will help.'

'Maybe you weren't as bad those times.'

Relenting, Father Duffy took the glass, observed the whisky for a moment, then swallowed it as though it were poison. Bill waited for it to hit the bloodstream.

'This guy from the past you recognised?'

'It's him in the photo.'

'You're sure?'

'I'm sure.'

'Tell me about him.'

The priest held out the glass for a refill, resistance melting like snow off a dyke.

'I met him in Bradford about five years ago. He came to confession. Told me he knew what I needed and wanted and he could make it easier for me.'

'How did he know?'

'I was taking chances.' Father Duffy paused. 'When I came to Glasgow, I thought I'd seen the back of him.'

'But he turned up?'

'July last year. I didn't recognise him at first. Then he asked for confession. And it began again.'

'How?'

'He brought women to the chapel house. I paid. Sometimes he watched. Sometimes he took photos.' He looked sickened by what he was saying. 'I told him I didn't want to do it any more. He threatened to send the photos to the bishop. Every day I prayed to God he would leave me alone. And then he disappeared.'

'When was that exactly?'

'September or October.'

'And he reappeared when?'

'Only once, last Sunday evening.' Father Duffy looked as though he wanted Bill to tell him it was all a bad dream. 'He must have seen me bring Leanne to the chapel house on Saturday night. On Sunday, I gave him her number.' Father Duffy avoided meeting Bill's eye. 'I'm sorry. I've put Leanne in danger, haven't I?'

Bill tried to remember that the priest had helped Leanne pay off Minty. That he'd come here of his own accord, knowing when he spoke out it would be the end of his priesthood. Duffy wasn't an evil man. Just a bad priest.

59

MCNAB TRIED RHONA'S mobile on his way to the car and got no reply. When he rang the lab Chrissy answered.

'I thought she was with you, strolling down the Molendinar.'

'I left there over an hour ago. She's not been in touch?'

'Nope.'

The uncomfortable thought that she might have gone back into the culvert crossed McNab's mind. Surely even headstrong Rhona MacLeod wouldn't be that stupid . . . but then, it wouldn't be the first time her curiosity had put her in danger. For now, he had to assume she'd let common sense prevail.

'I'm headed for Rhu Marina. Looks like we found the yacht. Bill wants Rhona to take a look.'

'I could come . . .?' Chrissy sounded cautious.

'Okay,' McNab answered with equal wariness. 'I'll pick you up.'

McNab had never known Chrissy so quiet. He'd expected the usual acerbic wit known to shrivel a cock at a hundred yards. Even the look she'd given him as he drew up outside the lab, hadn't included the usual daggers. Ever since he'd become obsessed with Rhona – McNab had finally admitted it to himself – Chrissy had been his number one enemy. This new mellow Chrissy, sitting next to him, was something else. He was wondering what sea-change had occurred, when Chrissy broke the silence.

'I'm pregnant.'

Chrissy's blunt announcement took McNab's mind off the road, generating a horn blast from the Audi behind.

'And I'd like to stay alive long enough to have my baby.'

McNab gave the finger to the guy in the Audi, who'd just realised to his consternation that he'd honked his horn at a police car.

'Sorry, but it was a bit of a surprise.'

'That's what fucking does, makes babies. Men like to forget that.'

McNab held his tongue on that one, and tried to work out who the father might be. Chrissy had been seeing that bloke, Sam Haruna, during the Nigerian case. McNab did a quick calculation and decided it had to be Sam.

'You're keeping it, then?' He made his voice neutral.

'It's not a dress I brought home to try on.'

McNab suddenly remembered the scene in the Necropolis when he'd suggested Chrissy was putting on weight. How Rhona had changed the subject and removed him from the scene.

'Who else knows?'

'I figured once I told you, everyone.'

'I won't mention it, if you don't want me to.'

'I don't give a fuck what you do.'

McNab decided Chrissy was either very brave or very foolish. Haruna was on the run from the law and the entire Suleiman tribe. Hardly a stay-at-home, financially supportive father. Chrissy was about to enter the world of the one-parent family. The single mothers' society the *Daily Mail* liked to blame for the world's ills.

'My mum had me on her own.' McNab surprised himself by saying it. It wasn't something he normally broadcast.

'And look how you turned out.' Her tone was sharp, but the look Chrissy gave him was conciliatory.

Daniel Bradley was one nervous man, but McNab was used to honest citizens taking fright when faced with an enquiry from the law. Bradley had brought up the database on the screen and was doing a search with trembling hands.

'Look. He's not there. He should be under the "G"s.'

There was no 'Gordon'.

'Who put him on the system?'

'I did it myself, when he booked yard space to work on his boat.'

'Could Gordon have had access to the database himself?'

Bradley looked suitably affronted. 'The office is strictly off limits to anyone except staff.'

McNab brought out the Atlantic City photograph.

'Is this Gordon?'

Mr Bradley took a quick glance and shook his head.

'It's not him?'

Bradley avoided looking again. 'No, that's not him.' A nerve twitched at the corner of his mouth.

McNab decided to go for the jugular.

'Mr Gordon is wanted in connection with the Necropolis murders.'

All the blood drained from Bradley's face. If he hadn't been sitting, he'd have fallen down.

'Murder. I thought . . .'

'You thought what?'

Bradley chewed on his lip.

'This is very serious. I shouldn't have to remind you . . .'

'He gave me photographs,' Bradley mumbled, 'and some DVDs.'

'Porn?'

Bradley nodded.

'You wiped his name from the system?'

'I thought it was about the photographs. I didn't want to get involved.'

McNab indicated the picture again. 'Take a good look. Is that Mark Gordon?'

This time Bradley did look. 'It might be.'

'What do you mean, might be?' McNab's tone was icy.

'I told you, I don't want to get involved. I've got a wife and two kids.'

'And pornographic material from a murder suspect.'

Bradley's face went white.

McNab was getting pissed off. 'Protecting the identity of a murder suspect . . .'

'Okay. Okay. The photo could be Gordon, but he looks different now.'

'How different?'

'He's smarter dressed and his hair's shorter.'

McNab went in search of Chrissy and found her suited figure at the hull of a wooden yacht.

'This the one?'

She lowered her mask. 'It is.'

McNab admired the sleek lines.

'Got what you need?'

Chrissy nodded. 'Enough to be going on with. How about you?'

'The photo is Mark Gordon, even if he has changed his hair style.'

'So where is he?'

'Bradley wiped his file, or thought he did. Seems Gordon was supplying him with porn and Bradley took fright at our interest. I'm taking the computer to Tech. Let's hope Gordon gave a valid contact address when he joined the yacht club.'

'And if he didn't?'

'We're no nearer picking him up.'

60

'NO LUCK IN locating either Irvine or Forbes,' said Janice. 'Lothian and Borders are watching Forbes' work and home. Apparently he hasn't been seen in either place for the last couple of days.'

'And Irvine?' Bill asked.

'According to a neighbour, he's gone on holiday. At least that's what he told her.'

'Where?'

'Somewhere hot and sunny, away from the rain.'

'They know we're on to them.'

'Looks like it, sir.'

The leads were shutting down as quickly as they opened up. McNab had already called in from Rhu Marina with the Bradley story. He was on his way back with the confiscated computer from the repair yard, and the one holding the yacht club members' list. The CCU would have no problem recovering Gordon's deleted details, but there was no guarantee he'd given a true address and phone number anyway. Chrissy had taken some samples from the yacht and a team would descend on it tomorrow. McNab had voiced his concern about Rhona's whereabouts during the call.

'Chrissy checked with the lab,' McNab had told Bill. 'Rhona's not there and her mobile's switching to voice-mail.'

It was after six. Rhona might have gone home or to the Jazz Club. Bill decided to check both places before he panicked. There was no answer from her flat, so he rang the club. The barman answered and immediately handed Bill over to Sean.

'What's wrong?'

'Nothing, so far. I wanted to check up on Rhona. Is she with you?'

'I haven't seen her since she left for work this morning.'

'Okay, I'll put a call out for her car. She was at the cathedral with DS McNab earlier on, but no one's spoken to her since.'

'She showed me the photo on her mobile. If that bastard Magnus harms her . . .'

Bill cut him off. 'We have no reason to believe she's in any danger. And certainly not from Magnus.'

'That's what she said last night. I didn't believe her then and I don't believe you now.'

Superintendent Sutherland was incandescent with rage.

'Why wasn't I shown this before?'

'Rhona received it by phone late last night. I haven't been able to get hold of you until now.'

'The girl's alive in this.'

'Yes, but it could have been taken up to twenty-four hours ago. CCU believe that's an underground stream in the background. McNab and Rhona were checking the Molendinar culvert this afternoon, but eventually had to abandon because of high water levels. The council is identifying points of access, but according to them, there could be buried manholes under a number of buildings, predominantly north of the Necropolis.' Bill didn't add that it was like potholing without a map during a flood.

'You checked the phone's location?'

'It was definitely Magnus's phone, and came from the Glasgow Green area. The mobile hasn't been used since.'

'Who else knows about it?'

'Myself, McNab and Rhona.' Bill decided not to mention Sean.

'Keep it like that until we find Professor Pirie and hear his explanation.'

Bill didn't believe for a moment that Sutherland thought finding Magnus was a forgone conclusion. The Super had ordered Magnus not to involve himself with the online auction, but Magnus had chosen to ignore the command and made contact with the killer, with some stupid notion he could play him at his own game. Bill didn't like to have his theories on involving Magnus proved right. But textbook psychology wasn't real life – you couldn't understand a killer's mind just because you'd read the right books. Solid policing was the only way to catch him. Solid policing, forensics and luck.

Bill outlined the developments on Mark Gordon. The prospect of a suspect went some way to mollifying

Sutherland. The Super would have questions to answer on this one, just like Bill.

'He's the one?'

'Looks like it.'

Sutherland allowed himself a nod of approbation.

An hour later, the report came in that Rhona's car had been located in Duke Street, not far from where Cathy's body had been discovered. There had been no sign of Rhona.

'A CSO came into the main culvert from the east, close to where we found Cathy,' McNab said.

'A CSO?'

'Combined sewer outlet. Where the sewer overflows into the burn, if its capacity is reached. Rhona took a look but it was encrusted and impossible to search. She thought the injuries on Cathy's body might have been caused by the encrustation.'

'Rhona wouldn't have gone back in alone?'

'I wouldn't have thought so. Not without proper equipment.'

McNab's expression didn't mirror his words. Rhona's car had been found near the culvert. If she wasn't planning another look, why would she go back there?

Bill went to the wall map. The route of the underground burn had been highlighted in blue, running from west to east, north of Alexandra Parade. Culvert 5A was tucked in the triangle between Millbank Street and the Parade. Then a big gap before manhole 6, where the Parade met Wishart Street. The council hadn't been able to locate any manholes between 5A and 6 and thought they were probably buried under buildings or covered by tar.

After 6 the burn ran southwards under Wishart Street, west of the Necropolis, the line of manholes down the centre of the road. Then the manhole McNab and Rhona had used, near the boundary of the Necropolis. That was believed to be the last one before the burn emerged above ground. But was it?

Minty had said he left Cathy standing outside the Great Eastern. They had forensic evidence to show she'd been in Cardross, but her killer had brought her back to Glasgow. They'd searched the Great Eastern and found nothing. Rhona had been concerned about the CSO coming from the east, the direction of the old hotel. What if they had missed something in the building, like an opening on the culvert? The hotel had been an old cotton mill in the time when the burn was used to supply a variety of works. It would be logical to assume it had some access to the water. Maybe Rhona went in there to take a look for herself?

'Okay. We hit the Great Eastern again,' Bill told McNab. 'This time we make sure there's no access to the culvert from the basement.'

61

HE'D TOLD HER she would be dead soon, but she wasn't dead yet.

Rhona dragged herself into a sitting position, feeling the ground wet beneath her and knowing it was blood from the sharp, metallic smell. She felt the chilly weight of manacles and followed their chains to the wall. Someone had already died in this place. Trussed up and tortured.

A wave of nausea hit her as she tried to move away from the wall. When he'd shoved her down the manhole, she'd slipped on the wall irons and fallen heavily, her right leg twisted beneath her. He'd jumped down behind, spitting curses through the mask, calling her a 'stupid fucking bitch'. Rhona was glad she'd pissed him off, despite the searing pain.

She reached down, feeling the extent of the swelling. She had no chance of straightening the leg without help. Rhona rolled onto her front and attempted to crawl towards the sound of running water. The CSO was her best chance of getting out before her tormentor returned. He hadn't restrained her, thinking she wasn't going anywhere with a broken leg. She would prove the bastard wrong.

She was almost at the water when she realised he was back. Her ragged, laboured breathing must have covered his approach. A footfall brought her to an abrupt halt. She lay perfectly still, her eyes probing the darkness, her heart hammering in her chest.

'Going somewhere, Dr MacLeod?'

She could smell him, a musky mix of oil and sweat. Magnus had said a serial killer fed off the scent of his victim's fear. She would deny the bastard that, at least.

Rhona waited, sensing his slow walk around her. If he still held the gun, she didn't stand a chance. But if she was going to die, she would go out like Cathy, fighting and kicking.

Rhona felt a slight movement of air and made her move, reaching out and grabbing his leg. The speed of her attack caught him unawares. He tripped and fell, screaming curses.

But his recovery was too swift to roll out of the way. Rhona let out a howl of pain and protest as his body pinned hers to the ground. Then his hands were around her throat.

Rhona clawed at the air, trying to inflict damage on him before the darkness took her.

'Say you're fucking sorry, Dr MacLeod.'

He tightened his grip.

'Say it.'

Rhona drew in her last breath and spat in his face.

When she came to, her brain buzzed with light and sound. She knew where she was, what was happening to her, yet no longer seemed to care.

Pain had been replaced by pleasure. Ripples of it ran across her body, like a lover's fingers. Rhona tried to pull her mind back, anchor it in reality, but this *was* reality, this strange mix of pain and joy.

The rules of torture. Hurt the victim, then give them pleasure. Then bring back the pain. For now she felt only peace.

An arc light held her in its heat and glare. In her drugged state she imagined it to be the eye of God, watching her. Every nerve in her body tingled. An all-body orgasm, that's how addicts tried to describe the effects of crystal meth. Somewhere inside the haze, Rhona's rational brain told her that was what coursed through her body.

Then a face loomed over her. A voice breathed her name.

'It's time, Rhona. Time to teach you what I like.'

Searing agony broke through the pleasure as her right leg was moved roughly and placed at an unbearable angle. Rhona imagined her body being split apart, bone prised from bone. She blacked out again.

62

MEN WERE SPREAD out in a line across the waste ground, their torch beams reflecting the steady fall of rain. A small team of firemen, wearing breathing apparatus, had already been led up the culvert by a thrilled Kenny to check the CSO Rhona had been concerned about.

Inside the building, Bill had split his force. A team was working from the top level down. He and McNab had stayed with the second team, moving from ground level to basement. The discovery of Rhona's mobile beneath an old sink in the back laundry had been the moment of truth.

When McNab had handed him the phone, he'd found his number on the screen. Rhona had been about to call him when something had happened to make her drop the phone.

Bill left McNab searching the laundry and went further in. Above him, the building resounded with noise. There was no way they could search the place quietly, so he'd made the decision not to try, hoping that if the killer heard them, he would try to escape. If Rhona and Magnus were still alive, maybe that would help them stay that way.

They were in the basement now. Bill remembered it well. The first team had been over it with a fine-toothed comb, looking for anything that might be linked to Cathy's death. What they hadn't considered was the possibility of a level beneath this one. Nothing in the plans of the building had suggested it. They'd checked every floor visible from the outside. But not the dunny, if it existed.

The team in the culvert were sending a crawler along the floor of the CSO. A guy from CCTV Surveying was already working this floor, attempting to pick up the whereabouts of the crawler by a sonar detector. He'd already explained the crawler wasn't good over rough surfaces, a problem if the floor of the CSO was badly encrusted.

'A man can pick his way along, a crawler just gets stuck.'

Bill hadn't even thought of dousing for the pipe, but Kenny, who'd taken McNab and Rhona down the culvert, had brought along an old guy they used, called Hunter. 'Don't ask me how it works, but it does,' Kenny had said mystified.

Bill was counting on good search techniques and an eagle eye, but he watched with interest as Hunter unfastened the catch on his wooden box and unpacked the L-shaped brass rod.

Hunter paid Bill no heed and made no attempts to explain what he was about, just began his slow walk across the floor. Bill knew there had been experiments using dowsers to find buried bodies, documented in the work of The Body Farm, the scientific facility set

up at the University of Tennessee to study human
decomposition. Bill prayed that if the old man de-
tected anything, it would be running water and not a
body.

He took a call from Margaret an hour later, when
they were no further forward in their search. Bill heard
his wife's worried voice and the words she spoke, but
his brain refused to register them.

'I said she wasn't to go to the bloody concert!' he
shouted.

There was a terrible silence at the other end.

'Margaret, I'm sorry. How long have you been
waiting?'

'Half an hour.'

Bill could hear her voice shaking.

'You tried her mobile?'

'Yes, but she would have switched it off during the
performance, so maybe she forgot to turn it on again?'
she said hopefully.

'What about Susie?'

Then came the bombshell.

'She's here with me. She says they got split up in the
crowds coming out of the Barrowland. When she
couldn't find Lisa, she came to the rendezvous point,
hoping she would be here already.'

Bill let it all sink in. His daughter had disappeared, in
an area where three women had been killed and three
were missing. He tried to steady his voice before he
answered.

'Call Susie's parents and ask them to pick her up.
You stay where you are. I'm on my way.'

He could feel Margaret's relief. 'I'm sorry. I shouldn't have let her go,' she said, her voice breaking.

Bill couldn't find the words to answer, so he pretended he hadn't heard and ended the call. In the few moments the conversation lasted, Bill had convinced himself the killer had his daughter. It all fitted – first Magnus, then Rhona, then, if not him, a member of his family. Rapid images of Terri, Lucie, and the unknown victims flipped through his mind, like shots from a snuff movie, only this time the face on each body was Lisa's.

Bill felt a need to vomit. He made for the stairs and the nearest cubicle. As he emptied his stomach, he could only think he was contaminating a possible crime scene. Afterwards, he stood near the broken window, letting the cool air hit his face and tasting the bitter rain on his lips. A final full moon, one hemisphere already on the wane, broke through the clouds. The Gravedigger would kill again before the period of the full moon was over, Magnus had promised. And the victim might be Lisa.

Bill told himself to get a grip, otherwise he was no use. When he'd composed himself, he went looking for McNab and told him a teenage girl had been reported missing after a concert at the Barrowland ballroom, slap bang in the middle of the killer's playground. They would have to transfer some of the search party to look for her.

McNab was confused at first. 'Leanne was seen at a concert?'

'Not Leanne. Lisa, my daughter.'

63

'RHONA?'

Magnus's voice sounded far away. She imagined him on a distant shore, a large stretch of water between them.

'I'm going to straighten your leg, before the drug wears off.'

She made no response, no longer sure what was real and what wasn't. There had been pain, then pleasure. Rhona wanted only pleasure from now on. She felt hands on her ankle and cried out, thinking it was her tormentor. Then a face resembling Magnus's swam before her eyes. Rhona wanted to kiss him, because he was alive.

A sudden jerk twisted her around, and she felt bones grate horribly inside her broken leg. A scream emerged from deep within her. The return of pain was a terrible thing, made more awful by its previous absence.

'Please,' she sobbed. Something was being wedged against her leg, something else wrapped tightly around it. Rhona collapsed back, exhausted by the effort of dealing with the agony.

'I'm going to carry you.'

Her body rose heavily. She was a child again, being lifted by her father, her face close to his, the scent of his skin in her nostrils. He stumbled, readjusted her weight against him, walked more steadily. Rhona heard the splash of water and imagined being carried into the sea off Skye. The scream of the gulls above them, the cool breeze from the water, even on the sunniest day. She wanted to float on the tide, taste its salt on her tongue.

'I'm going to pull you through behind me.'

Rhona listened to the voice that wasn't her father's, yet had a similar lyrical quality. She was being lowered, she hoped, into the sea. The sudden shock as the cold water met her body broke through her dream. Magnus was staring down at her, his face creased with worry. Rhona wanted to reassure him she could swim. There was nothing to worry about.

Her buoyancy improved as the water grew deeper and Rhona knew she was moving out to sea. The thought didn't frighten her. She would be carried across the Sound to Raasay. She would come ashore there. She would show Magnus her favourite island. Rhona wanted to reassure him about the chill of the water. Explain it was always this cold, that she was used to it.

It was the booming sound that worried her, not the depth and movement of water. The thunder and the darkness. The water was moving faster now. Her head kept bumping against Magnus's legs. She wondered why he was walking and not swimming, because the channel between Raasay and Skye was deep. And why was it dark? Chrissy had called him a Norse God. Maybe Magnus could walk on water?

They had come to a halt, although the current tried desperately to carry Rhona onwards. It sounded as though Magnus was pounding rock with his fists, cursing. The sound dragged Rhona into the horror of reality. She found herself staring up at the encrusted ceiling of the culvert.

'Magnus.'

He turned from his fight with the stalactite. The look he gave her was like a man who'd just seen Lazarus rise from the dead.

'Thank God, you're conscious.'

Rhona winced as the flow bumped her bad leg against the rough wall. 'I liked the drugs better.'

'We'll have to turn back. We can't get through and the water's rising.'

Trying to break the forest of stalactites had reduced Magnus's hands to a bloody mess. When Rhona had fully regained consciousness, the water had been up to his thighs. Now it was at his waist. The Gravedigger knew they couldn't get out this way, that's why he'd let them escape. He had no need to kill them when the rising water would do it for him. The torch Magnus had taken from the upstairs room was still functioning, but there was no guarantee how long it would last.

'We could go back to the chamber we passed. Maybe the water won't fill it?' suggested Rhona weakly.

She could tell from Magnus's face that he was trying to calculate how long he could keep her head and his own above water. He was a strong swimmer.

So was she, but in her current state she might pull him under.

The ugly wound on his forehead was black with flies. Magnus had given up brushing them away. He anchored Rhona to him and turned her as gently as he could, keeping her injured leg from hitting the side walls. Now they were fighting the current, not walking with it. If Magnus failed to keep his feet, they would both be swept away.

64

HUNTER CALLED MCNAB OVER.

'A water course crosses under here.'

The elderly man looked certain, both his hands and the brass rod quivering with excitement. They were at the end of the building furthest from the burn.

Hunter walked slowly forward, stepped left, tried again, met a brick wall.

'Below here. Definitely.'

It occurred to McNab that Hunter had probably found a water pipe that served the building. Just as likely as locating some access to the Molendinar.

The brick fireplace the old man indicated was a remnant of the building's former glory. At its base was a heavy metal fire grate. There was no manhole visible. McNab hunkered down and pulled the grate back for a better look. There was nothing there but dirt.

McNab's desperation showed itself as frustrated anger. 'This is shite!' he exploded. 'New-age rubbish.'

Hunter didn't flinch. 'The culvert is beneath us.'

McNab called Kenny over and asked what he thought.

'The Molendinar doesn't run in this line, not as far as we're aware. But there are CSOs we don't know about. Sections we can't reach.'

If they hadn't found Rhona's mobile in the old laundry, McNab would have said they were in the wrong place. But Rhona had wanted to go back into the culvert, despite the rising waters. Her intuition, if not her scientific mind, had convinced her they'd missed something.

Hunter ignored McNab's discussion with Kenny and continued to walk outwards from the fireplace, checking, turning back, moving around by a few degrees, trying again.

Then he found it.

Tucked under a narrow metal stairway ending abruptly short of the upper level. The floorboards beneath the metal rungs, even to a good eye, looked undisturbed.

Hunter stuck the edge of a brass rod between the boards and lifted a section clear. McNab got down on his knees and shone the torch through the resulting hole. An open space lay below, criss-crossed by supporting beams. McNab dropped into the darkness and began to crawl, sweeping his beam in front of him, finding nothing but damp filth and the skittering sound of rats.

He realised he'd moved far from the hole and turned. This part of the foundations hadn't been crawled on for decades. He could tell by the sedimentary layers of undisturbed grime that rose, choking him.

'Any luck?' Kenny called down.

Fucking luck. They hadn't had much of that.

'Come back to the opening.' It was Hunter this time. 'Try directly west from there.'

McNab did as he was told. He would have danced naked down Sauchiehall Street if it meant their luck would change.

There. An opening, some two feet in diameter. The metal of the manhole lay a foot below the surface. McNab whooped for joy.

He called to Kenny for a manhole key.

As McNab pulled the metal lid clear, he heard the blessed sound of running water.

Margaret stood beside the car, scanning the street, looking for her husband. The crowds leaving the concert had dispersed and the road in front of the famous flashing neon sign was empty. Bill had composed himself on the drive. The Gravedigger did not know his daughter, had never seen Lisa. It was nonsense to think she'd been targeted. Both Rhona and Magnus had put themselves in view and challenged the killer. Magnus with the auction, Rhona by going into the Great Eastern. The killer could not, did not know, Bill had a daughter. Yet a niggling fear lingered. That the killer had been watching them all the time they were looking for him. That he knew everything about them, including the fact Bill had a seventeen-year-old daughter.

Bill tried to quell such flights of fancy.

The most sensible explanation was Lisa had gone to the wrong place, given up waiting and gone home. And just in case that wasn't true, his men were searching the area around the ballroom.

Margaret turned on his approach and Bill read fear in her eyes. So Lisa hadn't been in touch yet.

'I checked the house. Robbie says she's not there.'

'That doesn't mean she's not okay.'

Bill put everything he knew, and everything he'd learned from Magnus, into his gestures and voice. If he sounded as though he believed what he was saying, then Margaret might too.

'I want you to go home. Leave this to me.' Her body seemed to crumple in his arms. 'Leave the car here. I'll have someone drive you.' Margaret regarded him with troubled eyes. 'Please, Margaret. Call me as soon as Lisa appears.'

When the squad car left, Bill checked in with the station and put the wheels in motion for another missing girl. Only it wasn't just another missing girl. This time it was his worst nightmare come true.

65

THE LINE OF the CSO curved, exposing a wide opening to the left. McNab flashed his torch over the still waters of the underground lake. Kenny appeared behind him.

'It's an overflow chamber. It floods when the culvert is under pressure. There are several throughout the water system. The Victorians knew how to manage water.'

The frantic noise of the culvert was left behind as McNab stepped up and under a vaulted roof. The full circle of light from his camera torch shone on motionless water, like moonlight reflected in a dark loch. He might have missed them entirely had he not swung his torch over the entire surface.

They were lying together, arms entwined, in a few inches of water near the rear wall. Some childhood memory brought back an image of 'Babes in the Wood' and McNab silently willed them to be asleep, or at worst unconscious. His hope didn't last as long as the few steps from the culvert. For him, death had become something instantly recognisable, even without blood.

McNab wondered how long they had been there. Had the water risen and drowned them in their underground prison, then subsided again? Closer inspection told him a different story.

The MO hadn't changed, only become more violent in its execution. Stab marks covered Terri and Leanne's bodies, not just in the pubic area, but on their thighs and breasts and upper arms. Despite the distance below ground, flies were already in attendance, clogging the girls' wounds, nostrils and eyes. McNab's approach made them rise momentarily in a buzzing cloud, then fall again to feast. He called to Kenny to stay where he was, while he moved in a circle around the bodies, capturing the scene on camera, guilty at his intense relief that neither body was Rhona's.

In the background Kenny was getting twitchy, not because of the corpses.

'We have to get out of here. The water's rising too quickly.'

Intent on his recording, McNab hadn't noticed. At this rate the bodies would be afloat before long. He'd planned to send Kenny back with news of their find, while he carried on alone to look for Rhona, but Kenny wouldn't even consider the suggestion.

He pointed to the tide mark close to the roof. 'We have ten minutes to get out of here.'

Bill was waiting as McNab emerged from the hole. The return journey had been terrifying, made worse by the thought Rhona was trapped somewhere down there. Kenny had been a hero, forcing his way against the current, sheltering McNab in his wake. They'd left the

chamber just in time. Any longer and there would have
been two more bodies floating in the culvert.

Bill was frantic. McNab had never seen his boss like
this before. Whatever they'd faced together in the past,
the DI had been in complete control. Now he looked
like a man drowning in indecision.

'There's nothing we can do,' McNab told him for
the third time, 'except wait for the water to go down.
According to Kenny, it can fall again quickly.'

They'd already discussed the possibility that Rhona
was underground and in danger from the rising water.

'Kenny says some chambers don't fill completely.
They provide an overflow lake, like a flood plain, when
a river breaks its banks. They also lessen the speed of
the flow.' McNab was clutching at straws and Bill
knew it. He threw McNab an anguished glance.
McNab realised that in the panic he'd forgotten about
Bill's daughter.

'Lisa?'

'Nothing yet.'

'What about other mates, a boyfriend?' McNab was
running through the standard questions asked on
missing teenager hunts. The majority of them turned
up relatively quickly, sulky and contrite – but not all.

Bill indicated he didn't want to discuss it. 'Terri and
Leanne's bodies. Will they stay in that chamber?'

'Kenny thinks it unlikely. If the CSO is encrusted,
they may get stuck further down.'

Six dead women. And little chance for Rhona, if she
was down there too. No wonder Bill didn't want to talk
about Lisa.

Word had arrived that the team with the crawler had also abandoned the attempt for the moment.

In Glasgow it never rained but it poured.

McNab couldn't shake off the feeling that it was as if the Gravedigger was pissing on them from a great height. He'd drawn them to the culvert, and while they were busy there he'd made his escape.

66

RHONA FLOATED HELPLESSLY behind Magnus as he laboured to keep his feet on the uneven surface. Torchlight gave the tunnel an ominous glow. On either side, discharge oozed from small pipes, creating a glacier effect of smooth red deposits. Above, chemicals seeping through the cracks between the bricks had produced long hard icicle shapes. To clear the tunnel of encrustation would take time and high-powered equipment. Magnus could never have forced a way through on his own.

The pungent smell of heavy rain and disturbed effluent reminded Rhona they were in a CSO. It was like immersing their open wounds in a septic tank. The bacteria must be having a field day.

By the time they reached the overflow chamber, Magnus was barely able to stay upright in the rapid flow. He managed to grab and hold onto the rough wall, steadying himself before stepping up and pulling her out of the current.

Rhona immediately felt the difference, like gaining a safe harbour after struggling through a stormy sea. Magnus shone the beam around. The vaulted roof was magnificent and at least a foot higher than the tunnel.

'No ledge.'

'The water won't reach the top,' Rhona said.

Magnus studied her quizzically.

'The Victorians knew their waterworks. That's why we're still using them.'

He decided to believe her. 'So we wait it out here.'

He pulled her towards the back wall and anchored her behind him.

'You're bleeding,' she said, seeing his face and hands clearly.

'So are you.'

Their words echoed around her as though she were in some ghostly fairground attraction. Rhona's head still swam with the after-effects of the drug. The pleasure she had felt seemed infinitely preferable to this harsh reality.

In their attempts to escape there had been no time to discuss what had happened in the cellar. Now that her head was clearing. Rhona wanted desperately to know.

'Is Terri alive?'

Magnus looked stricken. 'I left her to try and find a way out. When I got back she'd disappeared.'

'A photo was sent to my mobile. Of you and Terri.'

'He was recording her torture. I saw the images on a laptop in the upper room.'

Rhona wanted to ask him what the image meant. Was it real? But she couldn't say the words. Magnus answered anyway.

'I don't know what I did.'

'You don't remember?'

'I remember he threatened to kill Terri. Then the light went out. He must have come up behind me. I felt something jab my neck, then nothing but . . .'

'Pleasure,' Rhona finished for him. She waited for a moment, listening to the boom of the rising water through the culvert, knowing she had to ask.

'What happened to me?'

She could see that Magnus was deciding how much to tell her.

'Please, Magnus. I need to know.'

They were so close, she could see the rapid pulse at the base of his throat.

'I was trying to force the lock on the door in the room above. Then I heard something. When I looked down he was there, with you. I switched off the arc light and made a lot of noise, hoping he would run.'

'What do you mean, *with me*?'

Before Magnus could answer, recall hit Rhona. She remembered excruciating pain, then unending pleasure; the drug entering her bloodstream, cruising her skin like a lover's fingers. Her body responding to touch. Whose touch?

She cried out, and to her ears it sounded shrill and distant. In her distress, she released her hold on Magnus and felt the current pluck at her, pulling her away.

'Rhona, no!'

Magnus lunged, caught her and wrapped her tightly in his arms as the culvert roared with the incoming rush.

The water entered the chamber in a great circular motion like an underground whirlpool, dragging relentlessly at Rhona's lower body, sending waves of pain through her injured leg. Magnus stood like a rock, holding her head above water, as the flood hit them.

67

BILL WATCHED AS a wall of water emerged below Duke Street. It topped both banks, using the waste ground and car park as its flood plain, before hitting the culvert under the goods yard. It reminded him of a highland river in spate, confined between rock walls, its force enough to take away a railway bridge. There was something both beautiful and terrifying about its power.

McNab stood next to him. Kenny and the rest of the team were further along, watching this scene from hell. Almost as swiftly as it rose, the water began to fall, leaving the waste ground behind the Great Eastern resembling a paddy field. Someone had been foolish enough to leave their car parked overnight behind the business park. Now it stood a foot deep in water.

The old hotel was a blaze of light and activity. They'd located the lower basement and found the execution room, manacles attached to the wall, dried and fresh blood soaking the floor. The room above had contained a camera and computer system set up to broadcast the images captured in the chamber of horrors.

The watercourse running alongside the dunny would meet the Molendinar, but where exactly they didn't know, and couldn't check until the water subsided. Their only remaining hope was that Magnus and Rhona had got out and were hiding somewhere in the underground system. Bill knew the likelihood of that was tiny.

Of their killer, they had had no sign. And there was no sign of Lisa either.

'Go home, sir.' McNab's voice broke through Bill's fog of despair. 'There's nothing more you can do here, and Margaret needs you.'

The storm had deserted Glasgow, heading south, leaving a bruised and battered sky. The moon, swimming into view, did little to lighten Bill's heart. He'd spoken to Margaret, sitting up waiting for her daughter's return. Bill thought of Nora Docherty, waiting in hope for Terri. He felt near to breaking point and wondered if he was fit to drive.

When his mobile rang he drew in at the edge of a deserted street. His heart soared when he saw Lisa's name on the screen.

'Lisa?' There was no answer. 'Lisa. Is that you? Where are you?' There was a click, then a droning sound. Bill ended the call and tried to phone back. When he got the message service, he shouted in frustration, then made a swift U-turn and headed for the police station.

68

MAGNUS'S ARMS REMAINED tight about Rhona's body as the water subsided. How he'd withstood the deluge, she had no idea. More than once, she'd felt herself slip away. Each time, Magnus had somehow clung on, keeping them at the outer edges of the turmoil.

The water was leaving as quickly as it had come, as though a plug had been pulled out. Rhona imagined it pouring into the Clyde and wanted to shout for joy. Then she sensed something wrong and turned. As he'd released her, Magnus had tipped forward, his face submerged.

'Magnus!'

He didn't react. His body had become a piece of flotsam rocking with the water. Rhona grabbed his long hair and yanked his head back. His eyes were half-closed, as though almost asleep. God knows how much he'd swallowed in his determination to keep her head above water.

For a moment Rhona contemplated the fact Magnus might die, drowned in his attempts to save her. The swiftly receding water was at her shins and she was forced to balance on her good leg. Rhona sat down heavily, eased Magnus's head onto her lap and pressed his neck, seeking a pulse. The stillness beneath her fingers terrified her.

She put her mouth on his, watching his chest as it rose with her breath. They were one now, lips together, lungs together. She wanted desperately for Magnus to live.

When she could find no pulse, Rhona pounded his chest, willing his heart to beat.

Then he coughed, and water gushed from his mouth. Rhona said a prayer of thanks to the God of this Underworld as Magnus's eyes opened.

'Am I on the other side?'

'Of what?'

'The River Styx.'

'This is no time for Greek mythology.'

Magnus gazed about him. 'This looks like Hades to me.'

They followed the noise back up the culvert. Rhona figured only a search team could make such a commotion. When they waded into the cellar, Magnus propping her up, the place was a blaze of light. The excited barking of a police dog alerted McNab to their arrival. God knows what they looked like, soaked and streaked in sewer mud, but McNab rushed towards them, a grin splitting his face. Rhona thought for a moment the DS would scoop her up in his arms.

'Her leg's broken. We need an ambulance.' Magnus's announcement couldn't put a dent in McNab's wide grin.

'Dr Rhona MacLeod, I could kiss you.'

'Don't you try it.'

While he supervised Rhona's transport to the main door, McNab filled them in on what had happened.

'We found Leanne and Terri together in one of the flood chambers.'

Rhona could see McNab was distressed. She imagined him and Bill above ground, knowing nothing of what was happening beneath.

'You found the upper room?' Magnus's face spoke volumes.

McNab's reaction, however well disguised, told Rhona what he'd seen.

'The CCU people have taken the computer.'

There was an uncomfortable silence before McNab told them about the contents of Ray Irvine's lock-up.

'The boss thinks Forbes and Irvine were on the periphery. The killer's disciples.' McNab left the worst until last. 'And Lisa's missing.'

'Lisa?' Rhona couldn't believe it.

'The boss had a call from her mobile about half an hour ago. He's at the station, trying to pinpoint a location.'

'Bill can't think the killer has Lisa?'

McNab didn't have an answer for that one.

The paramedic shut the ambulance door. It was as though Rhona had been waiting for this moment before she let go. Shock rippled her body and crushed air from her chest. The coldness of the water had seeped into her bones. She began to shake, her teeth knocking together. The insulation blanket did nothing but trap the cold that lay beneath. She forced words out between her chattering teeth.

'I've been drugged and possibly raped. I think the drug may have been methamphetamine. Don't give me anything that might affect the outcome of a police examination.'

69

BILL WASN'T THE only one who stared when Magnus entered the incident room. It was like a scene from a medieval movie. The professor was bare from the waist up, his hair wild, his body streaked with mud.

'Any news of Lisa?' he asked.

'They're still trying to trace the call.'

Magnus began to pace and talk at the same time. 'Okay, he's on a roll. Upping the stakes each time. Terri, then Leanne. She was important to him. He wanted them together. I reacted to the online auction, just as he planned. Rhona's intuition took her back to his lair, then her curiosity took over.' He paused and ran his fingers through his hair. 'He must have loved that – *Come into my parlour* – he wanted to prove he was better than all of us, especially me, more psychologically astute. And he did.'

The entire team stood around him now, listening. He went on pacing, oblivious to those watching him.

'We all played into his hands, at my instructions.'

Bill saw the agony on Magnus's face and realised he too was close to breaking down. Failure. Neither of them could endure it. They had put everything on the line and Bill was paying the ultimate price.

'Lisa,' Magnus glanced at Bill. 'Since we don't know where she is, we assume she's with him. He thinks Rhona and I are dead, caught up in the floods in the culvert. Moon and water. That aspect I was right about. He hit us all at our weakest points. Rhona's intuition and curiosity, my arrogance, and your love for your daughter. To get Lisa back, we must think as he thinks. This time I have to read *him* correctly.'

'What if he's already killed Lisa?' Bill couldn't believe those words had come from his mouth.

'No,' Magnus shook his head. 'This is way too important for him. He wants you to squirm. He wants you to acknowledge his superiority. McNab told me how you were one step behind him at the marina, and the wealth of forensic evidence against him. He's not willing to lose. His aim is to leave here and begin someplace else. His weakness is he can't leave without this one last humiliation.'

Bill's mind raced with a series of sickening images of his daughter being tortured by the killer. He staggered a little then felt McNab's hand on his arm, steadying him.

'Where would he feel safe, now that we've raided his underground lair?' Magnus addressed the team.

'Near water,' someone shouted.

'A boat.'

'A yacht.'

A constable came in with a phone location. Lisa's call had come from the area west of Glasgow Green, close to the river. A buzz exploded in the room.

'Okay, timing is important,' Magnus said. '*If* Lisa tried to make that call, then she was alive and still in the vicinity. If her abductor made the call, he wants to draw us there.'

Fear was hampering Bill's ability to think. He shouldn't be handling Lisa's disappearance. He was too closely involved. Remember procedure, he kept reminding himself. Follow procedure. It was the only thing that kept you sane. But still he felt himself turning to Magnus like a drowning man.

Magnus stood in front of the wall map that stretched from Calton to Inverkip. Everything was on there. The location of the graves, the marinas, the Molendinar. A geographical profile of the killer.

'Place is significant to him. He has never killed outside his zone. With access to the culvert gone, I believe he'll go back to the Necropolis,' Magnus said. 'He will end where he began.'

The fleet of cars moved quietly, seeing only the remnants of late-night revellers and the occasional street prostitute still touting for business.

Magnus sat in the back, his face like stone, silent after his outpouring in the incident room. He'd borrowed a shirt from McNab. It was too small, and he hadn't bothered to try to button it. His hair had been pulled back and secured with an elastic band, exposing the vivid wound on his forehead. When Bill had urged him to have it seen to, Magnus had refused, declaring it to be nothing. His hands were what concerned Bill most. They were swollen and black with encrusted blood. One finger looked broken. Whatever pain Magnus endured was being masked by adrenalin, determination and rage.

The river police had been alerted to Lisa's mobile location and were searching the stretch of water close by. Road blocks were set up surrounding the area. They were counting on the killer being inside the zone.

Bill hadn't told Margaret about the latest development. It would be too cruel to give her hope, when the call might mean the opposite. He'd also chosen not to tell Nora Docherty that Terri's body had been seen in the culvert. They would have to retrieve the two bodies and have them properly identified first. Bill had seen McNab's footage and there was little doubt, but they had to be sure. If Nora's link with her daughter was as strong as she claimed, she would know in her heart that Terri was dead.

The armed team circled the graveyard, planning their approach from all directions. Bill and McNab headed for the brewery car park south of Ladywell Street, entering without lights. As he climbed from the car, Bill felt as if the whole world was holding its breath.

Magnus was pacing up and down, tightly wound.

'Okay, our man has a thing about burial, so we need to look for disturbed earth, anything that suggests he might have been there.'

Bill's guts turned over. 'You think he's buried Lisa?'

'If he took Lisa, this is different. It's more about taunting you than his need to kill. Showing you what he can do. One man against authority and justice. Assumed invincibility is a trait of serial killers. He believes

he cannot be beaten.' Magnus paused. 'I think we
should assume he'll stay true to form. I think he'll
try and imprison Lisa underground, like he did Terri
and Leanne. We have to find that prison while Lisa is
still alive.'

'Jesus, Mary and Joseph.'

Magnus met Bill's eye. 'He hasn't won yet.'

The first flush of dawn was visible to the east as they
climbed the rear of the mist-swathed graveyard. Above
them was the steady beat of the police helicopter. If the
mist cleared, they would have an aerial view of any
disturbed ground. The dogs would focus their search in
the thirty-seven acres that constituted the Necropolis.

Magnus's conviction had relayed itself to the entire
team. He'd been closer to the killer than anyone, had
been one of his victims. The Gravedigger had effectively
ended his professional career. Now he was threatening
Bill's most precious possession.

70

RHONA OPENED HER eyes. The first rays of dawn warmed the room. She was completely alone apart from the steady hum of a machine. For a moment she thought she was in the lab, but couldn't imagine why she should be there at dawn, then in a rush, she remembered everything. From the moment she saw the man enter the old hotel, to shaking uncontrollably in the ambulance. And afterwards, weeping as the female police officer carried out the rape examination, and finally oblivion before they set her leg. Every part of her body ached with memory. She wanted to be asleep again, or dead, anything not to have such thoughts.

The door opened and someone entered, tiptoeing so as not to disturb her. Rhona thought it was a nurse, then recognised the rhythm of the walk and quickly closed her eyes. She didn't want to see Sean, not yet.

She heard him pull his chair close to the bed and felt his warm hand enclose her cold one. She could sense his agitation through the pulse in his fingers. He was muttering something under his breath. It sounded like, 'I'll kill the bastard.'

Rhona opened her eyes.

'Who?'

Sean started at her voice. 'Thank God you're conscious.' His voice was thickly Irish with emotion. Rhona realised how terrified he must have been.

'Who do you want to kill?' Rhona repeated, knowing Sean wasn't talking about the man they called the Gravedigger.

Sean didn't answer.

'You're talking about Magnus.' Rhona was suddenly afraid of the look in Sean's eyes. A brutal, incensed gleam she'd never seen before. 'Magnus Pirie saved my life in the culvert. I would have drowned but for him.'

'It was his fault you were there. The fucking bastard!' Sean's face was livid with fury. 'He put you in danger.'

Rhona clung to Sean's hand, but he shook her free and stood up. 'I was waiting for you to wake up. Now I know you'll be all right,' he said stiffly.

'Sean, stay with me, please?'

'Chrissy will be in soon.'

'Sean, promise me you won't go near Magnus.'

His eyes were like a stranger's.

'Why should you care what happens to Magnus Pirie?'

When she didn't answer, he turned away. Rhona wanted to call after him, ask him to stay with her so she could tell him what had happened in the cellar. She wanted to share her fear and her disgust. She wanted his arms about her.

The door banged shut behind him.

Rhona rang the emergency bell. When a nurse arrived, she asked to make an urgent phone call.

71

MAGNUS STOOD MOTIONLESS as the armed team moved silently among the headstones. Yards away, the team was almost invisible. But not their scent. Not to the dogs and not to him.

Magnus closed his eyes and concentrated. Sound and sight would be distorted in the mist, but his sense of smell was as acute as ever. The hot damp weather had caused an abundance of growth. Magnus sensed the earth writhing with life as the sun began to show its colours. He was seeking something else in the blanket of smells around him. Something different. Not the wall of decay he'd met on his first visit to the graveyard, but the scent of the killer. A scent he'd first breathed in at Rhona's lab, and again in the vaulted space of the cellar. The scent he'd picked up from Rhona's skin. The unique human scent everyone had. Like the dogs, Magnus knew he could find the guy in a crowded room, even though he'd never seen him clearly.

Every hair on Magnus's body stood to attention. Each vein and artery pulsed with blood. He could feel each beat of his heart. He knew if he came face to face with the man they sought, he could kill him. All thoughts on the sanctity of human life had departed him in those moments he'd watched the killer with Rhona.

If he could find and follow the killer's smell, he would find Lisa. He was convinced she was here. They were both here. Soon Bill would receive a call from Lisa's phone. The killer would reveal he'd tricked them. Laugh at them, revel in their despair.

But the game wasn't over yet.

The men were fanning out over the hill. Magnus aimed for the lower mausoleums. Digging a grave in open ground would be difficult. A mausoleum would be better.

Three vaults lay embedded in the hillside. Large, rusting hazard signs forbade him entry through their gates, due to their crumbling state. Magnus sniffed each padlock, checking for oil, but there was nothing but the dust of corroded metal.

His breathing was matching his heartbeat, fast and furious. Magnus forced it to slow, and tried to gather his thoughts. He'd roamed this place at night and during the day, after their initial find. Then, he'd been seeking to understand the killer's mind and his world. The map of the place was burned into his memory.

Magnus turned abruptly left and slithered down a grassy bank. Someone had been down here before him, while it was wet. In front of him were bent and broken branches.

Magnus let the smells wash over him. Gorse, the coconut scent of the flowers long gone, but the sharpness of the foliage still there. And something else.

Magnus smelt the killer; salt and oil and the scent of his skin.

The metal gate of the partially collapsed mausoleum was closed but not padlocked. Magnus pushed it open, his mind already computing the fact that the floor was stone and looked unmarked. Nothing had been buried there, but still Magnus was convinced the killer had been in, or near this building.

Magnus placed both hands on the wall. The stone was dry and surprisingly warm, as though it had been in full sun not long before. There was a rustling at his feet as a mouse, disturbed by his presence, made for the outside world. The crypt had been built with its gate facing east, so its occupants might see the rising sun and Jesus's second coming. Already dawn was swallowing the shadows.

Magnus stepped outside and examined the outer wall. The northern section was partially collapsed, the roof fallen in, its exposed tombs reminding him of the burial mound of Maeshowe in Orkney, plundered by Vikings, who had written graffiti on its internal walls.

He went back inside, knowing there was nothing there, but unable to leave. The stillness of the night was being replaced by the energy of dawn, heralded by a blackbird's bid to begin the chorus.

The rising sun now shone on the western wall. It was three tombs high, the divisions between them like a grid. Magnus saw the carving and knew he was in the right place. A full moon and a fish were scratched into the stone of the central tomb.

His fumbled attempts to open the sarcophagus lid were hampered by his swollen hands. Magnus gave up in frustration and used the radio. Bill answered immediately.

'The dogs found disturbed earth. We're checking it now,' Bill said.

Magnus gave his location and explained about the symbols. 'I can't get the lid off.' Even to his own ears, he sounded desperate.

Bill was there in minutes. Magnus was aware he must look like a madman, tearing at the lid of a sarcophagus. McNab and Bill immediately joined him, their combined efforts freeing it to scrape across its base.

The escaping air was full of the scent of dust and disuse. Magnus knew before he looked in, the sarcophagus was empty. Inside his head, Magnus could hear the killer's laughter. How many places had he scratched those symbols within the graveyard? Leaving his scent at each of them. He'd drawn them back here. Tricked them when they thought they were tricking him. Magnus could taste Bill's anger and despair.

'She's here. I'm sure of it.'

'Why?' McNab said. 'Why are you so fucking sure?'

Magnus concentrated on Bill. 'He was watching you. He followed you home. He saw your family. He followed Margaret to Barrowland. Lisa looks like the others. His victims all look alike. I said that didn't matter. I was wrong.' Magnus turned to Bill. 'Why would Lisa go with him?'

'She wouldn't.'

'But if she did?'

Bill thought for a moment. 'I've had police cars follow her before, when I knew she was walking home. I frightened her once. She didn't realise who they were.'

'Maybe he told her he was a cop,' McNab came in. 'That you'd sent him.'

'A perpetrator wants to be part of the action,' Magnus said. 'What if he's here with us now?'

Bill shook his head. 'Impossible.'

'Drivers?' Magnus tried. 'The guy who opened the gates?'

'We checked out everyone who had a key.'

Bill's look suggested he thought Magnus was rambling. 'You need to get checked over at the hospital. Have those wounds seen to.'

Magnus didn't argue. The adrenalin was draining from his body, leaving him weak and full of doubt. He'd been so sure he would find the killer, and save Lisa. A false belief, more about himself than the case.

McNab left them at the crypt to check out the road blocks. Magnus knew the sergeant's anger was directed at him. McNab thought him a fool. McNab blamed him for what had happened to Rhona, and believed Magnus had increased the danger by responding to the auction. And McNab was right.

72

MCNAB STOOD ALONE near the road block, thanking God he was no longer with his boss or Magnus. The DI's fear was too raw for McNab to cope with, and McNab's dislike for Magnus was too intense. McNab had secretly prayed for the Norse God to fail, but would never have wished for this to happen to Lisa.

He couldn't shake off the thought that if Rhona had stayed with him, she would have been safe. But you couldn't make Rhona do anything she didn't want to. If McNab had learned anything in the short space of their relationship, it was that.

The camera image of her lying helpless in the cellar had affected McNab deeply, in a way he was not proud of. To be in control of Rhona was a fantasy of his. A fantasy that could never be realised. Rhona could never be possessed. McNab had tried and failed. Maybe if he hadn't tried so hard, they would still be together.

A white van drew up. McNab watched as a constable moved to the driver's window and asked the usual questions. Routine. Endless routine, which – the boss never tired of telling his team – was good policing. McNab's eyes drooped with fatigue. The only thing that would keep him awake now was alcohol or the prospect of sex.

McNab's eyes ran over the van and checked the number plate. They'd had a half-dozen delivery vans through already, starting before the rush-hour traffic. This one was no different. The constable stepped back and the engine revved into action. Something in that sound alerted McNab. The guy was really keen to leave. Watch and listen, that's what the DI had told him.

The vehicle was pulling away.

'Stop,' McNab shouted without knowing why. Then his brain registered what his eye had spotted. A towbar on the rear bumper.

The van slithered to a halt. McNab immediately thought that a guilty man wouldn't stop. A guilty man would drive on. Knock them down in his effort to escape.

McNab checked out the occupant of the driver's seat. An ordinary bloke. Middle-aged. A face he didn't recognise under the lid of the cap. They had only one photo to go on. Bradley had said it might be Henderson, but couldn't be sure. He looked different now, Bradley had said. Smarter. This guy didn't look smart and he definitely smelt ripe.

'Lose the cap.'

McNab watched as the man reached up with his left hand. The exposed hair was thinning and mousey-blond.

'I'd like a look in the back.' McNab could have sworn the guy flinched.

'Be my guest.'

The guy got out of the cab and strolled around. Took his time about unlocking the door, then stood back for McNab to take a look.

McNab could sense something about him, something stiff and alert. The guy was cool, but McNab could hear a strange tension in his voice. No light came on when the door opened. The back was a place of shadows. The man stood quietly as McNab jumped inside.

A jumble of stuff, clothes, cardboard boxes. McNab picked up a set of stinking overalls.

'Sorry about the smell. I've been clearing a drain for a mate.'

McNab threw the offending garment to one side. 'Where did you say you were headed?'

'South.'

'Where south?'

'Bradford.'

Wrong answer, mate.

McNab surreptitiously prodded the remaining heap of clothes and his foot met something firm. Out of the corner of his eye, he saw the swift movement of the man's left hand towards his belt.

McNab flung himself to the floor of the van, shouting 'Gun!' to alert his colleagues. He felt something firm absorb his fall and began to hurl aside the remaining garbage, oblivious to the shots outside.

The shiny blue sleeping bag was zipped all the way around like a body bag. McNab cursed as the zip caught, then forced himself to go more slowly, imagining all the time the blue and lifeless body of his boss's daughter inside.

At last he had it open.

Lisa's face was like porcelain. McNab wondered if such beauty came only with death. Routine sent his fingers searching for a pulse. He caught it, lost it. Panicked. Found it again. Held it, faint but steady. With his other hand he pulled the gag from her mouth and leaned close. His heart leapt as he heard her suck in air and saw her chest rise.

'Lisa?' Her lids flickered at her name. McNab tried again. 'Lisa.'

The eyes slowly opened.

McNab would remember her look of fear for ever. Fear, then joy.

73

THE DISTURBED EARTH had turned out to be the grave of a dead dog, its corpse bearing the signs of a traffic accident. A Glasgow resident had deemed their pet important enough to take up residence in Glasgow's answer to the Père Lachaise.

There had been four other reports of scratched gravestones, symbols that might have been a fish, or a fish and a moon. Magnus had been wrong, although his conviction had brought them there, like disciples following a prophet. Desperation had made fools of them all.

The call came in on his mobile as Bill abandoned the search and headed for the Bridge of Sighs.

'I've found Lisa.' McNab's voice cracked with emotion. 'She's alive.'

'Where?'

'We stopped a van. Lisa was trussed up in the back. The driver ran, but we got him.'

Bill shook with relief. 'Is she okay?'

'Shaken, but all right. She's on her way to the Royal.'

Bill felt his legs give way under him and grasped a nearby headstone for support. 'I'll call home.'

Margaret answered immediately. He imagined her

waiting, like Nora Docherty, for the call that would pronounce her child dead.

'We've got her. Lisa's okay.'

Bill wished he could put his arms around his wife as he listened to her weep.

'She's at the Infirmary. I'll send a car for you.'

'Thank God.'

'She gave a pretty coherent account of how she was grabbed,' the doctor told Bill. 'But couldn't remember much after that. She asked to have a rape examination. There was no semen, but we found this.'

He produced an evidence bag. Through the clear plastic, Bill saw a small silver charm, shaped like a half-moon.

Bill felt bile rise in his throat. He wanted to cry out, but was struck dumb. He accepted the bag and put it in his pocket.

'The girl doesn't know about the charm yet. I thought I'd leave that up to you. You've informed her family she's here?'

Bill realised the doctor had no way of knowing he was more than just a policeman.

'Lisa is my daughter.'

The doctor's matter-of-factness transformed into genuine distress.

'I'm so sorry. I didn't know.'

Bill brushed his concerns aside. 'Where is she?'

Bill stood at the door, hardly daring to enter in case he woke her. He hadn't composed himself yet, hadn't perfected the lie he'd made up his mind to tell. Lisa suspected the bastard had violated her. She didn't need to know he'd left something behind to prove it.

Bill moved quietly to stand by the bed. His first-born. His wee girl. Now he knew what it was to be David Docherty. Understood why Docherty had prowled the streets. Felt the man's pain, anger, shame and impotence. And most of all, his desire for revenge. Only one thing separated them now. Bill's daughter was alive.

Lisa's eyes opened.

'Oh Dad, I'm sorry.'

Bill drew her into his arms, not wanting her to see his tears. Lisa was apologising to him, but he was the one who'd failed. Failed to protect his family, failed to protect his precious daughter, with all the knowledge and resources at his disposal.

'I lost Susie on the way out. I went back in to look for her, but she wasn't there. I panicked a bit because you didn't want me to go to the concert, and Susie's mum had only let her go because she was with me. She thinks because you're a policeman . . .' Lisa left the sentence unfinished. 'I went looking for Mum. There was a van with its back door open. I walked past and he just grabbed me.'

Magnus had been right. The killer had watched and waited and taken his opportunity when it arose. They'd all played into his hands, one way or another.

'We got him. He'll pay for what he did,' Bill said, knowing he wasn't interested in justice. He wanted Henderson dead. He would always want him dead.

When Margaret arrived, Bill left the two women alone together. Margaret would need to be told about the charm, but not yet.

Rhona lay still, a monitor beeping beside her. Bill thought she was asleep, but when he approached, she turned and looked at him, her eyes full of fear.

'We found Lisa. She's all right.'

Rhona grabbed his hand. 'Thank God.'

'McNab searched a van going through the road block. She was trussed up in the back.'

They stared at one another, both knowing how close death had come. Bill couldn't bring himself to mention the charm. Rhona had enough to think about without that horror. He felt as responsible for her as he did for his daughter, for Nora's daughter. For all the women the Gravedigger had tortured and killed before they caught him.

Accident and Emergency had a half-dozen people still waiting to be seen, but there was no sign of Magnus, either in the waiting room or the cubicles. An enquiry at the desk confirmed Bill's suspicions. Wherever Magnus had gone when he left the Necropolis, it hadn't been to the hospital.

74

MAGNUS MADE HIS way home through the early morning streets. He knew he looked a mess, by the shocked glances of the few people about at that time. One man offered to call an ambulance, but Magnus brushed his concerns aside. The pain from his wounds was the only thing keeping him upright.

The flat was silent and still. Magnus poured himself a stiff drink and took the bottle to the balcony. The sight of the river calmed him a little. Had he been in Orkney he would have immersed himself in the sea. Tried to wash himself clean, inside and out. Here, he had to be content with the river's close presence. The whisky entered his bloodstream like a transfusion. Magnus drank it down and poured another.

He swirled the measure around the glass, thinking of Rhona standing next to him that night on the balcony. The scent of her skin. The mind games they'd played.

He'd wanted to go to the hospital and make sure she was all right. But he hadn't, knowing it wasn't his place to be there. He wasn't her lover. Sean was.

When the buzzer went, Magnus glanced at the video-screen and opened the door without speaking. He'd been waiting for this moment. It was the first time they'd met since that night in the club. Then Sean had been relaxed, friendly, and rightly suspicious of Magnus's motives.

Sean walked into the sitting room, his steady stride belying the amount of drink he'd consumed. They stood facing one another, absurdly, over the chessboard.

Magnus waited in silence. Part of him wanted Sean to hurt. Maybe then he would break up with Rhona, leave the way clear. The rest of him hated himself for even thinking that.

'Is Rhona okay?' he said.

'What the fuck do you care?'

When Sean sprang towards him, Magnus didn't move. Perhaps he wanted to be beaten, punished for abandoning Terri and leading Rhona into danger. Sean caught him by the throat and forced him against the wall. They stood eye to eye.

'I saw you at the club. I saw the way you looked at her.'

'I didn't touch Rhona.' Magnus wanted Sean to know that, at least.

'But you wanted to.'

'Yes, I wanted to.'

His admission should have made Sean angrier, but seemed not to. He released his hold and stepped back.

Sean looked Magnus up and down, taking in the muddied torso and wrecked hands.

'What happened to Rhona in that place?'

Magnus knew then that he wasn't the only broken man in the room. He shook his head. It wasn't for him to say.

'What did he do to her? Tell me, you bastard!'

Magnus took the blow full on the face. On the second, he fought back, feeling his own knuckle hit bone. They were evenly matched. Two men, full of anger because they'd failed to protect the woman they both cared deeply about.

75

BILL WAS MET with a cheer when he entered the incident room. The night shift hadn't left and the day shift had joined them. Bill let their combined forces express their joy, his joy.

'Okay, where is he?'

'Interview room one, but the Super wants a word first.' Janice handed Bill the phone.

It rang only once. Bill imagined Superintendent Sutherland in his dressing gown, pacing the floor.

'Sir?'

'How's your daughter?'

'She's fine,' Bill lied.

'Good.'

There was a pause while the Super cleared his throat.

'You will not interview Henderson.'

Bill said nothing.

'DS McNab will do it.'

Bill remained silent.

'That's an order.'

'Yes, sir.'

Sutherland sounded relieved not to be argued with. 'Go home. Get some sleep. Be with your family. Come and see me in twenty-four hours.'

Bill put down the phone, aware of every eye in the room on him. Everyone knew what the conversation had been about.

He turned to McNab. 'Okay, let's go.'

Magnus had been right. He was ordinary. Henderson, or Williams, or Gordon. His hair was thinning on top, though still blond, grey at the temples. Eyes not empty, nor soulless, just calculating, with a hint of mocking superiority.

McNab sat next to Bill, awaiting orders to start the tape. Bill nodded and McNab did the preliminaries, listing all the pseudonyms. They were facing not one man, but three, and all of them killers.

'I demand a lawyer be present.'

McNab snorted. 'English law. Doesn't work that way in Scotland. We haven't charged you yet.'

A flicker of unease crossed Henderson's face. It was a small success, but tasted sweet nevertheless.

Bill fingered the plastic evidence bag in his pocket. The half-moon charm would go to forensic, but not yet. Bill drew out the bag and placed it between them on the table. He reported the exhibit for the tape. McNab had never seen the charm and had no idea what it meant. He threw Bill a questioning look.

Henderson glanced down at the bag and smiled. Bill's stomach lurched.

Henderson looked up. 'Shame. I planned to go back in for that.' He licked his lips. 'Bet you didn't know your daughter shaved her pussy. Who for, I wonder?'

McNab flinched, anger reddening his face.

Bill fought to control his own reaction and succeeded in keeping his voice steady, as he addressed the tape. 'Note, Mr Henderson has admitted to placing the charm inside Lisa Wilson and also to planning a further sexual assault on her.'

'You fucking bastard,' McNab hissed.

'Got in there before you, did I?' Henderson met McNab eye to eye, goading him. When he didn't respond, Henderson carried on. 'Pity about the flat shoes. Still, I used my own stiletto.' He held up two fingers and mimicked a fucking motion through the circle of thumb and forefinger. 'Daddy's little girl will never forget *me*.'

There was a second's silence, then the table lifted off the floor as McNab's boot caught Henderson hard between the legs. His face twisted in agony at the force of the impact. He grunted and slumped forward, gasping for breath, scrabbling to shield his crotch from further blows.

Bill grabbed McNab by the arm and addressed the tape. 'This interview is suspended at 7.15, on the request of the interviewee to visit the toilet.'

When Henderson got his breath back, he started doling out all kinds of threats. Ignoring him, Bill righted the table and motioned McNab outside. The commotion had brought a constable to see what was wrong. Bill sent him away with an angry wave.

'I'll kill that bastard.' McNab's body shook with fury.

Bill's voice was sharp. 'Neither of us is going back in there. Someone else takes over from here.'

McNab opened his mouth to protest, then saw the determination on Bill's face.

'If I can let it go,' Bill said quietly, 'so can you.'

McNab looked close to weeping. Whether he was upset for Bill, himself, or Lisa, Bill didn't know.

Throughout the day, they began to put the pieces of the jigsaw together. Bill watched as McNab channelled his anger into work. He owed his sergeant a debt he could never repay. But one thing he could do. If there was a problem over the incident in the interview room, it would be Bill and not McNab who would take the rap.

McNab had established Henderson's stay at the Great Eastern.

'The hostel began rehousing residents from 1994 and shut its doors finally in 2001,' he told Bill. 'Williams, then called Peter Henderson, lived there for a time in the late nineties before he went south. That's when he must have got to know Cathy.'

'And got to know the building,' Bill surmised. 'Any family?'

'He was fostered with an older brother when he was two and the brother three. They both went to live with a family in Bridgeton. No father's name on the birth certificate and Henderson and his brother apparently never saw their mother again. In some trouble as a juvenile, the social service record mentioned a caution for exposing himself. Was a gang member at one point, and had a reputation for using a knife. He cleaned up his act and got a job in a boat yard. It looked good for a while, or at least we don't know what he was up to, but we think he moved around a lot. Never married as far as we're aware. Then back here to the men's hostel.'

'When?'

'1997. Not sure how long he stayed, before he went to Bradford.'

'What about contacts in Bradford? Maybe there's more we can get him on.'

'We're checking.'

And it took time. Time they hadn't had when they were looking for Terri and Lisa.

'The hostel records gave his room number as eleven, in the basement. We're taking a closer look.'

Forensics had come a long way in a decade. If the Gravedigger had left traces of himself in room eleven, they would find them.

'CCU retrieved an address for a Mark Gordon from the commodore's computer. Six Riverside Gardens.'

'That's near Magnus's flat,' Bill said.

And a far cry from room eleven in the Great Eastern.

76

WHEN THEY REACHED the riverside apartment, Magnus was waiting for them.

'Thanks for calling me.'

'You deserve to know who your neighbour was,' Bill said. 'Whatever the boss says.'

Gordon's name was on the entry phone list at the front door.

McNab leaned on successive buzzers until someone answered and let them in. When they reached Gordon's door, Bill gave a cursory knock, then forced it.

The apartment was what you'd expect an up-market rental to be. Minimalist and functional. Magnus had said the killer would move between lair and hunting ground. This place looked like the respectable face of Dr Jekyll.

'Some smart stuff in the wardrobe,' McNab called from the bedroom. 'Bed's made. Room's tidy.'

Magnus stood in silence, expression intent. Bill had seen the same look at the scenes of crime, and in the graveyard when they were searching for Lisa.

'I can smell him. I can smell others too.' Magnus cast his eyes around the room, then followed McNab into the bedroom. Bill could detect nothing, but Magnus strode confidently to the bed and pulled back the cover.

The trophies were laid out, side by side, row on row, like a patchwork quilt. More than five, so it seemed more had been killed than they were aware of. Something had been removed from each victim. Mostly underwear, smeared with blood, urine, faeces. Now even Bill could smell it.

'He wanted them close,' Magnus said. 'When he lay among them, he could relive each precious moment of every kill.'

'Sir.' A shocked McNab pointed out what Bill had already seen. A small charm, shaped like a half-moon, had been attached to every item.

'He would never have left these behind through choice,' Magnus said.

They'd forced him to run. To abandon his trophies. His pride had been dented. What better way to restore it than to abduct Bill's daughter? Magnus had succumbed to temptation. Rhona's curiosity had been a bonus. But the ultimate prize would have been Lisa. Bill could hardly bear to admit to himself that if it hadn't been for his daughter's violation, they wouldn't have caught their killer.

On their way to the Great Eastern, Bill's concern for Magnus's physical state increased. In the close confines of the car, he could see fresh evidence of cuts and bruising. Had Magnus been in a fight since they last met?

Number eleven was at the far end of the lower corridor, next to the stairs, close to the room Bill had taken refuge in when he'd learned Lisa was missing.

At first glance the cubicle looked the same as all the others. Little more than an empty cell, containing a metal bed frame and broken chair. A torn curtain shivered in a faint breeze from a broken window. A SOCO knelt close by, examining spotting on the wall below. The outermost wooden partition had already been removed, exposing the gap between it and the concrete retaining wall behind. The SOCO working there indicated some of the items already extracted from this hiding place. Souvenirs of Henderson's earlier days. His training for what was to follow. Grimy bras and pants, stiffened by old blood and semen, evidence of the Gravedigger's past.

Bill sat in his swivel chair, knowing it might be the last time he did. He was struck by how little that bothered him. Maybe it was time to go and live in a cottage somewhere in the west. Or the Orkney Isles. Where there were no crackheads like Minty, no monsters like Henderson. If any such place existed.

'Beattie's waiting in room two, sir.'

Bill thanked Janice and lifted the forensic report on the third body they'd found. He gave the chair a spin before he left the room. His way of saying goodbye.

Bill could tell by Beattie's smug look that news had reached him of Henderson's arrest. Beattie, or Atticus, was in the clear.

'Thank you for coming in, Mr Beattie.'

Bill laid the brown envelope between them on the table.

'It was inconvenient but . . .'

Bill drew out a photograph. 'Do you recognise this girl?'

Beattie gave the image of a fresh-faced schoolgirl a cursory glance. 'No, I'm sorry, I don't.'

Bill studied Beattie's complacent expression for a moment.

'That's strange. Angela Sweeney was in the care of your local authority. She attended your school for a period of time, before she ran away. According to records, Angela was assigned to you for guidance purposes.'

'I see many children . . .'

'But you don't fuck them all.'

Beattie flushed scarlet. 'How dare you. I will complain to your superior . . .'

Bill shoved a second picture in Beattie's face. This one was of Angela's body.

'She was fifteen years of age when he did this to her. She was also four months pregnant.'

Bill saw Beattie flinch.

'When you fucked your former pupil, you left a little something of yourself behind, *Atticus*.'

There was a moment's horrified silence.

'What are you suggesting?'

'We ran some tests on the foetus. Guess who the father was?'

'That's nonsense . . .'

'You were having illegal relations with a minor, Mr Beattie.'

Fury suffused Beattie's face. 'I had sex with a prostitute, so what?'

'You had sex with a fifteen-year-old girl.'

Bill sipped his congealing coffee, pondering how life could change in a split second. Magnus, with his bid in the online auction. Rhona choosing to go into the Great Eastern. McNab's decision to look inside that van.

Bill wondered whether he could have done something differently and perhaps saved Terri and Leanne, and spared Lisa. He was seized by a terrible feeling of powerlessness. Even with the full weight and might of the law behind him, he hadn't been able to protect his own daughter. He'd brought evil into Lisa's life. Evil that would stay with her for ever.

From the window, the Glasgow skyline looked as big, brash and uncompromising as ever. A city that bred good people. A city that bred monsters.

It was DC Clark who delivered the message. His team watched in silence as he crossed the incident room en route to the Super's office. DI Bill Wilson had captured a killer, but those who upheld the law were not permitted to break it.

77

'HEY.'

'Hey, yourself.'

McNab looked rough. Two days' growth, which couldn't be described as designer stubble, and dark shadows under his eyes.

'You're looking good.' He gave her the once-over. 'Not too sure about the hospital gown though.' He admired her plaster. 'Dr MacLeod, in bed and immobile. Just the job.'

'Stop it.'

'Stop what?'

'Stop flirting with me.'

'Okay. You look terrible. The gown's a fright and I don't fancy you at all. How's that?'

Rhona pulled a face.

'All of which you know is untrue.'

Rhona changed the subject. 'Tell me what's happening.'

'How long have you got?'

'I get out after the doctor's round, in an hour's time.'

'Sean picking you up?'

Rhona hesitated, a fraction too long. 'He's gone south.' She didn't add 'with Sam'. As far as she was aware, no one but Chrissy, Sean and herself knew that Sam had been in Glasgow.

McNab raised an eyebrow. 'So you require a chauffeur?'

It seemed churlish to refuse.

They settled into talking about work, much safer ground. McNab told her the bodies of Terri and Leanne had been recovered from the culvert. There was to be an internal enquiry into Magnus's role in the case. And he, McNab, was not going to let the DI take the rap for assaulting Henderson. He'd confessed to his role, of which he was proud.

Rhona already knew McNab had kicked the killer in the balls. The grapevine stretched as far as the Royal Infirmary, especially with Chrissy on one end.

McNab's final revelation was that Chrissy had told him she was pregnant.

'What?'

'She told me when we went to Rhu Marina together, while you were in the underworld. I thought pregnancy was mellowing her, but I'm not so sure.'

'She rebuffed your advances?'

'I didn't advance.' McNab looked affronted.

'I bet you didn't get the chance.'

They laughed together. Laughing was good. Rhona realised she hadn't laughed for some time.

Rhona returned to more serious things. 'Does Nora Docherty know about Terri?'

'Bill went down to see her. He didn't let on to the Super he was taking Magnus with him. Seems Nora knew already. Had written down the time she says her daughter died.' McNab looked spooked. 'She wants to bury the two girls together, if we can't find any family for Leanne.'

They were discussing it as though it was all over. Maybe the killing spree was, but the repercussions had only just begun.

'We took room eleven at the Great Eastern apart. The partition walls were packed with Henderson's souvenirs. Pants, bras. Photos. There was blood on the wall under the window.'

'I thought I heard Terri in that room, but when I opened the door, it was empty.'

'Henderson had rented a flat near Magnus under the name of Mark Gordon.' McNab's face darkened. 'He had trophies from all the women he killed. The creep had them in his bed.'

Rhona remembered the feeling she'd had in Magnus's car park. The sense that someone was watching her.

McNab waited outside, while the doctor checked her over and gave her the okay to leave. Rhona was surprised to note that she was glad it was McNab taking her home and not Sean.

Chrissy had been the one to tell her Sean had driven Sam to London. Rhona suspected Sean's silence meant he'd confronted Magnus despite her wishes. Anger and hurt had stopped her calling him. The longer the silence between them, the more difficult it would become, but she needed and wanted the space. It wasn't the first time they'd parted after an argument, but, deep inside, Rhona sensed it might be the last.

McNab helped her into a wheelchair and whisked her out of the door.

'No racing. I'm not a police car.'

'As if.'

In fact, McNab turned out to be a model porter, providing Rhona didn't mind him eyeing up the nurses and making them blush with cheesy compliments.

Settled in the car, she told him she wanted to go to the lab. McNab didn't seem surprised. Chrissy greeted her arrival with sarcastic comments about slackers, and a wheelchair she'd commandeered from somewhere. She and McNab bantered as usual, but Rhona sensed there was no antagonism. McNab bid her farewell at the door, after informing Chrissy how sexy she looked pregnant. Chrissy couldn't think up a suitable reply.

'It's not like you to be at a loss for words.'

'Well, that's pregnancy for you.'

It was good to be back in the lab, even if she was immobile. Sitting in the flat all day, albeit with Tom for company, would have been unbearable. The hospital had discharged her with strict instructions to put no weight on her leg. It sounded easy, but in practice was more difficult. Chrissy made a joke of it, moving her around in the wheelchair or bringing work to where she was sitting.

Normality was what Rhona needed. In the isolation of the hospital room, she'd had too much time to think.

The rape tests had found no evidence of semen in her body, but every time Rhona closed her eyes, the fractured memories of her time below ground returned. Eventually she hoped she might piece them together and know the truth.

The doctor had told her the methamphetamine in her system had probably been administered by injection and she was lucky with the amount. First-time users had been known to die if given an addict's dose. Occasionally, in her worst moments, Rhona wanted to be back in its grip, feeling nothing but pleasure.

She'd been right about Magnus. He hadn't raped Terri. None of his DNA had been found inside her body. He was innocent, but he wouldn't see it that way.

Chrissy had been working on material recovered from Lisa, the tape used to gag her, her bonds and clothing. Microscopic details that put Henderson firmly in the frame, even without his gloating admission in Bill's interview. McNab had saved Lisa's life. If he hadn't challenged Henderson, they would have lost Lisa, and the killer would have escaped. Procedure, attention to detail, gut feeling and a little luck had caught him.

Rhona contemplated, not for the first time, phoning Magnus. But she sensed it wasn't time yet for them to talk. Both had their demons to confront first. They were like soldiers after a battle, unsure how to treat their comrades.

Rhona settled to the task of sifting through her email correspondence. One in particular caught her eye. Her idea to look for non-perfect matches between the killer's DNA and samples stored in NDNAD, had resulted in eighty candidates, one of whom might be significant. A Joseph Henderson had a number of convictions for petty crime, including burglary. But of more interest was his Bradford address. He shared enough of Henderson's DNA to be a relative. Rhona gave Bill a call.

He listened to her findings. 'Send a list to McNab. He'll let Bradford know.'

There was a moment's silence before she brought herself to ask.

'How's Lisa?'

'Okay.'

Rhona knew he was lying. 'I'll come and see her once I'm mobile.'

'She'd like that.' Bill changed the subject. 'Terri and Leanne's bodies have been released for burial. The funeral's on Monday. Magnus is going down with McNab and me. Are you fit to go?'

The thought of meeting Magnus again, perhaps reliving what had happened, stopped Rhona from immediately saying yes. Bill must have read her mind.

'You don't have to.'

'I don't think I can.'

After the phone call, Rhona was morose. Chrissy must have sensed it from afar. Maybe sorrow moved through the air like scent. Not for the first time Rhona thought Chrissy a capable, even ideal, disciple for Magnus.

'Enough for one day. You need a drink. I can't join you, but I can watch and dream.'

The club was quiet. Too early for the after-work regulars. No music and no Sean. The stairs had been an obstacle Chrissy refused to let bother her. Rhona had ended up in a fireman's hold between the barman and the pianist. The young musician seemed unfazed by the experience.

Propped on a bar stool, Rhona sipped chilled wine while Chrissy watched like a child deprived of chocolate.

'Sam and Sean are in London,' she told Rhona. 'I had a text.'

Rhona said nothing. London was the end of the universe as far as she was concerned.

Chrissy regarded her with concerned eyes. 'What happened between you and Sean?'

'Ask me again in a month's time.' Rhona found her voice breaking.

Chrissy put her arm around Rhona's shoulders. 'That bastard Henderson will get what's coming to him. I feel it in my waters, which have become a dominant force in my life.'

Rhona laughed. Thank God for friends. Thank God for Chrissy.

McNab arrived an hour later. 'Your carriage awaits.'

A glance at both faces revealed what Rhona feared. She'd been ganged up on. Chrissy, at least, had the grace to look sheepish.

'You didn't fancy staying with me.'

An understatement. Chrissy's mess could not be lived in, even though Rhona loved her for offering.

'I thought you might not manage the stairs, and McNab's stronger than me.'

From Chrissy, that was an amazing admission. Rhona knew she was beaten. McNab looked awkward, fearing a rebuff. Rhona felt mean and useless at the same time. She managed a thank you.

McNab turned the journey and subsequent stair climbing into a joke. No easy feat. By the time they reached her level, Rhona could have kissed him for his efforts, but didn't.

'What about food?'

'I'll phone out for pizza.'

'Eight thirty tomorrow morning okay?'

Rhona wanted to hug Michael McNab, to thank him for saving Lisa and for helping her now.

'That'll do fine.'

He waited as she moved inside with her crutches. The relief as she shut the door was overwhelming.

Tom was inordinately pleased to see her, immediately forgetting his abandonment. The kitchen was as it had always been. It was this room that had made her buy the flat, before Sean, before Tom, before Magnus, before what the Gravedigger had tried to do to her in the cellar. It was both her refuge and her strength.

Rhona listened to the sound of silence and welcomed it, like a long-lost friend. She didn't venture through to the bedroom to check the wardrobe, knowing instinctively that Sean had removed his things. He'd done what she'd asked him not to do. He'd made that choice knowing her well enough to understand what it would mean.

Rhona sat in the gathering darkness, relishing each quiet moment.

78

Two months later

RHONA TOOK THE plane, a journey lasting an hour from
Glasgow to Kirkwall. The aerial view of Caithness and
Sutherland reminded her she'd been too long away
from the wild places of Scotland. The further she
travelled from the central belt, the more Rhona's spirits
lifted. She had no idea what she would say to Magnus
when they met, but she knew it was time to see him.

The taxi ride from Kirkwall Airport enveloped her in
a landscape she'd often imagined. The fertile fields of
the mainland, and across the deep harbour of Scapa
Flow, the purple-black island of Hoy.

Rhona knew Magnus lived west of Kirkwall, in a
house surrounded on three sides by the incoming tide.
She believed someone like Magnus would be well
known to the locals. She was right. The taxi driver,
hearing Magnus's name, set an immediate course for
Howden Bay.

The house was just as he'd described it. Built by
fishermen on free land below the high-water mark,
the afternoon tide was already lapping a trio of its
walls.

Now she was there, Rhona stood outside, incapable of knocking on the door. Instead she took to the nearby beach, and walked the golden sand, seabirds wheeling overhead and a wonderful view across to Ward Hill on Hoy.

On the western side of the house, two black smoking sheds stood on stilts in the water, fronted by a small jetty. A small boat bobbed alongside. Rhona thought of Magnus's flat in Glasgow, the balcony jutting out over the river, and understood why being close to water had meant so much to him.

She spotted a figure emerge from the house and look in her direction. Rhona stayed where she was, like a child caught in some misdemeanour, hoping Magnus would come to her. And he did.

As he strode towards her, Rhona was struck by how much he looked a part of the landscape. A Norse God come home. Magnus's face lit up in recognition, his broad smile quelling Rhona's fears that she wouldn't be welcome. He opened his arms to her, wrapping her so tightly, he lifted her off her feet.

'Rhona, I can't believe you're here.'

She couldn't believe it herself.

He released her and looked her full in the face.

'You came to see if I'd regained my sanity?'

Rhona examined his eyes and saw, with relief, there was humour in them again.

'Well, what do you think?'

'You're the psychologist. You tell me.'

Magnus turned to the water, and a shadow briefly darkened his face. 'I can sleep again. A good sign.' He put his arm about her shoulders. 'Come and meet Olaf.'

Olaf turned out to be a big grey cat that looked more wild than domestic. Sitting on the jetty, he pricked up his ears at their approach.

'Olaf catches his own fish, so is an easy house guest when he chooses to stay.'

'He's yours?' Rhona reached out and Olaf disdainfully allowed her to stroke him.

'Olaf belongs only to himself.'

Magnus briefly showed her the house. Sturdily built of grey granite, with walls two feet thick against the weather and the sea.

'You can hear the salt spray hit the seaward windows during the winter.'

'Like being in a ship?'

Magnus smiled. 'Exactly.'

Each deep window ledge was cluttered with spoils from the beach, sea urchin shells, dried starfish, and bleached, knotted driftwood. Scattered here and there were pieces fashioned further by carving. In the sitting room a chess game sat centre stage.

After her tour, Magnus served up home-brewed beer on the jetty. It was sweet and cloudy and tasted delicious.

'I decided it was better to do, than to think. Hence the carvings and home-brew – and I spend a lot of time out on the water.'

Rhona was surprised at how easy it was to be with Magnus. All her misgivings about awkwardness between them seemed ludicrous in that place.

'You'll stay a couple of days at least.'

Of course she would.

Magnus cooked fresh fish for their evening meal – 'only five hours since it was swimming in Scapa' – and they drank more home-brew. Its light sweetness was unlike anything Rhona had tasted before, except perhaps in Africa.

It was Magnus who brought up the subject of Sean.

'He came to see me. He was very hurt and angry. He had every right to be.'

'Sean cared more about punishing you than about how I felt.'

It was the first time Rhona had voiced what she had felt since that night. 'He's in London.' She didn't add that he might never come back, or that she might not want him to.

There was a moment's silence.

'Sean was very angry at himself for not protecting you.'

'That isn't his job,' Rhona said firmly.

'What is his job, if not to protect the woman he loves?'

He seemed agitated. She put her hand on his arm.

'Magnus, this isn't just about Sean, is it?'

He sighed and shook his head. She waited. Eventually he spoke.

'Anna was the love of my life, and I killed her through my arrogance and thoughtlessness.' Magnus looked at Rhona. 'I thought I'd learned my lesson, but I hadn't, had I?'

'What happened?'

'We were rock climbing. The weather was poor, she was frightened and didn't want to go on. I persuaded her. Told her there was no problem. I didn't want to be beaten, by the weather, by her fear.' He looked down. 'If she'd been on her own, or climbing with someone else, she would be alive today.'

Just before midnight, Magnus took her out in the boat. Gliding through the silky water, Rhona felt herself in a different universe, made up of only sky and sea and the soft swish of bow through water. A waxing moon lit their way, although it wasn't dark enough to need it. Magnus saw her glance upwards.

'According to legend, the waxing moon is a time for spells, for good luck, and for love.'

Rhona knew Magnus wanted her to forget, or at least replace any memories the sight of a full moon might bring.

She was seized by a moment of happiness. She'd thought meeting Magnus would make her remember, that she could never look on his face without recalling the face of her tormentor. She'd been wrong.

'Victims are not only those who die,' Magnus said.

For once, Rhona didn't care that he could read her thoughts.

Later, he showed her to her room, overlooking the water and the distant hills of Hoy. Left alone, Rhona, like Magnus, slept soundly and well.